Shadow in the Pines

PJ Nunn

OTHER BOOKS BY PJ NUNN

Angel Killer: A Shari Markham Mystery

Private Spies: A Jesse Morgan Mystery

PRAISE FOR *ANGEL KILLER*:

Angel Killer: A Shari Markham Mystery

Praise for Angel Killer:

"Dr Shari Markham demonstrates skills Charlie Fox would be proud of in this tense hunt for a deranged serial killer. Crackles with romantic suspense."
  – Zoe Sharp, author of *Die Easy* and the Charlie Fox Thriller series

ANGEL KILLER by PJ Nunn had me riveted. As a Forensic Psychologist, I tend to be critical of such characters, but Ms. Nunn's lead character Forensic Psychologist Shari Markham hits the mark! I was immediately hooked when a child's body is found and Shari begins the "magic" of a Forensic Psychologist. More bodies add to the suspense and a love interest adds to a realistic feel. I was right there with Shari, as PJ weaved her words into a thriller. Captivating! Delightful! A+
  – Dr. Cynthia Lea Clark, Psy.D., Ph.D., MHt. CHS-IV Forensic Psychopathologist, Actress, Writer

Tense and enthralling, *ANGEL KILLER* is a first-rate story of nail-biting suspense and unpredictable mystery. From page one it grips the reader and never lets go. Bring on more of Shari Markham, Dallas PD profiler. She's a winner!
  – Joanne Pence, author of the Angie Amalfi mysteries

For anyone that loves a well written and thoroughly developed murder mystery, I recommend PJ Nunn's *Angel Killer*. This book is dark and not for the faint of heart. It deals with a serial killer murdering the most innocent people in our society – our children. But don't despair, the protagonist Shari Markham is on the case!
  – Michael E. Witzgall, Law Enforcement Consultant, Charlie-Mike Enterprises

PRAISE FOR PRIVATE SPIES:

In what will hopefully be the first in a series the author has created a contrast to the typical super-competent detective with stellar self-defense skills and whose impulsiveness would be frustrating were it not for the fact that Jesse is completely aware of her flaws. Her emotions frequently override her thoughts, but what does become charming is that she actually grows and learns from her mistakes. Humor remains central to the core of this very complex and well-written mystery and readers will enjoy a heroine who manages to defy the odds and survive, often despite her best attempts to get herself killed. It's impossible not to somehow fall in love with this character who both exasperates and delights readers with her impetuous but always well-intentioned behavior.
      – Cindy Chow

Maybe a little too much back-story slows the beginning of this novel, but don't let that stop you. Once the action starts, it is non-stop.
      – Pat Batta

I enjoyed this very much. Kept me guessing. I had a hard time putting it down once I started reading. Great characters, especially Jesse. I would like to see them again in another book.
      – Leslie

This is an engaging twisted private investigative thriller starring a wonderful rookie and the veteran trying to keep her out of trouble though she is a magnet for tsuris. Fast-paced from that first call, readers (and the sleuths) wonder what is going on as nothing is what it is supposed to be; the refreshing reason will stun the audience.
      – Harriet Klausner

I loved the main character and the quirky way she gets the job done. There were lots of plot twists that kept the story interesting. I look forward to reading more. Very enjoyable!
      – Marcia

"Because we focused on the snake, we missed the scorpion."
– Egyptian Proverb

ACKNOWLEDGMENTS

From the time I was small, I was taught that if I could say it and believe it, I could do it. Like so many children of my era before technology took over our lives, I grew up in worlds of make believe and imagination, worlds created with my siblings and friends. My parents taught me to love reading; my Grandma Ford taught me to transition my pretending into becoming. I'm ever so grateful for that. And of course there have been countless others who made deposits of wisdom and knowledge into my life until I ended up surrounded by friends who were, like I am, writers.

There are far too many of you to mention, but in particular as this book goes to print, I have to thank Earl Staggs, Jan Christensen, Pat Reid, Charlene Truxler, my clients, and so many others who daily remind me what a joy it is to be part of the widespread mystery writer's community. I love coming to work with you every day.

Then there's Mike Witzgall, my partner in crime. He's endured endless phone calls, text messages and emails while I try to make sure I don't write anything that will make a cop throw the book against the wall. I promise if I messed something up it was my doing, not Mike's.

And of course I have to thank my family, especially my husband David and my two sons who are still at home, Dave Jr. and Caleb. Thank you so much for keeping things going around the household while I spent countless hours after work on the computer. I couldn't have done this without any of you. Thank you all.

CHAPTER ONE

Maneuvering the Taurus as close to the front walk as she dared, Dani Jones got out and surveyed her surroundings. It was still daylight in town, but here, about three miles down a winding road, the dense foliage and canopy of trees cast eerie shadows and blotted out the early evening sun. What happened to the comfy and cozy the realtor promised? Visions of a cozy log cabin nestled among the trees with smoke trailing from the chimney while she snuggled on a sofa in front of a roaring blaze vanished as quickly as the smoke would in a burst of cold air. A quick glance at the back seat of her car reminded her she'd exchanged the thrill of buying her first house and starting a new life for the agonies of packing and moving. That might have tempered her enthusiasm just a little.

Before her stood a log cabin. Her log cabin, now. Two stories of history, planted firmly in the midst of overgrown pine trees and an assortment of scraggly shrubs that reached out spindly limbs and grabbed her jeans as she walked by. The sidewalk was a collection of stones arranged in a semi rectangular pattern and pounded into the earth. The shadows and piles of fallen leaves and debris hid whatever grass there might have been. Since it was only late August, the fallout testified to total neglect of the landscape for at least a year. Uncovered portions of the yard were cracked and dry, with only a few sprouts of weeds scattered about to prove that it had once sustained life. The front porch would creak, she knew that before she set foot on it.

The wind, whistling and rustling through the trees, gave her a chill even though it wasn't cold. Dani scurried up the steps, digging in the snug fitting pocket of her jeans for the key. If she hurried, she might just get the car unpacked before it was really, truly, totally dark.

Heaving the last box through the door almost an hour later, Dani sank down on it and kicked the front door closed, wrinkling her nose at the onslaught of stale, musty air that replaced the fresh, cedar scent of the outdoors. Home. From now on, this was it. Wearily, she pulled the cap off of her head and ran long fingers through her short blonde hair and wondered for the millionth time if she'd made the right choice. But this was no time to dwell on the wisdom of her move, or lack thereof. Even though the boxes were inside, she had miles to go before she could sleep.

The house came furnished; Dani bought it lock, stock, and barrel. At the time, it seemed preferable to making arrangements for all her things to be transported here from Austin, but now, looking at it close up, she wasn't so sure. From the looks of it, most of the pieces had come from garage sales. One man's trash, as they say. Outside, the logs gave the place character, but they weren't visible inside. There wasn't much character visible either, she mused, surveying the four white walls. Not even a nail hole interrupted their monotony. The only variation was a light smoke stain around the edge of the ceiling. It could be worse, though. It could be covered with hideous wallpaper she'd have to remove before she could redecorate.

The stone fireplace, tucked away in the corner, showed promise. At least it would, if she patched and refinished the mantel. Oh well, she sighed, getting to her feet. She had a bed to sleep on and a table to set up her computer. She could replace it all, piece by piece, if she had to. Hadn't she decided this was her chance to start life all over? Besides, out here in the boonies with no friends or relatives, what else did she have to do after work?

Life for Dani, or Danielle Elisabeth Jones as she was legally known, hadn't always been easy. Still, she'd managed to do okay. Raised alone by a single mom from the time she was six, she knew what it was to do without, but somehow, Mom worked hard and got her through college. When she married her college sweetheart and he graduated from medical school, she thought she'd made it. At least Mom died before things went bad.

Mark Bridges was every mother's dream for her daughter, according to him, anyway. That should have tipped her off a long time ago, but she was too intoxicated by his attention. Tall, dark and handsome, he imagined himself a real life clone of George Clooney on ER, and even started a first year residency in emergency medicine. Less than a month into it, he bailed, begging his way into another residency spot specializing in plastic surgery. After all, that's where the real money was.

At Mark's suggestion, Dani postponed graduate school and went to work full time so they could afford the glamorous lifestyle of a doctor in spite of a resident's salary. A chic townhouse in a high-class neighborhood. A used, but very flashy Porsche. All the right clothes to wear to all the right cocktail parties. How could she have been so blind? She'd heard all the stories, too, of women who worked to put their husbands through med school, only to get divorced when they made it. She just never believed it could happen to them. To her. He'd actually had the nerve to tell her that the reason he was first attracted to her was her blonde hair and the fact that she was just the right height to wear on his arm. Instead of complacently accepting it and understanding like he fully expected her to do, she experienced a wake up call that was long overdue. Their divorce was final almost a year ago.

It wasn't until she saw his wedding announcement in the Austin paper that she realized how deeply it had changed her. Whether it was a rebound reaction or a sudden taste of reality, she didn't know, but suddenly, she had to get out of there. Two weeks later, she'd submitted an application for admission to grad school at the University of Texas in Tyler, secured a position in the lab there, and started a search for a house.

The divorce settlement was surprisingly generous, awarding her the townhouse and all its furnishings, not that any of it held fond memories. Fortunately, she found a buyer right away and made a tidy profit on the sale. A couple of yard sales later, she was on her way, leaving Mark Bridges and her old life behind, and picking up the dreams she'd shelved for him almost ten years ago.

Real estate in east Texas was considerably less pricey than in the elite Austin neighborhood they'd inhabited. Maybe she was naïve, but when the real estate agent tentatively suggested an old fashioned log cabin located outside of town, it seemed perfect. When she heard the price, it seemed better still. She paid cash for the house and still had enough left in the bank to support herself for a year or so, even without a job if she kept her budget under control.

Hauling her suitcases upstairs, she dropped them on the four-poster bed and turned, catching a glimpse of herself in the dresser mirror. Moving closer, she peered at her image. Did she look thirty-four? She'd gained a few pounds since college, but she hadn't lost her girlish shape. She'd always been lean. Faded blue jeans hugged her hips and thighs, still shapely and firm. Her waist was proportionately smaller than her hips, leaving a slight gap between the waistband and her waist. Her breasts were firm and full enough that a bulky sweatshirt didn't quite conceal their presence. It was her face that drew her attention, though.

Leaning closer, she examined herself critically. The makeup she'd applied this morning was long gone, but bright blue eyes looked back at her, large and wide. The beginnings of a few wrinkles were there, but it was nothing alarming. At least not yet. She could still pass for a coed, she thought. She was no prom queen, but she didn't consider herself unattractive, either. Not that it mattered much. Attracting a new man was dead last on her things to do list.

She'd been in shock since the night Mark first told her he wanted out. Her friends had encouraged her to start dating again, to get out and socialize. They'd even set her up a couple of times, but Dani could think of few things less appealing to her right now. It was time for her to learn how to function alone, to be self-sufficient. Time enough for men later, if ever.

Opening the suitcases, she pulled out her clothes and sorted them into musty dresser drawers that smelled of cedar. When she was finished, she took a look in the bathroom, enchanted by the claw-footed tub that had intrigued her on her first visit. Finished in deep blue porcelain, it was by far the most attractive piece in the house. Promising herself to make a shopping list later, she filled the tub full with warm water, dug a novel out of her bag, and sank slowly into the soothing water.

She stayed there until the water turned cold, half attending to her book and half allowing the gentle lapping of the water to wash the troubled thoughts from her mind. Toweling off and slipping into some sleep shorts and a tank top, she climbed beneath the handmade quilt that covered the bed and fell fast asleep.

***

The first thing Dani noticed in the morning, aside from the bright sunlight streaming through the window, was the sound of the birds, so close they might have been in the room with her. A little disoriented at first, she sat in the bed, allowing the atmosphere of the house to sink in. So far removed from the city noise of Austin, it would take some time to adjust. Even though it was August, her feet were cold when they first hit the hardwood floors. Throw rugs, lots of throw rugs, she added to her mental shopping list. Come to think of it, she hadn't even touched the air conditioning controls last night. The house must be well insulated, both by the logs and by the huge shade trees that surrounded it. No matter what part of Texas it is, it's hot in August. Making another mental note to bring a coffee maker upstairs, she padded into the bathroom to get ready for the day. Dressing in jeans and a jersey T-shirt, Dani spent about an hour taking inventory and adding items to her growing list, then fired up the Taurus and headed into town.

Tyler was small, compared to Austin. It would take some time to learn her way around. With the whole day dedicated to turning her house into a home, she drove up one street and down the next, stopping wherever the urge struck. Her first stop was a bookstore where she came out armed with a new stack of mysteries for late night reading. Next, she wandered into a Pier 1 Imports store and rapidly acquired an assortment of candles and doo-dads to make the place seem cozier. Moving deeper into the store, she selected a variety of throw rugs and pillows. Captivated by the sight of a huge basket swing, she immediately envisioned herself curled in its plush green cushion on the front porch with a tall glass of iced tea and a good book. By the time she'd checked out and made arrangements for delivery, she'd already exceeded her self-imposed spending limit for impulse items, but went happily on her way.

After stopping for a sandwich, she adhered more diligently to her shopping list, filling the wagon with necessity items like a coffee maker and vacuum cleaner, pots and pans, eating utensils and a small grill. To Dani, nothing tasted better than homemade hamburgers or a rack of ribs barbecued on the grill, but Mark thought cooking outdoors was tantamount to caveman behavior. Maybe his new wife was more civilized, Dani thought, giving the grill a shove to make it fit.

By the time she'd finished at the grocery store, she was barely able to find room to squeeze in the bags. Content that she'd done enough damage for one day, she turned the car toward home, but a nursery outside of town beckoned and she surprised herself by turning into the lot. The cabin yard was really a garden waiting to happen, and she couldn't resist the thought of replacing the neglected spidery shrubs with fresh new foliage and flowers.

In the townhouse she shared with Mark, she'd been restricted to a window box and a couple of indoor ferns, but here there were no limits. Rationalizing that a vegetable garden would be cost efficient, she indulged herself, finding a sales clerk who was only too happy to help her select everything she'd need and then some.

Dani spent the rest of the afternoon happily puttering around the house. Cleaning, placing shelf paper, arranging furniture accompanied by lilting music from her favorite CDs. When the delivery from Pier 1 arrived, she decided to take a breather, finding her new porch swing every bit as comfortable as it looked. Swinging gently in the evening breeze, she put a pencil to paper and spent the better part of an hour plotting out her new landscape in anticipation of a morning delivery from the nursery. Whether it was the calming effect of the country air or the exhaustion from the day's activity, by ten o'clock she could barely keep her eyes open. Snug in her bed, freshly made with soft new flannel sheets, Dani slept like a baby.

CHAPTER TWO

Eager to get started on her gardening chores before the temperature got too hot, Dani plunged in, trimming and cleaning the flowerbeds. Withered weeds and cracked dry ground gave way to freshly turned earth, darkened by the generous sprinkling of a new hose. Slowly, but surely, the yard took on the appearance of a prized possession in process, complete with a growing pile of debris that Dani planned to eradicate with her first incineration effort when the evening sun sank behind the wall of trees.

By the time the panel van from the nursery rattled down the asphalt drive, it was almost noon and Dani was more tired than she'd been in years. Typing papers and examining microscope slides didn't do much for muscle tone. Fortunately, the driver, probably a student all of twenty years old, seemed captivated by her smile and happily carried the railroad ties she'd bought to border her gardens, placing them, and waiting while she stood back, considering whether their location was exactly what she had in mind or not. Once she was satisfied, he cheerfully positioned the heavy bags of soil and peat moss in the appropriate places with a lopsided grin that told her he was glad to do it. Smiling, she shaded her eyes and watched as the truck pulled away.

Tomorrow, she'd have to show up at the college for late registration, and then check in at the lab for her work schedule. From here on out, she wouldn't have much opportunity to spend all day working in the yard. As she looked around at all she had yet to do, she knew it was too soon to give up. Funny, it didn't seem like such a huge chore when she selected the plants yesterday. But now, surrounded by piles of soil with shrubs and plants all over the yard, it looked like an interminable task.

Thinking the vegetables would be the fastest place to start, she dug in, emptying the bags of soil and peat, then mixing them by walking through it all in bare feet, enjoying the squishy feel of mud between her toes. An hour later, her small plot of vegetables actually looked like a garden and she took a minute to congratulate herself before moving to the shrubs that lined the front of the house beside the porch. She'd already spent most of the morning clearing the debris and, with the ground dry as dust, it didn't take too much effort to just pull the dead ones up by the roots. Grateful that the huge trees protected her from the glare of the afternoon sun, if not from the heat, she plunged ahead. There were only two shrubs remaining with any signs of life, so Dani used the pruning shears to cut them back to nubs, then started mixing the potting soil and peat into the newly vacant areas. By the time the sun set, she had all the new shrubs firmly planted and surrounded by seedlings of blue phlox that the nurseryman assured her would spread quickly, covering the ground and effectively preventing the re-growth of weeds.

She still had a variety of flowers to plant around the yard and in barrels that bordered the porch stairs but she was too sore to do it and too tired to care. For a moment, she sat, rocked back on her heels, and surveyed her handiwork. There was nothing but trees as far as she could see on all sides. As she surveyed the tree line, a glimpse of color caught her eye in the trees across the road. Shading her eyes with one hand, Dani squinted and thought she saw movement. Was someone watching her from the woods across the street? Suppressing a shiver despite the heat, Dani got up and dusted her hands.

With frequent glances across the road, she gathered her tools and got things ready to go inside. Standing at the front door, she looked over her shoulder once more, then shook herself. She was surely imagining things. Washing her hands in the kitchen sink, she put a potpie in the oven then trudged up the stairs for a therapeutic soak in the tub.

Marginally revived an hour later, she sat down at the kitchen table with her dinner, a University of Texas catalog, and her day planner. After making a careful list of everything she needed to accomplish on campus, and adding notes to stop by and open a local bank account and change the address on her driver's license, she trudged wearily up the stairs to bed. So far, that bed was the thing she liked best about her new home. For the third night in a row, she fell almost immediately into a deep sleep, with lingering thoughts of how nice it would be to actually talk to someone again.

***

A medley of chemicals, disinfectants, and caged animal smells met Dani at the door of the lab, completely overriding the cheerful, professional decor of the office. Had she been away from it too long, or not long enough?

"Hi," she said, hoping her voice would prompt the gum-chewing receptionist to look up from her Glamour magazine. Academic fervor. "I'm Dani Jones, here to see Dr. Abraham," she forced a smile, staring down at the girl until she looked up.

"Oh, sure…down that hall and to the left," the girl shrugged, pointed, and went back to her reading. Dani raised her eyebrows and bit her tongue. It was all coming back to her now. She could only hope the students she worked with here were a little more enthusiastic about their work than the ones she remembered from UT in Austin. Their careless attitude about lab procedures was one of the reasons it was so easy for Mark to convince her to leave school and go to work. Since most of her coworkers in the lab were headed for medical school, she didn't want to know if their neglectful behaviors followed them into their chosen profession. In some cases, ignorance really is bliss.

The hall was narrow and undecorated, probably a back entrance to the labs that opened to student halls on the other side. She passed several doors, hoping to find one marked with Dr. Abraham's name, then paused and stuck her head into a lab filled with students.

"I'm looking for Dr. Abraham," she whispered to a nearby young man who was diligently trying to open a mussel shell. Amused, she watched as he tried to hold the shell still with a pair of dissection tweezers while he attempted to slide a scalpel inside. It slipped out of the tweezers twice while she watched, skidding across the tabletop like he was skipping stones.

"Huh?" he squinted up at her through glasses that slid halfway down his nose after his second unsuccessful endeavor.

"Dr. Abraham?" she said again.

Using the back of his gloved hand to shove the glasses back up on his nose, he nodded in a manner that looked more like a twitch, not daring to let go of the mussel he'd just retrieved. "That's him."

"Thanks," Dani smiled as she spied a tall, slender man in a white lab coat, leaning over a table across the room. "You'll have better luck with that if you'll just hold it in your hand and pop it with the probe," she suggested before she moved on. She'd never tried opening a mussel with tweezers, but doubted it would ever be successful.

"Probe?" the boy parroted with the blank stare typical of severe ignorance or insurmountable boredom.

"Here," she reached for the needed tool and handed it to him. "Just slide this in at the joint, it'll pop open," she instructed. Must be a freshman lab, her least favorite.

Making her way carefully between the tables, the looks of intense concentration and occasional aversion on the students' faces as she passed made her feel right at home. She stopped and stood watching as the doctor leaned over and helped a studious young man crack open his specimen.

"Dr. Abraham?" she interjected when he straightened up.

He turned toward her, a pleasant face with piercing blue eyes behind wire rimmed glasses, probably not a day older than her own.

"Yes, and who are you?" A smile softened the blunt words.

"Dani Jones, sir, one of your new lab assistants," she offered her hand.

"Oh, thank God!" he said, waving gloved hands to decline her handshake. "Two of my new assistants backed out! I didn't know if I'd have anyone this semester." He cocked his head as if to say 'follow me' and started weaving his way through the tables toward a desk at the end of the lab.

"Nice to know I'll be needed, then," she answered. "Do you have a schedule ready for me, or should I come back for it?"

"Well…" he searched through stacks of papers scattered randomly across the desk. "I did have one, but I'll probably have to change it…labs are always in the afternoon…"

Dani waited patiently, well acquainted with the absentminded mode of her previous lab instructors. When he started going through the same stack for the third time, she said, "It's okay. I've made sure all my classes are in the morning. Want me to just come in at one tomorrow?"

He looked confused for a moment, then nodded. "That would be great. Why don't you do that…"

"Okay," she smiled. He was kind of cute, but definitely existed in another realm. "I'll see you then."

"Thanks," he said, still nodding as he wandered off toward a student who'd called his name.

Feeling a little washed out after a long day on campus, Dani fixed a quick sandwich when she got home and rewarded herself by ignoring the awaiting chores and heading for the porch. At least in the front yard there weren't boxes and stacks of papers screaming for attention. She'd just settled in when she was interrupted by a smooth, deep voice floating across the yard.

"Danielle Jones?"

Dani looked up from the book she was reading on the porch swing and felt a twinge of apprehension at the sight of a strange man strolling casually down her driveway. Against the backdrop of trees, he reminded her of a lumberjack, tall and brawny. Shaggy light brown hair and a three-day growth of beard made it hard to see his face in the shadows, but the tank top displayed muscular arms and shoulders and tight blue jeans left little to the imagination. Self consciously running a hand through her hair, Dani stood up, eyes fixed on a black band strapped around his right thigh. As he moved closer, she saw it was part of a holster that held a large gun.

"Yes," she said uncertainly, suddenly feeling incredibly isolated and vulnerable.

He stopped at the foot of the stairs and handed an envelope up to her. "Guess they delivered this to me by mistake."

"Oh," she took the envelope from him. It was something from the realtor's office. "Thank you."

"I've been out of town. Didn't know I had a new neighbor," he continued. "Looks like you've been busy," he glanced around the yard.

"Yeah," she agreed. Up close, he was disturbingly attractive, but her eyes didn't stray far from the gun on his hip. "You live next door?" There was a house on the next lot, the only one for at least a mile in either direction, but she hadn't seen anything to make her think it was occupied since she'd been there.

"Sorry! I guess I forgot my manners," he smiled sheepishly, extending his hand. "I'm Noah Russell, I live next door."

Her hand felt small clasped inside his big one, but she couldn't help noticing how strong and warm it was. "Nice to meet you, Noah," she smiled awkwardly. She didn't know what to do. She wasn't about to share the close proximity of the swing with this stranger and his gun. "I'm Dani. Have you lived here long?"

"Mind if I sit awhile?" he asked, easing down on the porch steps before she answered.

"Not at all," she lied, sitting back down on the swing. The neighbors she'd pictured were a nice retired couple that might occasionally send a home baked pie her way. Not someone who looked like he belonged in a biker gang. Just her luck, her one and only neighbor might be some kind of armed felon.

"I moved here in March," he said. "Transferred in from Austin."

"Austin?" That got her interest. "I came from Austin, too."

"No shit!" He looked at her curiously. "Small world, huh?"

"Yeah, it is," she said, wishing she knew why she found him so intriguing. "Very different."

"It's good different, though," he said. "It grows on you," he smiled, causing her heart to skip a beat. As if sensing her discomfort, he got to his feet. "It's good to meet you, Dani Jones. Don't get up," he looked at her intently before he turned to walk away.

"You too," she said, watching him go. His gait was slightly uneven, with just a hint of a limp. She jumped when he turned to look at her again and caught her still staring.

"Hey," he said. "I have no food in my house. Would you consider getting a burger or something with me?"

The thought of having dinner and an actual conversation with a neighbor she couldn't afford to offend overrode the qualms she had about the gun strapped to his thigh. In Austin, she'd been surrounded by people, and three days of solitude was enough. "Sure, if you'll give me a minute to change."

His face broke into a smile that made him look a lot less intimidating. "Great! I'll pick you up in fifteen minutes, how's that?"

"Great!" she answered, hoping she was right.

Less than an hour later, she followed him between the tables in a heavily populated diner called "Pop's."

"It's a little loud, but the food's great," he spoke loud enough to be heard above the dull roar of conversation and country music. Dani smiled, sliding into the red vinyl booth directly across the table from him.

She couldn't help noticing the waitress, who patted Noah on the shoulder fondly and offered him a smile that livened up her tired face. "Whatcha want tonight, big guy?"

"Why don't you give us some menus and I'll try to act civilized for company?" Noah winked up at the woman who cackled at that.

"You? Civilized? That'll be the day!" She was still laughing as she went in search of menus.

Noah turned his attention back to Dani and offered her a wry smile and a shrug. Dani returned the smile, but wondered again what kind of neighbor she'd inherited.

"There you go," the waitress returned, dropping menus in front of each of them. "What can I get you to drink? You on duty?" Dani was surprised to hear her voice drop to a whisper.

"Nah," Noah shook his head. "Beer, straight up and cold," he smiled at her.

"I'll have the same," Dani said when she looked over at her. "On duty?" she asked when the waitress walked away.

Noah shrugged again. "She knows I don't like it broadcast."

Dani wondered what she'd missed. "Don't like what broadcast?"

He looked genuinely surprised. "I'm a cop."

It was Dani's turn to look surprised. She'd imagined all sorts of reasons why he might have a gun strapped to his thigh, but somehow that wasn't one of them. "Oh," was all she could say.

"Guess I … forgot to tell you, huh?" he grinned sheepishly.

"I guess," she smiled again. "I hate to tell you what I was thinking…"

Noah laughed out loud. "I'm sorry. It's a small town. Even though I do some undercover work, I just assume most people know."

Unconsciously, Dani breathed a sigh of relief. By the time they'd finished their meals, the two were chatting like old friends.

"You know," Noah pushed his plate back and slumped down more comfortably in the booth, "I've always been interested in the details of biological warfare but I just never took the time to study. Barely passed college chemistry," he chuckled.

"You either love it or you don't," she mused, with a growing awareness of just how attractive this man was and how long it had been since she'd felt like that. Too long. Too risky, she straightened up in her seat and warned herself not to get too comfortable.

"You ready to go?" he asked, as if sensing her mood.

"I hate to, but, yeah," she said. "I've got to go in early tomorrow."

Dani spent the ride home in his truck trying to remember the best way to end a first date when she didn't want to get too close, but needn't have worried. Noah pulled into the drive but didn't turn off the truck.

"Need me to walk you to the door?" he asked, watching her from behind the wheel.

"No," she answered, feeling a little let down as she reached for the door handle. "Thanks for dinner."

He smiled at that. "First of many I hope."

The next few weeks were hectic as Dani readjusted to campus life. She hated to admit she wasn't as young as she used to be. Even though the graduate classes had several students who were considerably older than she was, she was keenly aware that the majority of the student body was at least ten years younger. Even so, she was enjoying the freedom and making a few new friends.

The last student had exited the lab, leaving her with nothing to do but clean up and get ready for tomorrow's activities. Dani looked up with a smile as one of the other lab assistants burst through the door with exaggerated exhaustion.

"All done for the day?" Dani asked.

"Finally!" Beth said in her own unique melodramatic manner.

Dani grinned. Beth was like a breath of fresh air.

"So, how'd it go last night?" Beth asked with a knowing grin. She'd joined the Biology Department as a last minute addition a few weeks ago and Dani took an immediate liking to her. With a smile as perpetual as her frizzy, reddish brown halo of curls and a laugh that reminded Dani of Tinkerbell, the two had fallen into the habit of policing the labs together after the last class each day. It meant each of them cleaned up in six labs instead of three, but it really didn't take any longer with two of them working and the time passed much faster with someone to talk to. As ditzy as Beth seemed sometimes, she was twenty-four and in her second year of grad school, working on a degree in zoology.

"It was nice," Dani said non-committally, spritzing the table with disinfectant before wiping it up.

"Details!" Beth demanded, doing the same. "I want details!"

"What details?" Dani suppressed a smile. "We went to dinner, then we went home." Ever since Noah stopped by the lab last week, Beth had been smitten. He was, in Beth's words, infinitesimally dreamy.

"Come on! Give it up!" Beth looked up from her scrubbing with an impish grin and mischief sparkling in her clear green eyes. "Your home or his?"

"Mine," Dani smiled, putting her supplies away. "He came over for coffee after," she admitted.

"Oh, my God, it's so romantic!" Beth pretended to swoon. "Why couldn't I have bought the old Bailey house and moved in next door to Prince Charming? No wonder you're not afraid of ghosts!"

"Girl, you're nuts," Dani laughed, helping Beth put away her supplies so they could lock up the lab and get out of there. She didn't dare say so, but Noah was coming over for dinner again tonight and she still needed to stop at the store. "And what do you mean 'old Bailey house'?"

"You don't know?" Beth turned wide eyes toward her as they locked the door and headed for the parking lot. "I thought everybody knew about the old Bailey house! It's haunted!"

"Yeah, right," Dani laughed. She should have known Beth would be thinking like that.

The scorching summer heat had been replaced with cool, fall breezes. With Halloween only a few weeks away, the campus was ablaze with the colorful riot of changing leaves while the building interiors had been invaded by witches on broomsticks chasing ghosts and avoiding cobwebs.

"I've lived there for over a month. It's not haunted."

"No, I'm serious," Beth insisted. "Why do you think it was empty for so long before you bought it?"

Dani shrugged. "Cause nobody wanted to live way out there?" She'd wondered the same thing, especially since the price was so low, but it never occurred to her to ask.

Beth's voice took on a confidential tone as she launched into an explanation while they walked toward the parking lot. "You know the snake farm?"

"You mean Ophidian?" The Ophidian Research facility was the pride and joy of the science department and apparently responsible for collecting hundreds of thousands of dollars in grant money for the University.

"Yeah, yeah, whatever. Anyway, Dr. Atkinson used to own that house when he worked there and sometimes he'd take a bunch of kids out there and they'd go all out in the woods looking for snakes." Beth's eyes were wide as saucers and Dani suppressed a shiver at the thought of snakes slithering around her house.

"I suppose there are always snakes in the woods," Dani shuddered. "That's not haunted."

"No," Beth said, stopping beside Dani's car. "Wait! Two of the students that went out there to find snakes disappeared!" Her voice shrank to a stage whisper. "They went out to your house and they never came back!"

Dani tugged her keys out of her pocket and unlocked the car, then turned to face Beth. "Where did you hear that?" Surely she was just repeating some old East Texas folklore, but Dani felt an unexpected cold chill remembering the times she'd been working outside and looked up suddenly with the feeling that someone was watching her.

"Dano," Beth said, using her own preferred nickname for Dani, "I am serious as a heart attack! Ask anyone. It was five or six years ago…no, six… I was a senior in high school. There was a big deal in the paper about how they were bringing in more kinds of snakes to make the lab bigger. Anyway, if I remember right, just a handful of kids went out there that day, then a girl and a guy disappeared in the woods. Some people said they probably eloped or something. But, they never found them anywhere, Dano! After Dr. Atkinson moved away, some of the kids would still go out there to look for snakes, but they said someone was watching them in the woods. It's really creepy."

"Yeah. It is," Dani agreed, rolling her eyes. Beth's gullibility made her feel ancient. "Thanks for sharing."

"Oh, you!" Beth nudged her arm. "I gotta run, big date tonight! Talk to you later!"

"Later," Dani echoed, smiling. Beth could shift gears faster than anyone she knew. Maybe she was getting old, she thought, putting the car in drive and heading for the store. Still, what Beth had said made her think again about the feeling she'd had that someone was lurking in the woods across the road, watching her house. It had only happened a couple of times, and each time she managed to convince herself she was imagining things. But now, the idea might be a little harder to dismiss.

CHAPTER THREE

Fortunately, traffic to the store was light, so she got in and out in record time, but found herself looking around cautiously when she got out of the car at the house. Great. Now Beth had her spooked. She didn't know whether to worry more about watchers in the woods or snakes slithering around on the ground. The whole thing made her even more glad she had Noah for her closest neighbor. Even if he wasn't as handsome as any man she'd ever known, it was comforting to think there was an armed police officer living next door, just in case she might need him.

Turning the music up loud once she got inside, she busied herself cutting up veggies for salad and stir-frying chicken strips for fajitas. She wasn't much of a cook, really. The coconut pie on the counter, fresh from Kroger's bakery, was testament to that. But Noah loved Mexican food and would eat almost anything as long as it was accompanied by a huge helping of salsa.

The thought of him brought a smile to her lips as she worked. He'd scared her to death the first time they met, striding into her yard with a big gun strapped to his thigh. She hadn't learned he was a detective until later that night. Noah didn't look like any police officer she'd ever seen, except maybe in the movies. He was big enough, that's for sure, and she suspected he could be mean enough if someone provoked him, but he sported a perpetual three day growth of beard and his shaggy brown hair was longer than hers and always looked like he'd just been in a big wind. As the weather turned cooler, it seemed appropriate to see him wearing plaid flannel shirts.

They'd seen each other a couple of times a week at first, and Dani was leery of falling into a deep relationship too soon, but she was older than most of the guys she knew from the school and it was nice to be with

15

someone who didn't make her feel like an old maid. Lately they'd fallen into a pattern of seeing each other almost every day.

At first she told herself it was just practical. She hated to cook for just herself and he didn't cook at all. Since they lived out here with no one else nearby, why wouldn't they trade off? But it was more than that. The way she responded when he kissed her good night last night was proof of that. For the first time since she'd moved here, she would have traded her warm bath for a cold shower.

"Anybody home?" Noah called through the screen door.

"Come on in," Dani called. "I'm in the kitchen."

"There you go," he joined her, dropping a package of flour tortillas on the counter, then helping himself to a beer from the fridge.

"Hungry?" she smiled as he sat down at the table. Whatever the reason, her house seemed cozier when he was around.

"Starved! I worked through lunch," he took a big swig of beer from the bottle.

"Well, here then," she handed him the tortillas and reached for the grated cheese, which he accepted with a smile. "What'd you do today?" she asked, gathering the salad and croutons and placing them on the table.

His comparisons of life in a small town PD as opposed to the force in Austin were hysterical sometimes. It didn't take long to figure out that his perspective on people's motivations and life in general was significantly different from anyone else she knew, but she was learning to appreciate his insight and ability to read people.

"Oh, the usual, you know," he popped some cheese in his mouth. "Sweeping the scum off the street, shit like that," he joked.

"Right," she laughed, "we all know Tyler's full of scum." The daily paper was filled with high school and college events and news about the endless flower shows. After a few more trips to the kitchen, she had everything they needed on the table and he was already filling his plate.

"Hey, you'd be surprised," he winked at her as she sat down beside him. "Scum capital of Texas, I'll bet."

"Maybe I would," she agreed, stuffing a tortilla with chicken and onions. "Beth told me today this house is supposed to be haunted."

"Oh, really?" he looked mildly curious. "She's full of good information, isn't she?" His dry wit had escaped her at first, but she was getting used to that, too. It reminded her of the early days with Shelly, her first roommate at college. A time when she liked herself a lot more than she had lately. It was a comfortable feeling, like finally coming home after a long absence.

"Have you heard anything about students disappearing out here?" she asked, trying to sound casual. The whole thing bothered her more than she cared to admit.

"No-o," he said around a mouthful of chicken. "She was serious?"

"I think so," Dani said. "Something about the guy who ran the Ophidian Colony. She said he brought students out here to catch snakes and two of them disappeared... ...about six years ago."

"You know, I did hear something about that when I first moved here," he shook his head. "Pretty weird shit, as I recall. They don't get much of that around here."

"I think it's pretty creepy," she said, concentrating on her food. When she looked up, he was watching her intently.

"Does it bother you?" he asked quietly, shifting into his cop mode.

Shrugging, she said, "A little, I guess. I never lived alone before..."

That wasn't exactly true. She'd lived at home until she went to college. Then she'd married Mark right out of the dorm. The time she'd spent alone in Austin after they separated, she didn't really feel alone. Surrounded by Mark's things and the neighbors, it didn't seem the same. He was hardly ever home even before he moved out and she could always hear the neighbors thumping around behind a common wall. But out here, the quiet at night seemed to take on a presence of its own.

"I'll look into it if you want," he offered.

Dani was quiet for a moment and Noah waited. Finally, she asked, "Have you ever seen anyone out here? Walking around in the woods, I mean?"

Noah's eyes narrowed. "No. Why?"

She shrugged. "A couple of times, I've thought I did...across the road. Then I thought it was probably just a shadow or something. But after I talked to Beth about it, I started to wonder. It's probably nothing."

"There's not another house for miles," he said, like she didn't already know that.

"I know. I'm sure it's my imagination."

"I guess maybe hunters might wander this way sometimes," he offered. "I haven't lived here during deer season before."

"Whatever," she shrugged again, wishing she hadn't brought it up. She didn't really want to think about it. "Wanna watch a movie tonight?"

"I guess 'Silence of the Lambs' is out of the question," he teased, relaxing a little.

Dani rolled her eyes and got up to clear the table.

They ended up watching a rerun of "Face Off" on TV, sitting together on the couch while he gave a running commentary of why things weren't done right in the movie. A big fan of Nicolas Cage, she'd seen it several times before, but it was fun to hear Noah's take on the whole thing. Still, she sighed softly when it ended, knowing he'd leave soon and she'd be alone again. Maybe it was his police training, but he had an uncanny knack for knowing just what she was thinking.

17

"I better go," he said, contradicting his words by pulling her close and kissing her soundly. The touch of his lips sent a jolt of electricity coursing through her body. Mark never kissed her like this. "You okay?" he asked, so close to her face she could smell the remnants of the cologne he'd probably splashed on in a hurry this morning. Aramis, she thought, smiling as she mentally compared him to the pretty-boy Aramis man in the commercials.

"Yeah," she said, wondering if it was possible to fall into the warm brown eyes that stared back at her. This man was trouble.

"You know I'm right here if you need me," he whispered, caressing her with his voice.

"I know," she said softly, reveling in the feel of his strong arms around her. "Thank you for that."

He leaned forward and kissed her again, exploring her lips gently with his tongue. "I really better go," he groaned, pulling away.

It took all of her willpower to resist the impulse to pull him back and beg him to stay. She followed him to the front door, holding fast to the shirtsleeve near his elbow and wondering if it would be too forward to ask him to leave his shirt. Maybe if she had something that smelled like him to keep close at night, the dreams and the dreaded feeling of loneliness wouldn't plague her when she awoke.

"I'll see you tomorrow," he said, jerking her back to reality.

"Night, Noah," she smiled as he touched her face gently with one finger before going.

It only took a few minutes to tidy up the kitchen and she ran a hot bath, hoping it would still some of the restless feeling stirring inside of her. The bath felt good, but the feelings were still there when she turned off the light and climbed into bed. Sometime, she'd have to sort through all the emotions, but right now she just wanted to enjoy the feeling of being wanted by someone like Noah.

He couldn't be more different than Mark, and that surprised her at first. If she stood the two of them side by side, Mark would look like a pasty faced, insignificant wuss. He'd never been muscular and he detested working outdoors with his hands. That was one of the reasons he'd bought a townhouse. He didn't want to mow a yard. On the other hand, Noah was physical labor personified. She'd seen him heft huge logs and fifty pound bags of potting soil without straining. Although she'd never seen him at work, she doubted there were many criminals who'd resist arrest when he was involved. And it wasn't just the gun he carried either, he looked pretty intimidating without it.

He had his own issues though, everybody did. He hadn't said much about it, but she knew he'd been shot several times in the line of duty. In fact, that was the main reason he was here now. He'd been shot in the knee during a bank robbery in Austin. Recovering after surgery, he'd decided to move to a small town where he'd have less to deal with that way. He told her seeing all the violent crime tended to change people after a while. She knew he'd been married once, a long time ago, and that he was nearing forty. Maybe he was really ready to settle down now. Maybe…no, she better not start thinking that way.

Punching her pillow, she tried to get comfortable, then jumped when the phone rang. It was almost midnight! "Hello," she said tentatively.

"Not asleep yet?" Noah's voice spilled through the phone like a drink of brandy, warming her all the way to the core.

"No," she smiled. In those few seconds, the darkness that seemed cold and lonely was transformed into a warm and cozy place.

"I just wanted to make sure you were okay," he said. "You seemed a little nervous tonight." He was smiling too, she could hear it.

"I'm fine, thanks," she said, wishing like hell he was close enough to touch.

"You've got my number, right?" he asked.

"Yes, it's right here," she assured him.

"Good. Sweet dreams then," he said.

"Night."

***

For some reason, Dani couldn't get the thought of the missing students out of her mind. Every chance she had, she asked coworkers and fellow students what they knew about the story. Most of them had no idea what she was talking about, but occasionally she got lucky and mentioned it to someone who lived in town at the time. The general consensus was vague. Some thought Dr. Atkinson had something to do with it. Others thought it was Dr. Crane. Still others thought it was some wandering serial killer passing through on his way to who knows where. When she started getting strange looks in response to her questions, Dani tried to exercise more caution about bringing the subject up. She didn't want it to seem like she was obsessing, but it was never far from her thoughts.

Plagued with a vague sense of uneasiness, Dani broke down and went shopping at the local animal shelter, arriving home with an adorable mutt that hung on her every word. He was probably worthless for protection, but his spotted hair and happy brown eyes made her feel less alone immediately. He welcomed any and all attention with a happy bark and a quick doggie kiss if she wasn't careful. She named him Bandit because of the mask of gray hair around his sparkling eyes, and he promptly made himself at home by her feet wherever she might be. Noah teased her about her big, bad, watchdog, but she caught him wrestling with the dog and enjoying his company too when he didn't know she was watching.

***

Finally, darkness closed in, surrounding him, bringing with it the comfort of anonymity. He'd waited, impatiently, for Dani to arrive then watched in hidden silence as she unloaded her car. The woods offered no threat to him, they were his home. He could navigate them easily in the dark, even without the help of the full moon that shone down on him now. If he'd known about the sale of the house sooner, he could have taken care of everything before she arrived, but no matter. It had been six years and the Tyler police had bumbled the case from the beginning. They'd never pin anything on him after all this time.

Just to be sure, though, he wanted one last look at the cellar. Biding his time as he caught occasional glimpses of Dani through the windows, he waited until the house was dark, then slowly, cautiously made his way across the road and behind the house, ignoring the subtle crunch of gravel beneath his feet.

Internally, his anger coiled and uncoiled, striking out like the reptiles in his beloved lab. Who did this woman think she was asking all those questions and bringing his name up again when he'd worked so hard? Obviously, the hope that he'd had about the passage of time was in vain. Somehow, he had to stop her before she got the whole thing stirred up again. All he had to do was pick the right time. But he was still undecided. If he killed her, there'd be another investigation and the location was just too coincidental. Especially after she'd asked so many questions. No, maybe all he needed to do was scare her. Scare her bad enough that she'd pack up and get the hell out of town without looking back!

CHAPTER FOUR

When Dr. Abraham closed the lab to attend a convention, Dani decided to put the time off to good use. She'd spent so much time working in the front yard to make the place look better, but she'd neglected all the land behind the house. Dragging her lawn equipment out of the garage, she went diligently to work. Once the yard area was cut and trimmed, hopefully for the last time this year, she picked up a rake and headed for the perimeter where the yard merged into a thick bank of cedar trees.

A fence didn't enclose the yard, but it was easy to make out the boundaries. At one point, grass ceased to exist, replaced by old leaves and debris that cluttered the ground under the line of pine trees. Dani spent most of the afternoon raking leaves and twigs and filling lawn bags, but she was surprised when she swung the rake into the center of a new pile and heard the clank of metal. Closer examination revealed two doors, at a slight incline, completely buried by leaves.

Casting a glance around at the shadows beginning to develop from the setting sun, she saw Bandit chasing a butterfly around the side of the house. Stifling a shudder, she tugged on the door handle until it opened, revealing a cavernous hole and rickety looking wooden steps that disappeared into blackness below. It crossed her mind that it might be better to wait for Noah, but it would be dark soon and curiosity got the best of her.

After a quick sprint to the garage for a flashlight, she sat down on the top step and shone it down into the hole. Too dark to really see anything. Resisting twinges of claustrophobia, worsened by the creaking and groaning of the steps beneath her feet, she carefully made her way down the stairs to the bottom. The air that assaulted her nostrils was cold and reeked of mildew. The darkness was so dense, it seemed to absorb the light from her flashlight, which illuminated only the things that were in its immediate path.

Dani shrieked when something brushed against her face, but a quick swish of the flashlight revealed a long string hanging from a bare light bulb in the ceiling. Giving it a tug, she was surprised to find that it worked. Not that it offered enough illumination to dispel the gloom. Instead, it cast an eerie, yellow glow that faded before it reached the stairs.

Cautiously, Dani made her way around a corner into the heart of the cellar. Bandit's barking sounded like it came from another world and Dani wondered if the sensation was similar to that of a book she'd just finished. One of her favorite protagonists had been trapped exploring the underground caves in New Mexico, something Dani hoped never to experience. She'd never allow herself to be caught in a situation where she'd have to test the possibility of severe claustrophobia.

The place was relatively bare, with a few boxes sitting open on shelves along one wall. Spider webs and dirt were everywhere, but it was a large room with planked flooring that was curved and warped with the dampness. Dani was around the corner from the stairs, shining her flash light beam into the boxes, when she thought she heard footsteps above and stood upright, listening intently.

"Noah?" Maybe he came over after work. Or maybe she was imagining things. She didn't hear it again, but she'd seen enough. Turning to go back up the stairs, she jumped like she'd been shot when the metal door clanged shut, cutting off the light from above ground, followed by a sharp scraping sound and the whish of leaves.

Damn! What the hell was that? She stood, frozen, willing her heart to slow down so she could hear something besides the incessant beating in her ears. Probably the wind blew the door shut, she told herself. She hadn't been able to lay it all the way back against the ground due to the pile of branches and leaves. A good gust could do that, couldn't it? Not likely, a voice inside her head told her. Well, she could believe it if she wanted to, she retorted in her mind.

Climbing the stairs, she reached up and gave the door a gentle nudge. Nothing. Another push, a little stronger this time. It didn't budge. Finally, she pushed on it with all her might, resting the flashlight on the step between her feet. The door was not going to move!

Pushing and banging with all the strength she had, and ignoring the rising panic that threatened to choke her, she was finally rewarded by the sound of Bandit barking steadily at the door. Collapsing on the top step, she dissolved into a shivering heap, terrified at the thought that maybe someone had locked her in. All of Beth's spooky insinuations came flying back, causing goose flesh to rise on her arms.

Breathing deeply, she tried to stay calm. Of course no one locked her in. It was the wind, nothing more. Noah would come over after work and find her and they'd laugh about it over dinner. She refused to even consider the fact that they'd made no definite plans for today, or that she didn't even know if he'd come over, much less look for her if he didn't find her right away.

Whistling, Noah cut a path through the trees between his house and Dani's. He'd been doing a lot of whistling lately. Relationships, at least good ones, were a rare commodity in his line of work. Most of the cops he knew were divorced, or acted like they were. After his first marriage ended in disaster, he'd endured a lot of years of dead end relationships. Either the girls were scared of what he did for a living, or they wanted too much too soon. Nearing the age of forty, with all he'd seen, he really didn't blame them.

He'd pretty much decided he'd live the rest of his days alone when he moved to Tyler, aside from an occasional outing and some casual sex. He had no problem getting dates, that part was easy. It was brain food he craved. Spending time with a woman who was thoughtful and intelligent. Someone who at least tried to understand why he did what he did.

When he first met Dani, he had to admit, it was the idea of convenience that appealed to him. An attractive woman, happily pursuing her own career, who made few demands on him and lived right next door. But one night with her shot that all to hell. Little by little, he found himself wanting to call her just to hear her laugh, or to tell her about something interesting he'd seen that day because she always seemed to know exactly what he was talking about, even when he didn't say it very well.

Of course the idea of joining her in her bed was never far from him, and he'd taken many a cold shower after leaving her at night. But what they had was too rare, too important for him to jeopardize it by moving too fast. Dani Jones was a very real part of his heart. He could wait until she knew that.

Exiting the trees at the low end of the driveway, his heart skipped a beat as he saw her car in the drive, much the same way it had as a child when he discovered the prize at the bottom of the Cracker Jack box. He knew it would be there, but it wasn't quite real till he touched it. Still whistling, he took the front porch stairs in one leap and called, "Anybody home?"

He already had the screen door open when he realized there was no answer. "Anybody home?" he tried again. "Dani?" Silence. She must be here somewhere. Creeping cautiously inside, he listened for any sound that might indicate her whereabouts. "Dani?"

Thinking maybe she was on the phone, he moved into the kitchen. Nothing. Her purse and Daytimer were there on the counter, though, along with her car keys. Maybe she was upstairs. It was odd that there was no music playing, and he didn't think she'd be working up there with the front door wide open.

"Dani?" he called a little louder this time, taking the stairs two at a time. The first door he came to was her spare room. He'd helped her move some boxes in there not long after they met. Opening the door carefully, he saw that it was dark and everything was just like he'd last seen it.

On full alert now, he moved back into the hall, calling her name again before opening the bathroom door. There was no sign of her in there, or in her bedroom either. A familiar feeling of dread crept over him as he headed back down the stairs and out the door.

"Dani!" he yelled full out, ignoring the fear that gripped his heart irrationally. She was probably just gone for a walk or something. "Dani!" he called again, breaking into a run when he heard Bandit's answering bark. Moving around the back of the house, he could see that she'd been there. The lawnmower and weed-eater were propped beside the garage door, and a stack of trash bags bordered the back of the yard. The rake was laying half buried in a pile of leaves like it had been casually abandoned.

"Bandit! Where's Dani?" he called, seeing the dog wiggling with excitement on the far side of the yard. "Where is she, bud?" he called, looking around the perimeter at the trees that bordered her land. Bandit barked again, but didn't budge from the spot. Odd, he usually had to brace himself for the onslaught of the little mutt flinging himself at his legs. A feeling of apprehension went with him across the yard and he stopped, listening, about ten feet from where the dog stood. Was he imagining things? "Dani?" he called, thinking he heard her call his name.

Faintly, so distant it sounded like the wind, he heard, "Noah!"

Two steps closer, he saw the metal under the dog's feet, almost completely covered in leaves. He was on it instantly, shoving the leaves aside to reveal two metal doors with a thick branch jammed under the handles. Removing the branch, he jerked the door open, revealing Dani's tear stained face.

She leapt at him, flinging both arms around his neck as she sobbed. Lifting her off the steps, he carried her effortlessly to a grassy spot a few feet away and sat down with her in his lap.

"What happened?" he asked gently, smoothing the hair back from her eyes.

"I don't know," she wailed, still shaken with sobs.

"I'm sure as hell glad you got that dog," he said, scratching Bandit behind the ears as he snuggled up next to his mistress.

"Me too," she said, pulling away from his chest as she tried to compose herself. "Did he help you find me?"

"Rooted to the spot," Noah answered, still feeling a little shaky. "I didn't even know this place was here. How'd you get in there? I could barely see the doors through the pile of leaves."

Dani rubbed the tears from her face and straightened her shoulders, already feeling foolish. "I know. I was raking when I found it so I decided to go in there and take a look around. But while I was down there, the door blew shut and I couldn't get out. Dumb, huh?" She tried to laugh, but inside she was still shivering.

"Not dumb," he reassured her, stroking a strand of hair from her cheek. "But I don't see how that door blew shut." Carefully, he eased her off his lap and got up to re-examine the door. When he turned to look at her again, his eyes were narrowed and a frown creased his face. "That branch didn't just happen to blow between the handles either. Did you hear anything?"

She tried to think. "I don't know. I thought I heard footsteps, I thought maybe it was you," she smiled briefly, "but when I called your name…" She didn't like the way it was starting to sound. "I'm sure it was just the wind, Noah. I couldn't get the door to lay flat because of the pile. It just blew shut."

"Uh huh," he didn't believe her. "Ready to go inside? I need to call this in."

Without speaking, she nodded and got to her feet with his help. Once inside, she sank down on the couch, too numb to argue with him. Maybe she was still in shock, but it didn't faze her to hear him telling someone on the phone that she'd been deliberately locked into the cellar. Fifteen minutes later, the place was crawling with cops, asking questions and examining everything in her yard. Dani didn't even begin to relax until it was all over and she sat snuggled up beside Noah on the couch with a steaming mug of Suisse Mocha in her hands.

"You don't have any idea who would do this?" he asked for the umpteenth time.

"Noah, I told you," she said, "I hardly even know anyone around here. Why would someone want to lock me in that cellar? I didn't even know there was a cellar back there. Besides, it was just a branch jammed under the handles, right? Probably Bandit was scratching up there and that's what happened." Utterly exhausted, she felt like her mind was frozen, refusing to even think anymore.

"Maybe," he didn't sound convinced.

"Probably," she argued. "You saw all those branches and leaves. There's no reason in the world someone would do that on purpose." She sounded so convincing she almost believed it herself. "The wind blew it shut and Bandit was scratching around, trying to get me out. That's all it was." Never mind that she didn't hear Bandit barking close by until considerably after the fact. She didn't want to accept anything else.

He studied her face for a moment, obviously not sure if he believed her or not. "You want me to stay tonight?" he asked. "No strings."

"Oh Noah," she hugged him. "I'll be fine, really."

A muscle worked hard, flexing rhythmically beneath his beard. "All right," he said, kissing her softly before he got up. "You call me if you need me, no matter what time it is."

"I will," she said, following him to the door and standing on tiptoe to kiss him again.

"I'll be by in the morning," he said, stepping out the door. "Now let me hear that deadbolt turn before I go."

After the evening's activity, the house seemed incredibly empty after he'd gone. Dani decided to forego her nightly ritual bath and climbed into bed. The mystery she was reading was a little too suspenseful for comfort so she put it up and decided a good night's sleep was what she needed.

Sleep didn't come easy, though, and was filled with bizarre dreams all night. At the crack of dawn, she was wide awake with a throbbing headache and an urge for caffeine. The last twenty four hours were a jagged blur in her head, taunting, tormenting, then moving just out of reach. When it became apparent that she wouldn't go back to sleep, Dani stumbled to the kitchen and started a pot of coffee, then went to retrieve the morning paper from the yard. Since she usually slept in a soft, old pair of sweats and a T-shirt, there was no need to change before going outside. She was halfway up the drive before she stopped and looked hastily over her shoulder.

The sunrise creeping up behind the house was bright and clear, with just a hint of the cold weather soon to come. She'd heard the winters here were more intense than in central Texas and was secretly hoping for the snow she'd rarely seen in Austin. There were still a few birds that hadn't flown south chirping happily in the trees above her head and Dani sincerely hoped she'd catch some of their cheery mood. Scampering back down the drive in bare feet that were starting to get cold, Dani stopped short when Noah emerged from the trees beside the drive.

"Noah! You scared me," she gasped.

"Sorry," he offered her a crooked smile. "You're not usually out this early."

"Oh, and you are?" she asked grumpily, scooting back up the porch steps.

"Always," he said in a voice that was much too cheerful, following her in the door.

"Whatever for?" she asked, pulling another coffee mug out of the cabinet.

"Seems a shame to waste good daylight," he smiled, sitting down in a chair beside her at the kitchen table. "What's for breakfast?"

"Coffee," she grumbled, sipping hers and willing it to work fast.

"I can see you're not a morning person," he observed.

"Brilliant deduction, detective," she grinned reluctantly. If left to her own devices with no early morning classes, she'd probably stay up till four or five in the morning, then sleep till noon or after.

"Investigator," he corrected her with a grin. "What's the plan for the day?"

"I don't know," she yawned. "I'll probably try to keep breathing…"

"Good plan," he nodded, watching her with an amused expression. "And then?"

She scowled at him, wondering if he was this cheerful every morning. "I need to finish up in the yard, then I need to go shopping," she groaned.

"Great!" he said with far too much enthusiasm.

She rolled her eyes and smiled again. Coffee was kicking in and she had to admit, he was cute when he was so happy.

"No eat, no work," he said, looking at her expectantly.

That made her laugh out loud. "Help yourself, the cook's not here." She left him searching the cupboards for something to eat while she padded into the living room and turned on the morning news. A few minutes later, he joined her on the couch with a bowl of cold cereal in hand.

"No wonder you're so scrawny," he mumbled. "No food in there!"

"Scrawny!" she punched his leg playfully, thinking he couldn't have said anything nicer considering the way her hips looked to her in the mirror.

"Picked you up like a feather yesterday, didn't I?" he teased.

"Oh, look!" she said, captivated by a film clip of the annual Rose Dance on the TV. "Have you ever been there?"

"Of course not, silly. I just moved here this spring," he said.

"They say it's wonderful," she said wistfully. Tyler's roses were famous and they made a big deal out of the whole festival every year. "Do you dance?" she asked shamelessly, suddenly aware of how long it had been since she'd been to such a formal affair and how much she missed them.

"I've been known to trip the lights on occasion," he admitted. "Wanna go?"

"Really?"

He shrugged. "I'm game if you are."

"I'd love it, really," she smiled, aware that she was falling deeper and deeper into this relationship with a man she'd known barely more than a month. She wouldn't admit falling in love. It was way too soon and too dangerous. Burn me twice, she thought, shaking her head.

"We better get started if we're going shopping later," he said, getting up and heading for the kitchen.

"We?" she asked, following him to refill her coffee mug.

"Yes, we. You don't think I'll leave you to finish the yard alone after what happened last night, do you?"

Dani felt her eyebrows shoot up in surprise. "I never gave it much thought," she said.

"Well, I won't. Many hands make light work and all that," he smiled. "But only if you'll let me have the rest of the day once we're done."

"Deal," she said before he could change his mind. "Let me get changed then." With that, she flitted up the stairs, vaguely aware that the morning birds' songs were playing in her heart.

Hurriedly, she exchanged her sleeping sweats for a tattered pair of jeans and pulled on her sneakers. Half an hour later, they were busily raking the yard and stuffing garbage bags with Bandit romping around the yard like it was all a big game. A couple of times, Dani looked up from the task at hand to find Noah watching her with an odd expression on his face. He always tried to cover up, or look away before she caught him, but that only made her smile. Maybe she was more ready for a full time relationship than she'd thought.

"That should do it," he said, heaving the last bag on the pile. "Looks good, don't you think?" he scanned the yard with a critical eye.

"You're really a big help," she smiled, her hand on her hip as she squinted into the sunlight that surrounded him.

"One more thing," he said, dusting his hands on his jeans. "Let's take a look in that cellar now that it's daylight out here."

Dani's smile turned into a grimace. She knew she'd need to go back in there sometime, but she couldn't think of anything she'd like less right now. Following him to the door, she saw the remnants of the fingerprinting activities from last night. "Did they find anything?" she asked.

"Not a damn thing," he said. "Not even your prints, from what I heard. Too rusty I guess," he pulled the door open in one swift jerk. With all the leaves and branches gone, it lay flat against the ground. "Ladies first?" he gestured toward the stairs.

"Not even," she shook her head. "You go."

"Chicken shit," he teased, but there was understanding in his eyes. "Watch my six."

"What's a six?" she asked, watching as he slowly descended the stairs.

"Six o'clock. My back," he called from below. "Cop talk."

"Gotcha," she said, not sure she did. "There's a string on the light," she called when she couldn't see him anymore. Instantly, the light came on.

"Hey, this is pretty damn big!" he called. "Must be an old bomb shelter or something." She could hear him moving around in there but had no desire to join him. A few minutes later, he shut off the light and came back up.

"See anything interesting?" she asked, relief flooding her as he closed the door behind him. She'd been worried he'd tell her she had to get back on the horse after she fell or something ridiculous like that.

"Nah. But it's a great storage place. Wish I had one of those."

"Want mine?" she kidded, walking beside him up the hill.

Together, they hauled the filled trash bags up to the road for pickup, then headed for their respective homes to clean up before shopping.

CHAPTER FIVE

Dani was late getting out of class and by the time she arrived at the auditorium for a mandatory staff meeting it was already in progress. Each department head spoke briefly about the planned activities for the upcoming school year and announced their grant applications in progress. Once again, Dani was amazed that the science department as a whole was responsible for such a large amount of grant income. As a Biology lab assistant, she wasn't privy to the financial details of her department, but she was impressed with the amount of funding they hoped to obtain and delighted with the new equipment they'd secure if the grants were awarded.

Once the meeting was adjourned, she made her way to the other side of the auditorium where Beth was the center of a small group. As the group broke up and began to move individually toward the exits, Dani approached.

"Last call! Notes for sale!" Beth announced again, waving a sheaf of papers over her head.

"Stop that, you idiot!" Dani laughed. She should have known. Beth was always looking for ways to make an extra buck.

It was the first full lab staff meeting of the year, and she found it stimulating. It was especially interesting to hear Dr. Crane talking about the upcoming projects for Ophidian. The snake colony was founded back in 1989 and it had gone through a series of ups and downs, but it was thriving now, according to his report. She'd hoped to get a chance to talk with him after the meeting, but he ducked out before they were dismissed. The thought of those students disappearing on her property was never far from her conscious mind.

"Hey, chicky," a gangly young man in wire rimmed glasses approached Beth. "Burn me a copy of those notes, will ya?"

30

"Five bucks," Beth retorted.

"Burger," he negotiated.

"Deal," she smiled. "Dani, this is Mike McKay, better known as the snake charmer. Dani's the one I told you about who bought the old Bailey place," Beth nudged his arm with an elbow.

Dani wasn't sure, but it looked like the smile froze on his face. "Hi, Mike," she smiled at him.

"Hey, what's up?" he said, not quite meeting her eyes.

"You'll have to take her over there and show her all your slithering friends," Beth said, stacking her books and papers. "Wanna go get a burger with us, Dani?"

"Ooh, I wish I could," she said. "I've got a student working on a research project I promised to help. Another time maybe?" she asked, looking up at Mike, who looked strangely relieved. "I'd love to talk to you about Ophidian."

"Sure," he said, shrugging. But his face said not if he could help it.

"Okay. Laters, Dano," Beth waved as they walked away.

"Bye, guys," she answered, doubting if they even heard.

With a sigh, Dani gathered her things and went back to the lab. As it turned out, her student didn't really need much help, but she had to stay in the lab to lock up when he was through. It was the ideal time for her to get started on a research project of her own, but no matter how hard she tried, concentration avoided her.

For some reason, the disappearance of those students really bugged her. It was years ago, and there was nothing she could do about it now, but she just couldn't shake it. Maybe she read too many mystery novels. It seemed like she was suspicious of everything these days.

"Daydreaming?" Dr. Abraham's voice broke into her thoughts. She hadn't even heard him come in.

"A little, I guess," she smiled as he perched on the corner of the desk. Even though she hadn't known him long, she'd become fond of him. His expectations were high, for staff and students alike, but she'd often seen him working with students, one on one, doing everything he could to help them succeed with their projects. It was nice to work with a professor who had a real passion for his work. "Is there something you need me to do?" she asked.

"No, I just saw you in here and thought I'd stop by," he said, looking casually around the lab. Dani waited, not sure what to say. It wasn't like him to have extra time on his hands. "You do good work," he said after a moment.

"Thank you," she said. "So do you."

"You're in master's classes, aren't you?" he asked.

"Yes, sir."

"Decided on a project for your thesis yet?"

"Not really," she said, wondering if he was leading up to something. "I'd like to do something that would appeal to the Center for Disease Control."

"Hmmmmm. I thought I might put in a good word for you with Dr. Crane," he said. "He's had trouble getting enough help over there this fall."

That caught her attention. "At Ophidian?"

He nodded, getting up from the desk.

"That would be great!" she said without a clue what she'd work on over there. She just knew it might help her get some answers.

"You'd like that?" he looked surprised.

"I would, yes," she nodded enthusiastically.

"Good, then," he smiled. "I'll give him a call this afternoon."

"Thank you, Dr. Abraham," she said as he walked toward the door.

"I told you to call me Joe," he smiled again before he stepped through the door.

Wow. She might have a chance to work at Ophidian! She hadn't even considered that it would mean being surrounded by snakes, just that she had to have some answers. She looked up to see David, her student, watching her with a knowing look on his face. "What?" she asked.

"Joe?" he smiled and wiggled his eyebrows.

Dani smiled back, rolling her eyes. "Get over it!"

"Uh huh," he grinned, clearing off the table. "I'm outta here! Thanks for staying late."

"No problem," she waved good-bye as he walked out the door.

Dani was on her own for the evening since Noah was working late and it gave her some much needed time to get caught up on housework and a paper she was writing for her microbiology class. Spending most of the day at the campus, then weeding her gardens as soon as she got in didn't leave much time for anything else. Not if she spent her evenings with Noah, anyway. It also gave her some uninterrupted time alone with her thoughts, but she wasn't at all sure that was a good thing.

For one thing, it made her much too aware of how much she'd come to enjoy having Noah around. Was it possible she was really falling in love with this man? She'd only known him a little while. Maybe she was just trying to replace what she had with Mark. Or what she thought she had.

Summoning what little will power she had left, Dani decided to continue the thought process while scrubbing the bathroom. She'd never resolve everything, but at least the bathtub would be clean. When she finished, she carried the broom into the bedroom and started sweeping up the dust bunnies that magically appeared overnight, but a gorgeous sunset called to her through the window. Fighting the urge to run downstairs and watch from the porch swing, she stood in the window, staring until the sun finally dipped below the tops of the trees.

She was just chiding herself to get back to work when a movement beneath the trees caught her eye. Stepping closer to the window and squinting against the last rays of the sun, she saw a shadow that looked like a man standing between two trees directly across from the house. She stared intently, hardly daring to blink lest it disappear. Was it really someone watching the house? No, it was just a shadow, she told herself. But, when she blinked, it was still there, and it moved! Shadows don't move. At least not when the trees aren't moving.

Realizing she was holding her breath, she inhaled deeply, hoping to slow her increasing heart rate. When it moved again, deeper into the trees, she took a couple of quick steps and grabbed the phone, then went back to the window. She'd already dialed Noah's number when the shadow vanished.

When his voice mail message answered the call, she hung up, not knowing what to say. Why would someone be standing over there watching her house? It was a vacant lot with no other houses for miles around. Could Noah be right about someone locking her in the cellar the other day? It didn't make sense. Just in case she needed it in a hurry, she slipped her cordless phone in the pocket of her sweats and put away the broom. Her cell phone didn't get any reception out here. Too many trees. Once she'd checked the locks on both doors and all the windows, she fixed a bowl of soup and determined she'd put the shadow out of her mind and get at least some of her paper written.

It was actually working, too, until she was interrupted by a sharp knock on the door. All the fear she'd felt earlier came flooding back. Noah never knocked anymore. Wishing she had a peephole in the front door, Dani tried to peek out the curtain, but couldn't see anyone there.

"Who is it?" she asked, keeping her voice low and stern.

"Joe Abraham," was the muffled response. Relief flooded through her as she answered the door.

"Hey, what brings you out here?" she asked, suddenly aware of her house cleaning clothes. The thought of her shabby appearance was followed immediately by the question of whether David was on to something with his teasing. Dr. Abraham wasn't interested in her socially, was he? "I'm sorry," she realized she was staring as he shuffled his feet on the porch. "Come in." She held the door open wide.

"I'm sorry I didn't call first," he said, looking like he felt a bit uncomfortable.

"Oh, no problem, I just wasn't expecting anyone," she said. "I've been cleaning. Would you like some coffee?"

"That would be nice, thank you," he smiled politely. She left him wandering aimlessly in the living room, glad she already had a pot made. In the kitchen, she ran fingers through her hair and tried to check for runaway makeup in her reflection on the side of the toaster. Running a finger under each eye to clean any stray smudges of mascara, she grabbed two mugs and called, "How do you take yours?" She still couldn't bring herself to call him Joe.

"Black is fine," he called, sounding pleasant but a little tense.

Dani filled two mugs and joined him in the living room. Since he'd seated himself on the overstuffed couch, Dani handed him a mug and took a seat in the tattered armchair nearby.

"So, what brings you out here?" she asked again. He hardly ever came in her lab, so it seemed totally out of character for him to show up at her front door unannounced.

"Well, I was out this way and thought maybe I'd drop by..."

Surely he was kidding. In the neighborhood? Dani coughed to cover a laugh that threatened to escape. "Oh." She didn't know what else to say.

He laughed nervously. "That's not true," he admitted. Dani was amused to see a blush creeping into his pale cheeks. "I wanted to ask you about something."

"Okay," she said, crossing her legs and trying to look pleasant while Bandit sniffed curiously around the legs of their visitor.

He sat nervously on the edge of the couch, resting his elbows on his knees. "I've heard you've been asking questions about the students that disappeared six years ago."

This was an unexpected development. It hadn't even occurred to her to ask him about it. Dani shifted, leaning forward slightly to get a better look at his face. "Do you know about that? Were you here then?"

"I started at the lab the year before it happened," he said, fidgeting in his seat. "You seem like a nice person..."

Never one to beat around the bush, she couldn't help herself. "Joe, just say it - tell me what's on your mind," she said bluntly, smiling a little to take the edge off.

"I'm probably making way too much of this," he said, "I just..." He pulled at his tie like it was choking him. "After those kids disappeared, there was another kid, a lab assistant...he reminded me a little of you," he smiled apprehensively. "He worked over in Ophidian, and he was a little older than the others and took his work very seriously. The whole thing bothered him a lot, and he kept asking questions."

"You mean about the students that disappeared?" she asked.

He nodded. "Just wouldn't leave it alone. He said the police weren't doing enough to try to find them. Anyway, the last I heard, he said he was going to comb these woods himself until he found something."

"That sounds logical," she said, her mind working overtime. She'd had the same thought.

"The best I remember, that was a Friday. Monday he wasn't there. By the middle of the week, I heard he'd moved away suddenly," he stared down into his coffee mug.

"I take it you don't believe that," she said solemnly, aware of a tightening in her chest. He looked genuinely distressed.

"I don't know what to believe," he shook his head. "I had a bad feeling about it way back then, but I never said anything. But now.........I just didn't want to risk the same thing happening to you."

Dani was touched by his concern, but didn't like the feelings it evoked. Pictures flashed in her mind of the shadow between the trees this afternoon, and being locked in the cellar last week. "Wow!" she sighed deeply. "So you think I should just stop asking questions and leave it all alone?"

Somehow, being here in her living room, talking like this, Joe seemed much more human, more real. At work he was almost like an automaton, never tiring, rarely making a mistake. Sitting here now, he obviously had feelings and concerns like everyone else.

"I don't know," he looked up at her, his blue eyes filled with concern. "Sometimes I wish I knew what happened, too. Those poor kids," he said. "And I understand the University wanting to keep everything quiet, but......... what are the chances of three students who all worked for Ophidian disappearing without a trace in a couple weeks' time and it wasn't related to the University somehow?"

"Didn't I hear that Dr. Atkinson left not long after?" she suddenly remembered something Beth had said.

"Yes, he did," Joe said, nodding. "That seemed a little abrupt, too, but I didn't have much contact with anyone over there," he shrugged.

"What about Dr. Crane? Was he there then?" she persisted.

He nodded again. "They were partners."

"Well, you know him. Couldn't you ask him about it?"

"No. I don't know him that well, and he made it plain back then that he didn't want to talk about it at all. In fact," he rubbed his chin, "seems like there was some kind of problem with him even talking to the police when it happened."

Already, the wheels were turning in her mind. Noah could get access to all those records, she was sure of it. Glancing up at the clock on the wall, she wondered what time he'd get home. It was already after nine.

"I better get going," he got to his feet. "I'm sorry to intrude. I hope you don't think I'm being too nosy," he smiled.

"Not at all," she said, standing. "I'm glad you told me. I'll be careful," she assured him.

"Good. Do you still want me to call Dr. Crane about you doing some work over there?" he asked as she opened the front door.

"Absolutely," she smiled. "Who knows? Maybe I'll get lucky."

"All right, then," he looked a little disappointed. "Good night."

"Night," she said, closing the door firmly behind him. What an odd conversation! First, he volunteered to talk to Dr. Crane about her working at Ophidian, then he acted like he didn't like the idea. What happened in a few short hours to change his mind? There must be something more he didn't tell her.

She'd already picked the phone out of her pocket and sat down at the kitchen table to call Noah when it occurred to her that she never heard a car start. Jumping up, she peeked out the curtain on the front window, but there was no car in sight.

CHAPTER SIX

The jangling of the phone in Dani's ear woke her from a surprisingly sound sleep. "Hello," she mumbled, reaching for the alarm clock to see what time it was. Three o'clock in the morning!

"Hey, sleepyhead," Noah's voice through the phone warmed her all over.

"Noah, hi," she smiled, snuggling back down under the comforter. Even though the weather was still reasonably mild and she hadn't cranked up the heater yet, it got down in the 40s at night and she liked to keep the window open a crack.

"I woke you, didn't I?" he asked.

"Duh," she chuckled. Like she would be awake at this hour. "It's okay, I missed you." It was dangerous to talk to him in this half sleepy state. Her defenses were almost non-existent.

"I saw your lights on and thought maybe you'd waited up."

"Oh, yeah," she'd forgotten. Feeling a little nervous after Joe left, she couldn't bear the thought of being alone with Bandit in a dark house, so she'd left the lamp on in the living room. "I guess I left the lamp on."

"Is everything all right?"

"I'm fine," she said. "I just felt a little nervous earlier. I thought I saw someone standing in the trees across the road, then my boss came over and I wasn't expecting him…" her voice trailed off.

Noah didn't say anything at all for a moment. "Want me to come over?" he asked finally.

"You don't need to do that," she answered. What she wanted right now was something else again. "Bandit would bark if anyone was out there, right?"

"Did he bark earlier when your boss showed up?"

37

She didn't remember Bandit making a sound until Joe knocked on the door. "No-o, not really," she admitted. She didn't even know where the dog was when she watched the sunset out the window, but she'd have remembered if he was barking at something.

"Let's try him out, then," he said. "I'll be right over. Don't get up till I ring the bell." With that, he hung up the phone.

Dani lay still in the dark, waiting. Bandit was asleep in his usual position at the foot of her bed. A few minutes later, she heard the crunch of footsteps on gravel, but Bandit didn't stir. So much for her theory that Bandit might not be big and ferocious but at least he'd warn her by barking.

Trying hard to stay motionless, she listened as Noah made his way around the front of the house, rattling the downstairs window. She even heard the porch boards creaking beneath his weight before he rang the bell, but Bandit slept on. When the doorbell pealed, she saw him lift his head and cock it like he was wondering if he'd really heard something or was just dreaming.

"Some help you are," she muttered, swinging her feet to the floor. She shivered when she opened the front door, this time from the burst of cold air that entered with Noah. The shiver was followed closely by a rush of warmth as he enveloped her in a hug, letting his hand linger near the small of her back as he followed her to the kitchen.

"He isn't barking yet," he observed.

"You noticed," she said wryly. She put on a pot of coffee, then led him back into the living room and curled up next to him on the couch, tucking her feet up under her to keep them warm. "Where have you been?"

He looked as fresh as if he'd just started the day. If she'd been working around the clock like that, her raccoon eyes would have told the tale.

"I covered a surveillance detail for a guy who got sick," he explained, pulling off his jacket and laying it over her lap. Draping his arm around her shoulder, he pulled her close. "Now, tell me what happened."

"You know, I probably just imagined it," she said, feeling foolish now that he was there. "Do you have to work early in the morning?"

"Nah. I'll go in around noon, probably," he smiled softly. "How about you?"

"My first class is at ten," she said, grateful for that fact now.

"So there's really no reason why you can't stay here with me awhile and tell me what the hell is going on, is there?"

Dani loved the way his brown eyes crinkled up when he smiled and almost seemed to twinkle.

"My boss, Joe Abraham, came over around nine," she said. "It was kind of weird, I mean, he's never said anything personal to me at work at all."

"So, he got personal?" he raised an eyebrow.

"No, not that kind of personal," she nudged him with her shoulder. "I mean talk about anything besides work."

"Just checking," he pretended to be jealous. Or was he pretending?

"Do you want to hear this or not?" she teased. "Okay, then," she continued when he nodded. "He worked here when those kids disappeared, and he said there was another lab assistant who thought they didn't look hard enough for them or something. Anyway, the guy asked a lot of questions and said he was coming back out here to comb the woods himself, then he never came back to school. They said the next week that he moved away suddenly, but it was in the middle of the semester."

His expression told her he was taking it all in. "Why'd he feel the need to come here and tell you all that tonight?"

Dani shrugged. "He said I reminded him of this guy, that I take my work seriously and all that. I think he felt bad because he never said anything back then and didn't want it to happen again. But you know what else? This afternoon, he said he could recommend me to Dr. Crane for some work over at Ophidian, then tonight, he acted like maybe that wasn't a good idea. Weird, huh?"

Dani watched a variety of expressions flicker across his face before it settled into his "cop" expression. To her way of thinking, it was a mask designed to keep anyone from knowing what he was thinking. She imagined there was a ticker tape of questions and possible solutions running directly behind his eyes. His appearance was deceptively casual but she knew his mind was always working.

"Interesting. Did you tell him you'd seen someone out there tonight?"

"No," she shook her head.

"Did you tell him someone locked you in the cellar?"

"No, why?"

"Don't," he said somberly. "Don't tell anyone."

"Noah," she pulled back a little and examined his expression. "You're scaring me."

"No," he shook his head, frowning. "I'm not trying to scare you. I just need to look into some things."

Dani laid her head against his shoulder and closed her eyes. She was tired and it felt so good to have him here.

With twenty minutes before her next student was due, Dani took a chance and laid her head down on her desk. Even though she'd slept later than usual, she didn't sleep well. Bizarre dreams kept intruding then receding from her memory, leaving her with vague feelings of unease and nothing real to blame it on. Every time the dreams came, she found herself alone in the woods running for her life from an unknown pursuer. To further complicate things, she'd awakened this morning tucked safely into her own bed with Noah fast asleep beside her. She must have dozed off on the couch talking to him last night. She didn't remember anything else. At least they were both fully clothed when she woke. There wasn't a chance in hell she could have slept through a session of lovemaking with him.

Lifting her head when she heard the door open, Dani smiled at Joe Abraham.

"Danielle," he smiled back. For some reason, he insisted on using her full name, even though nobody else ever did. "Your student called to cancel for the afternoon. Here's your schedule for Dr. Crane's lab." He laid a slip of paper in front of her. "You start tomorrow when you finish up here."

"Oh, thanks," she picked it up. Three days a week for two hours after her last Biology lab. Not bad. "This is great," she smiled.

He looked as though he might say something, then turned to walk back to the door. Looking back over his shoulder, he said, "You be careful over there."

"Yeah," she said softly, gathering up her things to go home. Maybe, if she hurried, she'd have time for a nap before Noah came over.

Things didn't go the way she'd hoped, though. After she'd changed clothes and let Bandit out for a quick run, she climbed into the bed, but lay wide awake for almost half an hour. Deciding finally that it was probably for the best, she went back downstairs to get a head start on dinner. If she slept this late in the day, she'd no doubt have trouble sleeping tonight anyway.

She'd stopped leaving the front door open after the cellar incident, and felt a rush of shyness when she heard Noah come up the stairs and ring the bell. Even though nothing had happened, it was still disconcerting to find him in her bed when she woke up. Carrying her dishtowel with her, she opened the door and headed back for the kitchen, turning around half way when she realized he was still outside.

"Aren't you coming in?"

"Sure," he wore an odd expression as he stepped just inside the door and stopped.

"What's wrong?" she felt her heart skip a beat.

"You've already started dinner?" he asked.

"Just getting ready to," she said, trying to read the expression on his face. "Is something wrong?"

He closed the door and rubbed a hand over his eyes as he moved to the kitchen table. "Nah," he shook his head, taking a seat. "It's okay. Can we go out to eat, though?" She saw the weariness around his eyes when he looked up at her.

"You sure you want to do that?" she asked. "You look tired."

"I'd rather, if you don't mind," he said. Looking past him out the window, she saw his truck parked behind her car. Usually, he walked over.

"Okay," she said meekly. "I'll just get changed."

She paused long enough to put away the vegetables she'd sat out on the counter, then dashed upstairs. Something was wrong; she didn't care what he said. Trading her jeans for a pair of khaki slacks and a soft sweater, she stopped at the bathroom mirror to touch up her makeup and run a brush through her hair. A spritz of perfume and she was on her way downstairs, but didn't find Noah there. He was waiting in the swing on the porch.

"Ready?" he smiled when she came out the door.

She nodded, following him to the truck after she flipped on the porch light and locked the door behind her. Sitting quietly, she stole occasional glances at his face as he drove into town. This was a side of him she hadn't seen before. Usually he was almost childlike in his openness with her, something she hadn't expected from a cop. But this, this was different.

"This okay?" he asked, pulling up in front of Steak and Ale.

"It's fine." Right now, it didn't feel like anything was okay.

The hostess that greeted them gave them forced congeniality and ushered them rapidly to a secluded room illuminated only by candles.

"How'd you rate the private room?" Dani asked, looking at all the empty tables in the center of the room.

"Gotta know the right people," he smiled, looking a little more like the Noah she knew. A waitress materialized immediately, taking their orders and returning with iced tea for both of them. Dani noticed the girl's eyes giving him the once over. He did look even more attractive than usual. Dark, and brooding. The tight jeans were the only pants she'd seen him in, but instead of the usual snug fitting T-shirt, he wore a dark blue plaid shirt, open at the collar to reveal a significant vee of deeply tanned chest covered with curly golden hair that beckoned for a touch. On top of that, he wore an old black leather bomber jacket that made him look like the quintessential bad boy every girl's mother warned her about.

"So, what's up?" she asked bluntly when the waitress moved away.

He surprised her again by pulling a pack of cigarettes out of his pocket. "Do you mind?"

"No," she shook her head, watching as he lit up.

"I've been checking things out, today," he said, exhaling slowly. "Looks like your boss was right to be worried."

"Really?" she perked up. "What'd you find?"

"Thaddeus Gregory was a lab assistant for Ophidian, and he went to the police several times with ideas, apparently. They did check it out, but nothing came of it. Then, I found a note in one of the files that said he'd moved out of town, so I called to see if I could find him," he looked serious.

"And?"

41

"He's gone," he said simply. "Never showed up anywhere. I ran his social and there's been no income or activity since he left here."

"Well, shoot! What does that mean?" Dani was afraid she already knew.

"I've requested his records from the university so I can get his family information, but according to what I saw, he'd been working steady from the time he was sixteen. It's not likely that he's alive."

Dani tried to process what she was hearing, staring absentmindedly at the smoke curling from the tip of his cigarette. "So, what's your professional opinion of all this?" she asked.

"I don't have enough to open the case back up, but I think I'll nose around a little bit."

She waited, but he didn't say anything. There was something else bothering him, though, she was sure of that. She'd eaten half of her meal, barely tasting it, when he finally broached the subject.

"About last night…" he said tentatively, causing her to look up from her plate. "I hope you don't mind that I stayed. I shouldn't have, but I was worried you wouldn't sleep…" his voice trailed off.

Funny, he didn't look like such an old fashioned gentleman.

"Noah, it's all right."

"No, it's really not," he argued.

"Noah," she reached across the table to take his hand. "Just say it, dammit."

His eyes were drawn to hers and he stared into them for a long time before he spoke again.

"I'm worried about you," he said, finally. "And I want to be there to protect you. But do you have any idea how hard it was not to touch you last night?"

In spite of the distress on his face, a smile tugged at her lips. If he'd seen her dreams, he wouldn't be asking that question. Time to lay the cards out on the table?

"So, touch me, then," she said softly, prompting a groan from him.

"You don't get it," he said roughly. "I could make love to you all night, but if I do, I'm done."

Dani wasn't sure what she expected, but that wasn't it. She didn't even know what he meant. "You're right. I don't get it."

"How can I protect you if I'm not objective anymore? Hell, I sat up half the night wondering if I should pay Abraham a visit, just to make sure he didn't mess with you! What kind of cop is that?"

Dani had no idea any of that would even be an issue. Secretly, she felt a little thrill at the thought that he was jealous but he was too distressed about it to dare say anything like that.

"So, what do we do?"

Sighing deeply, he said, "I don't know. I've tried to figure that out all day. Every time I decided I'd just back off so I could watch out for you, I'd remember how you looked last night, falling asleep on my shoulder. Then, when I saw you again tonight… I really don't want to back off."

Candlelight from the table flickered in his eyes as he held her gaze, making them look like warm, clear brandy.

Dani breathed out a sigh of relief. "Good. Then don't leave me," she whispered, fearing that's exactly what he had in mind. "I don't……… I don't want to be without you, Noah," she said, admitting it to him and to herself for the first time.

He closed his eyes and she waited, holding her breath again until he spoke.

"I don't want that either," he said softly. "Some tough guy, huh?" he grinned for the first time she remembered this evening.

"Can we go now?" she asked, knowing she'd be in his arms in another minute, no matter where they were.

CHAPTER SEVEN

Dani wasn't sure exactly when the decision was made, but she knew by the time they reached her driveway that she wanted to be with him more than she'd ever wanted anything in her life.

It wasn't really even a matter of choice, Dani told herself. It was more a matter of destiny. Any objections raised by her intellect were promptly overruled by her physical responses.

"What are you thinking?" she asked, rolling up on one elbow so she could see Noah's face.

"I'll never tell," he teased, smiling up at her in the moonlight that shone through her bedroom window. "Are you sure about this?" he asked quietly, tracing her jaw line with his finger.

"Make love to me, Noah Russell," she whispered.

***

"Girl! You look like something the cat drug up!" Beth laughed as Dani set her cafeteria tray down on the table beside her.

"Well, thanks!" Dani chuckled. "It's that damn microbiology class that does this!" It was the only class she had on Tuesday and Thursday, but she struggled more in there than in the other three combined.

"Ralston's a bear," Beth agreed. "I waited till I could get Deaver instead."

"Yeah, well Deaver's class was full by the time I registered," Dani said. "If I can't make Ralston happier than I am right now, I'll be sure to get Deaver for the retake."

"Oh, you'll do fine," Beth dismissed that idea. "Ralston's projects are a pain in the ass, but I hear he grades pretty lenient."

44

"I hope so. The instructions are nineteen pages. How am I supposed to remember all that?"

Dani chomped down on her burger, hoping to still the rumbling in her stomach that had gradually increased all morning long. Why was it she was never hungry until she sat down at her desk in the classroom?

"So, you never told me how you like the snake farm," Beth observed.

"I haven't seen much of it," Dani said between bites. "Crane has this system of breaking everybody in on file work for awhile before he lets them near his babies," she smirked.

Beth laughed at that. "That's the big secret," she nodded. "Those snakes aren't really reproducing, Crane is!"

Dani choked on her soda at the wicked gleam in Beth's eye. She'd thought the disparaging rumors about Dr. Crane were exaggerated until she met him. Tall and heavyset, his white lab coat was so tight that she feared the buttons on his belly might pop off at any moment and wondered curiously why he didn't just buy a bigger one or leave it unbuttoned. When she turned her attention to his face, she was taken aback by the intense look of displeasure he wore and studied his face carefully, trying to figure out just what was wrong with it. His once dark hair was now smattered with gray and his eyebrows were nearly white. She'd never seen such long eyebrow hairs and was momentarily mesmerized by the way the hairs seemed to stand up and wave in all directions each time he frowned, which was often. But, she finally figured out it was his eyes that captured her attention. Dark enough brown to look black from across the room, they were incredibly close set for such a large face and she choked back a laugh when she realized they reminded her of the gorilla poster hanging in the zoology room.

"He's a real prize, isn't he?" Dani snickered. Fortunately, after that first interview, she'd hardly seen him. What she'd heard from Joe, coupled with her own first impressions, convinced her she wouldn't learn anything from him about the students' disappearance.

"I don't know how you can stand it," Beth agreed. "He's creepier to me than those snakes."

"I hear you," Dani mumbled around a mouthful of fries. She only had ten minutes to get to the lab, but thankfully it was one of her short days and she'd be out by four instead of six. "I've gotta run," she got up, gathering her trash on the tray. "See you later!"

"Laters!" Beth's melodic voice followed her as she rushed to the door, stopping to drop off her tray.

She'd intended to get to the lab early today, but with her stomach growling and her microbiology paper lacking there was just no way.

"Hi, guys," she said to no one in particular as she hurried into the lab. Several of the students were already waiting patiently at their stations.

Without stopping to put on her lab coat, she dropped her stack of books on the desk and picked up a marker to start writing the day's instructions on the board.

"Okay," she turned to face them when she was finished. "Today's the big day," she smiled. This group was composed mainly of freshmen, most of whom had no real interest in Biology other than meeting the degree requirements for their diplomas. It was amusing at the beginning of the semester, but as the weeks turned into months and the work got more challenging, her amusement faded fast. "For the next four weeks, you'll be dissecting fetal pigs, mounting and labeling the organs, making wet mounts of each one, and writing a paper to describe your findings," she said. "Those of you who still haven't finished your frogs need to do so today. I want everyone's pig signed out before you leave here. Got that?"

Ignoring the murmurs and groans, she hoisted a plastic pail containing the specimens up on the table closest to the desk and said, "I'm ready when you are."

About half the students lined up holding large dissection pans with gloved hands and she watched as they each selected a specimen from the pail. Once everyone settled in, she started her rounds, observing each student in turn and helping out when it was needed. It promised to be a long and tiring day.

***

"I'll be right back," a frazzled young man called over his shoulder, exiting the back door of the office as Noah came in the front.

Scanning the office with a practiced eye, he noted the sparse furnishings and lack of storage. Only one small file cabinet in the corner gave any indication that it was an office at all. He stepped up beside the desk and placed a large hand on the calendar that covered it, twisting it until he could read the handwritten notes. Nothing of consequence there. With one hand in his pocket, he paced back and forth in the small waiting area, idly glancing at the photos of snakes that lined the walls.

He'd finally gotten Thaddeus Gregory's family records from the university's stored records office and the results were pretty much what he expected. Thad's father died last year of a stroke, but Noah reached his mother by phone late this morning. The last time she heard from Thad was six years ago. At that time, he was thrilled with his new job here at Ophidian and never mentioned anything about moving away. Noah's heart sank as he heard the hope in her quivering voice when he introduced himself. It made him all the more determined to find some answers and give the poor woman the closure she needed. The next stop, after getting the records he wanted from the lab, was the dorm where Thad was living prior to his disappearance.

"Sorry I took so long," the young man came back in the same door he'd exited a few moments before. "Can I help you?"

"Yeah, you can," Noah sized him up swiftly. Tall and gangly, his frame could pass for a teenager, but the lines on his face and the expression in his eyes made him seem plenty old enough to have been here awhile. "Tyler PD," he said, flashing his badge. "I need to see a list of employees and volunteers who worked here during these dates," he handed him a slip of paper and watched closely for any sign of recognition.

Narrowed eyes and a furtive glance told Noah he knew something. "What's your name?" Noah asked in a no nonsense voice.

"I'll have to clear this with Dr. Crane," he said, avoiding Noah's eyes.

"I asked for your name," he insisted, stepping between the young man and the door.

"McKay...Michael McKay," he said hesitantly.

"All right, Michael McKay," Noah said, stepping away from the door. "Go ahead and check with Crane if you want, but know this - I can get a search warrant if I have to, but you'll save us both a lot of time and grief if you just get me the list."

"I...I don't have access to the old employee files," he stammered, leaning toward the door like a runner waiting for the starter pistol.

"Then make it quick, would you?"

He didn't have to wait long before Dr. Crane burst through the door, forcing it open so hard it left a dent in the sheetrock where the doorknob struck.

"What the hell is this?" Crane bellowed, striding into the room in an imperial rage.

"Tyler PD, Crane," Noah said in a tone of practiced boredom. "You got a problem with what I need?"

McKay hung back in the open doorway, nervously fingering the slip of paper.

"This case was closed a long time ago! Why the hell should I waste my time digging up old records now?" Crane's face flushed bright red and he trembled with anger.

"Because I want them," Noah said simply, maintaining an even tone.

"I don't give a rat's ass what you want!" Crane shouted. "No warrant, no records!"

Noah took a step forward, staring him straight in the eye. "You got something to hide, Doctor? Is there something there you don't want me to see?"

Breathing heavily with nostrils flaring, he met Noah's stare for a moment, then turned away. "I got nothing more to say to you."

When he moved toward the door, Noah put a hand in the center of his heaving chest to stop him. "I'll be back with a warrant and those records better be here," he warned. "If they disappear, you and I will finish this outside, get it?"

He didn't wait for an answer.

Once he got outside, Noah used his cell phone to call the station and request the warrant. He lit a smoke, then glanced at his watch. It was after 3:00. Chances were good he wouldn't see the warrant before morning. With an exasperated sigh, he headed off toward the dorms. Half an hour and four offices later, he was standing in the same spot, knowing little more than he did before. The dorm director in charge when Thad lived there was long gone and the office wouldn't release his information until Noah produced a warrant. They needed to cover their butts, he knew, but his frustration was mounting and he was losing his edge.

Almost to the truck when he realized it was time for Dani to get off work, he turned and headed back to the labs. After spending a couple of incredible nights in her bed, she'd insisted he go home last night or she'd never get any work done. A smile tugged at his lips as he took the stairs two at a time. For someone who'd managed to successfully avoid romantic entanglements for fifteen years, he was in way over his head this time. No turning back.

Locating the lab quickly, he slipped in the far door and stood, leaning against the back wall, watching. She hadn't noticed him yet and looked like she'd about had it with this group.

"Agh! No way!" screeched a child-like waif with a mop of blonde curls while a trio of lanky young men looked on with amusement. They were crowded around something at the front table and Noah saw Dani's head jerk up with a pained expression.

"Get over it, Samantha!" Dani called from where she stood, stooped over, apparently engrossed in something another student was doing.

"But Ms. Jones, surely you don't expect me to put my hand in *there!*" she wailed, using all her innate abilities to play to her adoring audience.

Noah's eyes bounced back to Dani in time to see a flash of fire shoot from her cobalt blue eyes. "Only if you expect to pass this class," she warned.

The ball's in your court, kiddo, he thought, watching the display of emotions on the girl's face as she weighed her options.

"Ms. Jones," she whined again, "I'll cut up the stupid pig, but what difference does it make who gets it out of the bucket?"

Dani was already leaning over the student beside her and Noah chuckled under his breath at the expression she wore when she looked at the girl again.

"Oh, let's see," Dani said loudly. "How about the difference between an F and an A? Is that clear enough for you?" She didn't wait for an answer, but turned back to the boy she'd been working with. "Philip, you've sliced too deep on your initial incision and cut through half the organs showing. You'll just have to toss that in the incinerator bucket and start again next week," she snapped the gloves off her hands as she walked back toward the front desk. "Call me before you start next time and I'll help you not to do it again," she flashed a quick smile at Philip. "All right everyone, time's about up. Get your specimens labeled and stored in the fridge, then clean up your stations. You'll lose a letter grade if I have to clean up your mess!"

It was interesting to watch her work. The white coat made her look professional, more in charge, and her method of dealing with a roomful of rowdy teenagers told him she was stronger and more capable than he first thought. She still hadn't looked at him standing in the back of the room, even though several of the students had glanced his way, no doubt wondering who he was.

Noah started toward her desk when he saw her sit down, then stopped when a man in a white coat came in the door on the other side of the room and made a beeline for her. Her boss, maybe? Tall and thin with stylish black hair, he looked like a doctor out of a soap opera.

Adjusting his position so he could see the two of them talking through the group of students coming and going through the aisle as they cleaned their tables, his suspicious mind was rewarded when he recognized a look of veiled admiration in the doc's eyes as Dani smiled up at him. The guy had the hots for her.

Unwilling to just stand there staring, Noah stepped back out in the hall and waited until most of the students were gone. When he entered the room again, the last of the students were going out the other door and the doctor was nowhere in sight. Dani was putting the last of her papers in her book bag when she locked eyes with him coming through the door.

"Hey, why'd you sneak out of here like that?" she asked, stopping long enough to give him a quick hug and a kiss on the cheek.

"You saw me?"

"Yes, right before you left. Why'd you leave?"

He shrugged, feeling a little churlish. "I thought you might need a little privacy while your boss put the move on you," he said, half joking.

"Get real!" she laughed. "You're dreaming. Come on, let's get out of here." Crossing the room with books in hand, she turned off the lights and stood waiting for him by the door.

"You're in denial," he countered, holding the door open for her.

They walked together down the deserted hall to the outside door. "You're serious, aren't you?" she asked with a note of surprise in her voice.

"Did he ask you out?" he looked straight ahead as they walked to the parking lot.

"Well, not exactly," she hedged, studying his face. "He just said maybe we could talk over lunch tomorrow."

He didn't speak again until they reached her car and he could look her in the eye. "What'd you say?"

The confusion in her eyes made him wish he hadn't started this.

"I said okay," she said. "Geez, Noah, he's my boss for God's sake! He just wants to know how your investigation is going."

"Really? Then why didn't he want to take me to lunch?" he wished he could snatch the words back as soon as he'd spoken. "I'll see you later," he offered a tight-lipped smile then turned toward his truck.

CHAPTER EIGHT

What a lousy day! Dani frowned as she got out of the car. First her micro class, then whining students in the lab, and, whatever was the deal with Noah?

"Hey, Bandit," she bent over to scratch the scruff of his neck as he greeted her at the door. If only it was Friday.

Dropping her books on the table beside the computer, Dani trudged up the stairs to change clothes. Homework could wait. Right now, she needed to get outside and hope the wind would clear her brain.

Feeling a little more relaxed in an old pair of jeans and comfy V-neck sweater about three sizes too big, Dani called Bandit and headed outside. The day was crisp and clear, warm, considering it was mid-November. While Bandit scampered around the yard, leaving his doggie mark and chasing anything that moved, Dani knelt beside her tiny plot of vegetables, pulling weeds and picking a stray tomato here and there that just might be okay to eat.

The garden hadn't offered much in the way of bounty, which was a little disappointing, but she got a really late start and it was turning cold. Still, it gave her a feeling of being productive and semi-self-sufficient. When she moved to the other side of the garden, she was pleasantly surprised to find she had a good supply of okra ready for picking. She grabbed a basket from the porch and plucked everything off the stalk that looked big enough to cook.

Setting the basket back on the porch, she browsed the flowerbeds, pulling a stray weed here and there, then realized she hadn't seen Bandit in awhile. "Bandit?" she called, straightening up and scanning the yard. "Bandit!"

An answering bark drifted back through the trees across the road.

"Bandit! Come here, boy!" she walked toward the road.

It wasn't like him to run off like this. Crossing the road swiftly, she tucked her hands in her pockets as she entered the woods and felt the temperature drop several degrees. A canopy of leaves completely obliterated the sun and created an eerie, isolated feeling, even though the road and her house were still plainly in view. On impulse, she turned to her right and made her way over to the spot she imagined she'd seen the shadow watching her bedroom window.

Did she imagine it? A shiver crossed her back as she remembered the shadow of a man she thought she saw. There was nothing out here, not for miles. The whole time she'd lived here, she'd only seen a handful of cars pass by. If someone was over here, the only thing they *could* be looking at was her house. But why? It still didn't make sense to her. She didn't have anything anyone would want.

There was nothing on the ground to indicate that anyone had been there. Just the same mishmash of leaves and twigs and pine needles that blanketed the entire area. Using the toe of her shoe, Dani shuffled the piles around a little, not really expecting to find anything. With a last glance up at her window, she turned and moved deeper into the woods, headed in the general direction of the rustling noises she assumed came from Bandit's explorations.

About twenty feet further in, she spied a lone cigarette butt and stooped to pick it up. Newport menthol. Strangely enough, it was the only piece of trash she'd seen. No paper, no candy wrappers. Nothing. Just nature. She stopped with a gasp as a garter snake slithered across her path. Harmless, she knew, but it made her shudder just the same. Hopefully, she'd find the information she needed at Ophidian before she'd be expected to work inside the lab where she'd have to actually handle the reptiles. Dissecting a dead snake was one thing, but allowing it to slide over her arms and around her neck was out of the question.

"Bandit!"

It was really getting dark in the shadow of the trees. If she didn't locate him soon, she'd have to head back without him. The last thing she wanted was to get lost in here. She'd traveled far enough that she couldn't see the road or the house anymore. When she stopped and listened, there was no sound except for the slight rustling of the wind through the leaves. Shit! Would anything go right today? Keeping an eye on the ground in case that little snake had friends, she trudged wearily back toward the road. Bandit would have to find his own way home.

It was dark by the time she got her garden tools put away, and considerably colder than it was earlier. Inside the house, it wasn't much warmer. After several tries, Dani got the pilot light lit on the furnace, then wrinkled her nose at the acrid smell of heated air the first time the heater's turned on for the season.

A whine and a scratch at the front door told her Bandit found his way home and she opened the door, rebuking him soundly for running off as if he understood.

"Guess you're hungry, now, huh?" she smiled as the little dog looked up at her with adoring eyes, wagging his whole body with his scrawny tail. Wondering if a good grooming would approve his scruffy appearance any, Dani went to the kitchen and opened a can of dog food, emptying it into Bandit's dish as he watched eagerly. She sank down on a nearby chair and watched him devour his food like he hadn't eaten in weeks. With a sigh she looked up at the clock. It was after seven.

Determined not to let that last exchange with Noah upset her, and pointedly ignoring the fact that he'd ordinarily be here by now, Dani made herself a quick sandwich and a glass of Pepsi, then sat down in front of her computer. Maybe, just maybe, she could finish that microbiology paper tonight and be done with it!

With Bandit curled up on the kitchen rug, she got right to work and soon was immersed in note cards with library references and overriding the grammar check on the word processing program. The phone rang, abruptly breaking her concentration, and she was surprised to note it was almost ten o'clock.

"Hello," she said, expecting to hear Noah's voice.

Instead, a deep, gravelly voice said, "Get out of that house if you know what's good for you."

"Who is this?" she demanded, jumping up so fast her chair fell over backwards. The line was silent except for the random static that usually accompanied a mobile phone or a cordless reaching the outer edge of its range. "Who is this?" she asked again.

Click.

Following a hunch, she went to the front window and peeked out just in time to see taillights disappearing down the road. Was Joe Abraham right? Was someone upset because of all the questions she'd been asking? Suddenly feeling very apprehensive, she turned the music down on the CD player so she could hear if anyone approached the house before she sat back down at the computer. But the longer she thought about it, the more her apprehension turned to anger.

She'd been through a lot to get where she was today. And this house might not be perfect, but it was hers and nobody was going to scare her out of it! If they didn't like the fact that she was trying to find out what happened on *her* property, they'd just have to get over it!

Newly motivated, she attacked the paper again, determined to finish it before she went to bed so she could focus on other things. Then, tomorrow, she'd do some digging at Ophidian.

***

Friday lab was Dani's favorite. Partly just because it was Friday. But mainly because it consisted of graduate students who rarely needed her help and it gave her time to work on her own projects. And, since they were as anxious to start the weekend as she was, they were usually gone long before the four o'clock deadline. Consequently, she was packed up and ready to go to Ophidian by 3:30.

She'd had a little trouble sleeping last night, more because of concern about Noah than because of the stranger who'd called. The stranger, she'd written off to a prank due to her incessant questioning on campus. It took a little longer to convince herself that Noah was just wrestling with the closeness of their relationship and needed a little space. Truthfully, she could use some of that space herself. As much as she loved being with him, she'd not been able to shake that nagging feeling that maybe it was just too much too soon. Everything in her wanted to trust him completely. It was her own judgment she wasn't ready to trust.

With new determination to ferret out the facts and let the relationship with Noah work itself out in time, Dani got an early start on the day. Classes sped by uneventfully and she even looked forward to her lunch appointment. Purposely ignoring the fact that Noah wouldn't like it, she'd enjoyed eating lunch with Joe Abraham. He was a little hard to get to know, but the more she talked to him, the more she liked him. He was single, like her, but for a different reason. He'd married the summer after his college graduation and had high hopes for the future. Dani was surprised to learn that his wife, Paula, joined the university team the same time he did, but she took a job with Ophidian.

When he showed her a snapshot he had tucked away in his wallet, she smiled. They looked so perfect together, wearing their new matching lab coats and beaming at one another in front of the lab building. Tragically, she'd been killed by a hit and run driver just three months after they got here. No wonder he had a special interest in what went on at Ophidian. It was the last link he had with Paula.

Their lunch had been brief, and Dani couldn't help feeling a little guilty. But she couldn't believe Noah was right about Joe. He was just a lonely man looking for a little companionship. Somehow she'd have to convince Noah that he had nothing to worry about. When he finally called last night, she was close to finishing that paper she was working on and begged off, promising they'd get together tonight. He'd sounded disappointed, and was very apologetic for the way he'd acted earlier, but she knew if he showed up at her house they'd have wound up in the bed with her forgotten paper downstairs where she left it. Now, at least, the paper was done and they had the whole weekend in front of them.

The Ophidian office was deserted when she arrived. Dani stacked her books on the floor behind the desk, then hung up her jacket. Hoping she wouldn't cross paths with Dr. Crane, she ventured down the hall in search of Mike. Unofficially, he was the one she answered to.

"Oh, good, you're here," he said when he saw her. "Come give me a hand with something."

Before she could answer, he ducked back through the door. Swallowing her apprehension, she followed him tentatively into the lab.

"Over here," he called as she entered.

The room was dark, lit only by the hood lamps on the fifty-gallon aquariums that lined the walls, full of snakes, no doubt. Dani took a deep breath and let the door close behind her. Cautiously, she maneuvered her way through a maze of tanks until she reached his side.

"I take it you've never been in here before," he said, arms draped over the tank in front of him.

"No," she answered, trying not to sound as nervous as she felt. That little garter snake she saw last night had nothing on these guys.

"Meet Lamprophis fuliginosis, more commonly called the brown house snake," he pulled a four foot specimen out of its glass enclosure with both hands.

It took everything she had not to jump back as he held the writhing reptile out for her to admire.

"Wow," was all she could say.

With tiny beads for eyes and a disgusting tongue that flicked in and out of its mouth, the snake squirmed and undulated, trying to free itself from his gloved grasp.

"What are you doing?" she played nonchalant.

"Moving these into clean quarters," he gestured to the line of aquariums along the wall.

Oh God please don't ask me to do that, she thought.

"Kathy's sick today so I need you to help me finish up."

"Oookay," she drawled. "I've never done this. I assume they aren't poisonous…"

The quizzical expression on his face told her she'd made a mistake.

"Of course not," he said. "They'll bite, though, if you give 'em a chance. I don't want you to hold them; I just need help getting the lids on the containers. They're fast little critters," he laughed. "We've had to chase two down already this afternoon."

Terrific, she thought, stifling a groan. "Okay, just tell me what to do."

"Grab that," he nodded at a cover propped on another aquarium. "When I put her in there, hold it over the top and push down hard as soon as I pull my arms out."

She nodded, taking the cover in both hands.

"Don't budge," he warned, "she'll push against it and she's stronger than she looks."

Shit. She looks strong enough, Dani thought. Luckily, she was tall enough to reach it without trouble, and the first transfer went smoothly, even though her heart was pounding in her ears. Gradually, they worked their way down the line and her trepidation lessened as she got more accustomed to looking at the snakes.

"Not bad," he congratulated her as she snapped the last cover in place. "Not bad at all."

Dani didn't know whether to thank him or beg him to never ask her to do it again. She decided on the former.

"Thanks," she smiled. "Interesting work. Are there any more?" she asked hesitantly.

"Nope, we got it for today," he said, pulling off his gloves and shoving them in the pockets of his coat. "You guys 'bout done?" he called to the two men working along the other wall.

"Got it!" one of them answered.

"Hey, have ya'll met Dani?" Mike asked, walking to the other side of the room. Reluctantly, she followed him, hanging back as they snapped the cover on the tank in front of them.

"Nope," the tall one said, turning to look at her curiously. He was taller than six feet, and looked about twenty with a plain face and a lock of brown hair that persistently fell in his eyes.

"Dani, this is Jeff Dryden, and that," he pointed to the shortest of the pair, "is Emil Betancourt. Dani Jones, guys." Apparently Mike felt he'd done his duty because after he spoke, he just walked away and left her standing there.

"Welcome Dani," Jeff offered with half a smile before turning back to his work. Emil sort of grunted and carried on without so much as a look in her direction.

"Nice to meet you," she said in a flat voice that belied her words, then walked rapidly out of the room.

She found Mike in the file room and asked if there was something else that she needed to work on today, but he couldn't think of anything. While she was standing there, waiting, Emil stuck his head in the door.

"Mike, I gotta go, man," he said, pointedly ignoring her.

"Sure," Mike said without looking up from the file he was reading. "See you next week."

When she turned to look at Emil, he was already looking at her with narrowed eyes. Speculating about something. It was a strange environment for her. Usually, she got along well with just about anybody she worked with. But here at Ophidian, everyone she met seemed suspicious. Some of them were just plain unfriendly.

Without a word, he turned and she heard his footsteps pounding down the hall until he hit the exit door with a thud. It clanged shut a few moments later.

"There it is!" Mike said, more to himself than to her. Seconds later, he was out the door.

"I'm glad ya'll need my help," she muttered sarcastically under her breath. Oh well, if he didn't tell her what to do, she'd just find something. After all, she was scheduled to work until six.

Not sure exactly what needed the most attention, she decided to start right where she was. The file room was filled with clutter and the trash was overflowing. It wasn't a large room in the first place, and seemed smaller because of the dim light from a bare bulb in the center of the ceiling. The paint might have been off white once, but now it was all yellowed and peeling in some places to reveal splotches of gray.

Six four-drawer file cabinets were spaced erratically around the walls and a rickety table, accompanied by two wobbly, wooden folding chairs, was propped against a far corner. There were no labels on the file cabinets, but if the stacks of files sprawled randomly across every available surface were any indication, the filing system was in dire need of reorganization.

Once she'd removed the deteriorating coffee cups and wads of paper collecting dust on the table, she gathered the loose files and stacked them there. It was a miracle Mike was able to find anything in here. After looking through the individual folders, it seemed to her that they were grouped haphazardly by species. Rummaging through the overstuffed file drawers, she finally came up with a list of all the species maintained within the colony and painstakingly reproduced it in pencil on an available legal pad:

Colubridae
Checkered garter snakes (Thamnophis marcianus)*
Brown house snakes (Lamprophis fuliginosis)*
Trinket snakes (Elaphe helena)*
Chinese corn snakes (Elaphe rufodorsata)*
Radiated snakes (Elaphe radiata)*
Egyptian diadem snakes (Spalerosophis diadema)*
Madagascar Cat-eyed snake (Madagascarophis colubrina)*
Madagascar Giant Hognose snake (Leioheterodon madagascarensis)
Northern pine snake (Pituophis melanoleucus)*

<u>Pythonidae</u>

Brazilian rainbow boas (Epicrates cenchria)*
Spotted pythons (Anterisia maculosis)*
Mexican new world python (Loxocemus bicolor)
Calabar burrowing python (Calabaria reinhardtii)
Sunbeam snake (Xenopeltis concolor)

<u>Viperidae</u>
Southern copperhead (Agkistrodon contortrix)*

Those were further separated into the species that were actively breeding and those that were not. When she heard the exit door slam again, she glanced at her watch and was startled to find that it was almost seven. Time flies when you're having fun. Hoping that what she'd started would still be waiting for her when she returned on Monday, she left things where they were, gathered her books and took off. She still had to pick up some dog food from the store before she went home.

CHAPTER NINE

Noah was waiting for her on the porch when she pulled in, with Bandit happily romping in the yard.

"Sorry I'm so late," she called as soon as she got out of the car. "Have you been here long?"

"Nah," he shrugged, bounding down the steps to take her books.

She fumbled a minute and nearly stumbled in the door when Bandit rushed past her legs and made a beeline for his water bowl in the kitchen, slurping noisily.

"How was your day?" she asked, dropping her purse on the table and retrieving her books from him.

"Long," he said. "I'm glad it's over."

"You and me, both," she said with a sigh, giving him a quick kiss on the cheek. "I missed you, you know."

He smiled at that. "Yeah."

"If you'll give me a minute, I want to change before we go," she said.

"Sure," he plopped down on the couch as she headed for the stairs.

One good thing about Noah, she thought, scrounging for jeans in the closet, she never felt underdressed around him. Usually, when they went out for dinner on Fridays, it was for something casual like pizza or burgers, or his beloved Mexican food.

Dani heard him calling something up the stairs but she couldn't quite make out what he said.

"Huh?" she yelled, moving nearer the door.

"I asked, did Bandit get away again this morning?"

"No, why?" she answered, zipping her jeans and pulling a sweater over her head, obstructing her hearing again. "What?"

Dropping to her knees, she pulled back the comforter that had slipped off the edge of the bed, searching for her other tennis shoe. Making the bed in the morning wasn't something that happened often. There it was, under the foot of the bed. She reached for it, and almost had it when her hand froze, suspended in mid air.

To the left of her shoe, hidden by the comforter, a huge snake was coiled, watching her intently. She heard herself screaming maniacally inside her head, but no noise came out. *They're fast little critters*, she remembered Mike saying. *They'll bite.* She had no idea if it was the same kind of snake, but she wasn't thinking too clearly right now.

Dani started to retract her hand and back away slowly, but each time she moved, it moved, like it was playing with her. Stalking her. She had a flash of a movie she'd seen with a snake charmer playing a little dancing game with a cobra. She didn't want to play that.

Try something else, she told herself, listening to Noah holding a muffled conversation with Bandit downstairs and wishing desperately that he'd come after her. Leaving her extended hand still, she put all her weight on her knees and slowly lifted her left hand, hoping she could reach the comforter and slide it over, but the snake inched forward again when she moved. It was only two feet away; she didn't think she could get up and out of reach in time.

Terrified, she opened her mouth, holding perfectly still.

"Noah?" the voice that squeaked from her lips was too low for him to ever hear downstairs. It was good, though, the snake didn't seem to mind her voice. She tried it a little louder.

"Noah?"

"Did you call me?" he yelled.

One more time.

"Noah, come here," she said as loud as she dared, breathing a huge sigh of relief as she heard him get up. When she heard his footsteps top the stairs, she said, "Don't let Bandit in here!"

"He's asleep downstairs…are you all right?"

Out of the corner of her eye she saw him standing in the doorway with an incredulous expression on his face. Standing, bent over as she was with one hand extended, she must have looked like an acrobat that got stuck.

"There's a gigantic snake under here and it comes closer every time I move," she said, not daring to look away.

Lowering himself to a squatting position, he peered under the bed. "Whoa! Hold on," he said, disappearing as she heard him bounding down the stairs. He reappeared a moment later holding a broom. "I can scoop it, or I can shoot it," he looked at her seriously. "Which would you prefer?"

"Jesus! I don't know," she hissed. "Just get it out of here."

He crept toward her slowly.

"I thought if I dropped the comforter in front of it so it couldn't see me…but I can't reach it." Dani's back was starting to ache from crouching in the same position for so long.

"Okay," he said, standing beside and a little behind her. "Hold still."

It all happened so fast, she wasn't sure how he did it, but she saw the broom come over her head and knock the comforter to a heap in the floor. That was all she needed to see. She was out of the room and down the stairs in a flash. She stood shivering in the middle of the living room, listening to Noah cursing and banging around, and keeping a cautious eye on the floor around her feet. He emerged victorious minutes later, descending the stairs with a dead snake draped over the broom handle.

"Could you get the door for me?"

Mechanically, she moved to the door and opened it wide, shrinking back as he passed. When he came back inside, she was sitting on the couch with her feet tucked safely up under her.

"You okay?" he asked, sitting down beside her.

"Uh huh," she said numbly. She really wasn't, but he knew that. "Thanks."

"I'll get your shoes," he said, getting up. Bandit came out of the kitchen and joined her on the couch, nuzzling her arm with a wet nose.

"Hey! What were you saying about Bandit before?" she called.

"I don't know," he came back down the steps with her shoes in hand. "Oh, I asked if he got away this morning. He was outside on the porch when I got here."

"You're kidding," she said, taking her shoes from him and putting them on. "He was inside when I locked up like he always is. I thought you used the spare key to let him out."

Noah's eyes narrowed. "Come on," he said with a stern look on his face. He extended his hand to help her up, then bent over and scooped Bandit up with one arm.

"What?"

"Get your purse and pick me up at my house," he said, opening the front door. "I'm gonna take Bandit over there while we're gone."

Dani felt the color leave her face. "You don't think there's another one in here somewhere do you?"

"I don't want to take any chances," he said grimly.

She grabbed her purse and hurried out the door after him, locking it with trembling hands. He was waiting for her on his porch when she drove up. Putting the car in park, she got out.

"You drive," she said walking around to get in on the passenger side.

Laying her head back against the seat, she shut her eyes and tried to make some sense out of what just happened. Noah must have been doing the same because he didn't utter a word until they pulled into the parking lot of El Chico's.

"Still hungry?" he asked seriously.

She nodded, getting out of the car. "It was just a brown house snake, right?" she asked, walking through the door he held open for her.

"Yep."

Dani smiled, starting to relax a little. She was getting used to his moods, too. When he felt tense or unhappy about things, his vocabulary dwindled to sharp, one syllable words.

In spite of the Friday night crowd, they were seated right away in a red vinyl booth near the kitchen. With a cold beer and a bowl of fresh chips and salsa, he seemed more at ease.

Dani picked up a chip and munched on it, watching him expectantly. Already, the incident in her bedroom seemed far away – like it happened in another life. Not that she didn't know it would seem all too real again, once she was back there. Still, the time they'd spent apart made her all the more glad to be with Noah again, regardless of the circumstances.

"Well, I wish I knew what the hell that was," he said finally, his usually light brown eyes dark as thunderclouds.

"It was scary, that's what it was," she answered. "I don't know what I'd have done if you weren't there."

"I can fix that," he smiled, but the act didn't yet reach his eyes.

Dani's heart warmed as she watched the brooding frown deepen and the muscle working rhythmically in his jaw. It was a new feeling to have a man care about her the way Noah did. Even in the midst of terror, she'd been sure if she could just get him in there, everything would be all right. She couldn't help but be aware that ten years of marriage with Mark had never provoked the same feeling and shook her head to prevent that line of thought from continuing.

"I guess I better check the foundation and make sure everything's sealed up good," she mused, shifting in her seat so the waitress could set down her plate.

"That snake didn't crawl in through your foundation," he snorted.

"You don't know that," she argued. She really, really didn't want to think about the alternative, although, on second thought, neither one was good.

"Dani," his voice dripped sarcasm, "I suppose you'll tell me Bandit crawled out through the same hole."

She had a sudden image of a cartoon Bandit trying to squeeze out a hole in her foundation. Resting her elbows on the table, she dropped her face into her hands, then peeked at him between two fingers. "Do we have to do this?"

His mouth twitched with the beginnings of a real smile.

"Oh, all right. Talk to me," she moaned.

"I think somebody is not happy with you."

"Oh shit! I forgot I never told you!" she said, washing down a bite of quesadilla with a drink of beer. "Somebody called me last night!" She watched his face go from stern to granite as she filled in the details of the call.

"Damn, woman! Why didn't you call me right then?"

"Because I didn't know where you were," she snapped back at him.

"You're right," he conceded, raising his hands in mock surrender. "I'm sorry. I just can't figure out what they think you know…"

"I know," she agreed. "Or what they're afraid I'll find? And who the hell are they, anyway? I love my house, but I swear, it's like that place is cursed," she said, taking another bite of enchilada.

"What do you mean?"

"Like, today, when I was talking to Joe," she remembered too late that she wasn't going to mention that unless Noah brought it up. It was done now, might as well forge ahead. "His wife worked at Ophidian when they first came here," she said. "Then she died, three months later."

"How'd she die?" he looked up suddenly.

"Oh, it wasn't related. She got hit by a car," she said. "But still, it's like… I don't know…you know, I never have trouble getting along with the people I work with, but these guys all treat me like I have the plague or something."

"What was her name?" he asked, pulling a small spiral out of his back pocket.

"Paula Abraham," she said.

"And she died not long before those kids disappeared?"

"Yeah," she said, remembering the look on Joe's face when he told her about it. "It's sad."

"I don't like any of this," he said, pushing his plate aside.

"I know," she shook her head. "It just doesn't seem real - except when it's happening, I mean. Are you sure this isn't a bunch of strange coincidences?"

He looked straight at her with a cocked eyebrow and a crooked smile. "Right. Let's see… you've been here for three months. In that time, you've seen a man standing in the woods staring at your house…you've been locked in your cellar…you've had a phone call warning you to get out…and you found a huge snake under your bed," he said. "Oh, and you left your dog locked in the house, but when you came home, the snake was in and your dog was out, but the door was still locked. Yeah, I'm sure it's just a string of coincidences," he smirked.

"Well, if you put it that way," she joked with a sinking feeling in the pit of her stomach.

"And it's also a coincidence that you bought the house after it sat empty for years because six years ago, when it was owned by a doctor from Ophidian, two students…no, three students vanished without a trace," he continued. "Circumstantial, maybe, but coincidence? No fucking way." He dropped his napkin on his plate and pulled his cigarettes out of his pocket. "Want one?" he offered.

Dani shook her head. "No, but don't tempt me."

"Let me ask you something," she said slowly. "Do you think it's me? Or is it the house?"

"You know," he pointed at her, "that's a good question. I've asked a hell of a lot more questions about the case in the last couple of weeks than you have. Nobody's coming after me."

"Well," she laughed. "Look at you. Nobody in their right mind would come after you. You're armed and dangerous."

"Yeah, well, maybe I better make sure they know that. And make sure they know if they touch you they'll have me to deal with," he said sharply.

"I just wish I knew who 'they' were," she said, picking up her purse as he laid out money for the check on the table.

"It's only a matter of time, my dear," he smiled, getting up from the table.

"It looks a lot better from the outside," she smiled, walking into Noah's living room for the first time.

Bandit was right at home, curled into a fuzzy ball on the worn out olive green sofa. A tattered afghan covered some of the holes, but threads hung down from the arms that looked like they'd done double duty as scratching posts for an energetic cat. A blue ceramic lamp with a crooked shade provided the only light in the room, and a card table with folding chairs sat off to the side by the kitchen.

Noah grinned sheepishly. "I'm hardly ever here…"

"Now I know why," she laughed. "You *do* have a bed, don't you?"

After dinner, they'd gone to the movies and on the way home he insisted that she and Bandit sleep over. Tomorrow, he'd go through her house with a fine-toothed comb and make sure it was safe for them to be there. After meeting that snake under her bed and having subsequent visions of what might have happened if she hadn't lost her shoe, she didn't argue with him. Never mind that the snake wasn't poisonous, she'd have died of fright if she'd wakened in the night with it slithering across the bed.

"Come on, I'll give you the tour," he said, reaching for her hand. "You don't want to look in there," he nodded at a closed door in the hall. "That's where everything I don't know what to do with goes, you know, like boxes and laundry I don't have time to wash."

She smiled, looking up at his face and wondering how she got so lucky.

"Here's the guest bath," he opened the next door.

"Have a lot of guests, do you?" she asked.

"No, I don't have a lot of guests," he mimicked her teasing tone. "But if I did, I thought I should have a clean bathroom." He led her to the door at the end of the hall. "Ta da!" he threw the door open. In the center of the room was a king sized bed, unmade, but bigger than hers. Dani couldn't resist peeking under it, just to be sure. An end table resided on one side with a green banker's lamp, a phone, and a clock radio.

"The bathroom's in here," he opened a door with a sweeping gesture. "And, the closet's in here."

"So, where will *you* sleep?" she teased, screaming when he crossed the room and scooped her up, depositing her in the middle of the bed.

"I'm not letting you out of my sight," he growled, leaning forward to kiss the hollow at the base of her neck.

"Ooohhh, if only that were true," she sighed, reaching behind her and pulling a pillow up under her head.

When she looked back at him, the expression on his face caused her to catch her breath, and she reached up, stroking his face with her hand. What she felt for him at that moment was so intense, there were no words she knew to express it. He pulled her to him and hugged her so hard it hurt. She'd never felt so loved and protected in all her life, and she held tightly to his back, reveling in the feel of the muscles that rippled beneath his shirt.

"Hold that thought," he rasped, breaking away and jumping up. He dashed out into the hall, then returned, already removing his shirt. "All locked up," he said, flipping the light off and shutting the door. "Just try and get away now," he teased, dropping his jeans where he stood.

"Not on your life," she murmured, smiling, as he fell in to the bed and kissed her with a hunger she returned without shame.

CHAPTER TEN

When she woke, Dani was disconcerted momentarily. Struggling up on one elbow, she kicked a heap of covers off her feet and squinted at the sunlight streaming in the window as she looked around the room. Noah's house, she remembered. Yawning, she gingerly put one foot on the floor, smiling as she realized it was carpeted. Bandit had taken to dragging her throw rugs around the room and invariably, the first thing her bare foot touched in the morning was cold, hard wood.

Gathering her clothes from a heap in the floor, she headed for the bathroom. Noah had a shower, something she didn't think she'd miss until she didn't have one. As much as she loved long soaks in her tub, there was nothing like starting the day with a brisk shower to help her wake up. No matter what time it was, waking up was not one of her best things. When she emerged from the shower, she heard him banging around in the kitchen and called out to him.

"Can I borrow a shirt?"

"Help yourself," he answered. "In the closet."

It was surprisingly neat in there, and she was amazed to find a nice assortment of dress clothes. All she'd ever seen him in was jeans and casual shirts. It would be interesting to see how he decked out for the Rose Dance next weekend. Selecting a plaid flannel shirt that looked less enormous than the others, she buttoned it up and padded to the kitchen, still rolling up the sleeves that dangled to mid thigh.

"Morning," she smiled, grazing his cheek on tiptoe. "Whatcha making?"

He was fully dressed and had plates already laid out on the card table.

"Omelets," he said. "We actually eat breakfast at my house," he grinned.

"Long as you cook it, I'll eat," she smiled, searching for a coffee cup.

66

"Beside the sink," he read her mind. "Coffee's over there," he pointed to a pot in the corner.

"Can I help with anything?" she asked as she filled her cup.

"Nope," he said. "All done. Sit down."

She did as he asked, watching him with fascination. He was an odd mixture of rough and gentle, but she wondered how many people ever really got to see the gentle part. He never talked about friends or family, and she'd never seen him with anyone else. As witty and handsome as he was, that seemed strange. She was aware of the way the waitresses stole looks at him when he wasn't watching, and the men always treated him with respect. She'd never seen him really angry, either, but she'd seen enough to know she didn't want to be on the receiving end of that.

"There you go," he said, sliding an omelet onto her plate. A moment later he returned with a basket of hot biscuits and sat down beside her. "How's that for service?"

"Perfect," she smiled, taking a bite of one of the best omelets she'd ever had. "Hey, this is good," she said.

"But of course," he winked at her. "If I do something, I do it right."

She couldn't argue with that. "You know, it's Thanksgiving in a week and a half," she said, thinking out loud.

"So it is," he said. "You going out of town?"

"No."

Even when she was married to Mark, they rarely celebrated. Doctors took off on holidays and left their patients to the residents. "I love holidays, though," she said wistfully. "Even when we didn't have any money, my mom always made it special."

A small sigh escaped her lips as she remembered. When she and Mark were first married, she'd tried so hard to duplicate what her mom did for her growing up, but Mark thought she was being childish. He wanted cocktail parties and banquets instead of turkey dinners with homemade pies and tree trimming parties with caroling later.

"What about you?" she asked, shaking herself. "What do you do for the holidays?"

He shrugged, looking intently at his plate. "I don't know. If I'm not working, I just do...whatever."

"You don't have any family?" she asked, hoping it wasn't too rude.

"Well," he said, "I haven't seen my dad since I was six, and Mom died when I was twenty-two."

"I'm sorry," she said. "I didn't mean to pry."

"No," he took her hand. "You're not. It's just the way it is."

They ate in silence for a while. Dani didn't know for sure whether he wanted to talk about it or not.

"You know how to cook a turkey?" he asked, finally.

"I do," she smiled broadly. "Want to come over for Thanksgiving?"

"You think you can top this?" he held up a fork with his last bite of omelet.

"Damn straight," she said with a smile. "I've been practicing."

"Deal, then," he said, getting up and carrying his dishes into the kitchen. "Now," he said, looking at her from the sink, "Why don't you clean this up and I'll go on over to your house and check it out. You can come on when you're done."

"Okay," she said. It wouldn't take long to clear these dishes but she was in no rush to go back in her house until she knew there were no more snakes lurking in there.

When she'd finished the kitchen, Dani took the shortcut through the trees and got to the driveway just in time to see a truck pull back out onto the road.

"Noah," she called, climbing the porch stairs.

"In here," he answered, coming out of the kitchen wiping his hands on a dishtowel.

"Who was here?" she asked, glancing around the floor quickly as she entered. The house that seemed so comfortable yesterday morning seemed cold and unfriendly today.

"That was your sociable neighborhood locksmith," he smiled. "I had him change all the locks and check the windows."

"Oh." He sure didn't waste any time. "You really think someone came in here and planted that snake, don't you?"

He came closer and placed his hands on her shoulders. "Yes'm, I do. I have something else for you, too." Giving her shoulders a quick squeeze, he went back into the kitchen and emerged carrying a pistol. "Ever shot one of these?"

"No," she said, frowning. Last night's fears surged through her like she'd grabbed a live wire.

"It's just a precaution," he said. "Don't get all stressed."

"But, Noah…" Dani never even used mousetraps because she couldn't stand to see the disgusting little creatures killed like that. Did he really think she could use that thing on somebody? "I could never shoot anybody."

"And I don't want you to shoot anybody," he assured her, leading her to the back door. "All I want is to show you how to use this just in case you need it. That's all."

As she stepped through the back door, she saw that he already had some target cans set up along the far side of the yard and they spent the better part of the next hour getting her acquainted with a .38. It wasn't as bad as she feared, but it wasn't the gun that worried her. It was the target.

When they got back inside the house, she sat down on the couch and closed her eyes while Noah went to put the gun away. It was impossible to believe all this was happening to her. How could things happen so fast when time seemed like it was standing still?

The couch cushion took a little dip when he sat down beside her and she looked up at him. "What do you really think is going on here? I mean, you're not afraid I'll disappear like the other three, are you?"

Dani imagined all sorts of things running through his mind as he looked at her, things she didn't want to think about, much less hear.

"You want a professional opinion, or a gut instinct?" he answered a question with a question.

"Both," she said, suspecting they weren't at all the same.

"Okay-y," he said. "My professional opinion is, somebody thinks you're asking too many questions and wants to scare you out of it. The phone call, the big non-venomous snake. If someone wants to kill you, they don't usually warn you first. But, my gut tells me there's something more going on. I don't know what, but I care too much about you to take any chances."

"So, what do I do?" she asked. "I can't just quit my job and stay here all the time."

He wrapped an arm around her shoulders and pulled her close, tugging playfully on a strand of her hair. "You be careful. You let me ask the questions, and you don't go off anywhere by yourself."

"Okay," she said meekly, looking down at the floor.

"Or, you can move in with me and I'll be your chauffeur," he offered jokingly.

Rolling her eyes, she said, "Yeah, right."

She'd just come out of a ten-year marriage where her husband dictated every detail of her life. She wasn't about to go there again, no matter how different Noah seemed. If some coward wanted to play hardball, she'd just have to learn how to play.

**

Dani was putting the last of the file folders into the file cabinet when she looked up to see Mike standing in the doorway, watching her.

"Hi," she smiled, determined to be friendly despite the constant cold shoulder she got when she worked at Ophidian. "Need me for something?"

"Nah," he shook his head, glancing casually around the now spotless room. "You've done a good job in here. I've never seen it look like this in all the time I worked here."

That was high praise, coming from him.

Dani shrugged, not wanting to make too much of it. "Thanks. You guys work hard in there, you need someone to keep your reports organized."

In truth, she'd far rather be in the file rooms than in the labs with the snakes. Especially after the incident at the house last week. She swore, the first time she'd entered a lab after that she felt her skin crawling.

He nodded but didn't speak again. Dani waited a moment, then gathered her books off the table. It was already after six and Dr. Crane didn't approve of overtime unless it was his idea. Mike moved so she could pass into the hall, then followed her to the office.

"I heard you found a brown snake in your house last week," his words stopped her with her hand on the doorknob and she turned back to face him.

"Yes," she said. "How did you know?"

"Beth," he said. "She was pretty freaked."

Dani laughed at that. "So was I."

"Can I walk you to your car?"

"Sure," she shrugged.

He hadn't talked to her this much the whole time she'd worked here. Maybe she was finally gaining some ground. Her search through the files had been productive, at least for the lab, but it hadn't told her anything she wanted to know about the missing students. She'd tried to heed Noah's warning about asking too many questions, but it was hard when those questions relentlessly bombarded her brain.

Mike walked along beside her, nervously shoving his hands in and out of his pockets and keeping a wary eye on the surroundings. Dani was beginning to catch his uneasiness when he spoke again.

"What did you do with the snake?"

"I'm not sure, exactly. A friend of mine was there. He killed it and took it outside," she said. "Why?"

He stopped beside her when she reached her car and scanned the parking lot, not meeting her eyes.

"I had to come in Saturday to pick up something I left in the brown snake lab," he explained. "One of them was missing when I got here."

"You think it's the same one?"

"I'd like to check it, if you don't mind," he said. In spite of his wariness, there was a glint of determination in his eyes.

"Okay," she said, her mind reeling from the possibilities. She hadn't even thought about where the snake might have come from. "When?"

"How about now?"

Dani was going straight home anyway, so she waited for him to get his car and follow her. Once she got home, she called Noah to find out where he'd put the snake and was able to take Mike right to it. It didn't look near as scary sprawled on a bush, shriveled and crawling with ants, but Dani still had to suppress a shudder as Mike gingerly lifted it and laid it out flat on the ground.

"Is it?" she asked finally when he didn't speak.

"I can't be sure, but I think so," he said solemnly.

The gentle breeze and the crisp, pine scent did nothing to lighten the dread that hovered like a storm on her horizon.

"Mike," she said, unwilling to play games, "somebody put this in my house. Who would do that?"

"You don't know that," he turned angrily, stomping through the brush toward his car.

"What do you mean, I don't know that?" Dani struggled to keep up with him as he walked away. "You think that snake just escaped from the lab and crawled out here and let himself into my house?" Once they broke free of the trees, she hurried around and stopped in front of him, forcing him to look at her.

Running a hand nervously through his hair, he shook his head and stared up at the sky.

"Talk to me!" she demanded. He closed up the lab. He had to know something.

"I don't know what to tell you!" his eyes flashed with anger. Or was it fear? She couldn't tell.

"How long have you worked there, Mike?"

Pulling his keys out of his pocket, he sidestepped and got in his car, ignoring her question.

"Mike! I haven't done anything wrong! Why won't you talk to me?" she pleaded.

He put the car in gear and started backing out of the drive, then stopped, looking at her out of the open window. "I need to think about this," was all he said, then he was gone.

Completely frustrated, Dani picked up a pinecone off the ground and hurled it with all her might back in the direction of the snake. What was it all about, anyway? Her brain refused to process the data. It was simply too unbelievable. So what if she owned the land where they disappeared? It was six years ago, for God's sake. She didn't see anything!

CHAPTER ELEVEN

The funky cloud followed her into the house, hindering her evening activities and leaving her with a generalized feeling of depression. When Noah called and said he was working late, she decided to chuck it all and headed upstairs for a long soak. Maybe a glass of wine and a good mystery would take her mind off things for a while.

She had the tub filled with hot water, vanilla candles burning and was just pulling her shirt off over her head when the doorbell pealed. Hastily shrugging back into her shirt, she raced downstairs thinking Noah must have finished up sooner than he expected.

"Hey!" she said, smiling as she opened the front door.

But it wasn't Noah, it was Mike, and in his arms was a big, fluffy gray cat.

"What's this?" she asked, with Bandit sniffing and wiggling furiously at her feet.

"Snakes don't like cats," Mike explained, with a sheepish grin that smacked of repentance and made him look like an overgrown schoolboy.

"Are you serious?" she asked. "Come on in."

Shuffling awkwardly through the door, he stood in the living room floor and waited for her to shut it before handing her the cat. "I have some things for her in the car."

"You want me to have this cat?"

She'd never owned a cat in her life and wasn't sure she wanted one now. But if it helped assure she'd have no more reptile visitors, that was a definite plus.

"I thought it might be good," he said. "Unless you don't like her."

"No," she took the purring bundle, amazed at how soft and silky it felt. The cat settled right into the crook of her arm like she was used to pampering and looked up at her curiously with eyes that were startlingly blue. "I've just never had a cat before."

She sat down on the couch and watched, amused as Bandit sniffed the cat's tail. With an attitude she could only describe as haughty, the cat tolerated Bandit for a few minutes, then reached out a paw and tapped him soundly on the nose, sending him scurrying to the kitchen.

"She'll be fine with him," Mike said. "Her name's Charlie, like Charlie Baltimore."

"From that movie?" Dani asked, smiling. 'Long Kiss Goodnight' was one of her favorites. "Sit down," she urged, realizing he was still standing, restlessly shifting from one foot to the other.

"I can't stay. It's late," he mumbled.

"Mike, I really want you to tell me what's going on," she said.

Charlie slid off her lap and kneaded herself a comfortable place on the couch and proceeded to bathe right there between them.

"I don't know," he said, with the most honest expression she'd seen on his face up till now. "Friday, I locked the lab and everyone else was gone. What time did you get home that day, anyway?"

"I think it was just a little past seven," she said. "I stopped at the store to get some dog food and came straight here."

"I left right after you did, so that doesn't leave much time for someone to get back in the lab and get out here. I'll check around and see what I can find out, though," he shuffled toward the door. "Let me get her litter box and food, I'll be right back."

Dani stroked the cat absentmindedly while she waited. It was nice that he brought her a cat. It was nicer still that he was opening up to her and seemed willing to help her figure this out. She could use an ally at Ophidian.

"Thanks, Mike," she waved at him from the porch as he walked back out into the darkness. When she closed the door behind him, she felt a little less alone, and, after situating the cat dish and warning the two animals to behave, she went back to her bath.

***

For once, there was no one Dani knew in the cafeteria as she sat her tray of mystery meat down on a remote table. The week had been hectic. It seemed like she ran from one place to the next. From the looks of it, she might enjoy thirty minutes of uninterrupted time before lab.

It didn't take long to wolf down her food, some kind of turkey she hoped. Pushing her tray aside, she took out the spiral she kept close to jot down notes as they occurred to her. Noah had been busy most of the week. She'd only had dinner with him once. He'd finally got his hands on the old employee list from Ophidian and had been diligently tracking them down for questioning. As far as she knew, he hadn't uncovered any new evidence, but if there was anything there to find, she was sure he'd find it.

Dani was more interested in Mike's opinions about who might have put that snake in her house. At first, she'd thought it would be simple. Who had keys to the labs? Then she'd learned that almost anyone who passed through the lab could have picked the keys up. It's not like the snake labs were burglar magnets. Dr. Crane had keys, of course, and Mike. Emil and Jeff had keys, but master keys of all the labs were hanging just inside Dr. Crane's outer office, which was rarely locked. She'd checked and none were missing, but that didn't mean someone didn't take it and put it back later. Nobody should have had keys to her house, but Noah assured her the locks he'd replaced wouldn't have presented much of an obstacle to someone who knew what he was doing.

Mike had said something else that nagged at her. One day, when they were alone in the file room, he'd mentioned something about Dr. Crane's wife leaving him right after the students disappeared. From what she'd learned, Mrs. Crane still lived here in town, but they'd divorced later that same year. Dani couldn't think of a good reason to pay her a visit, but, since she was actively involved in the Rose Festival, she hoped maybe she'd get a chance to talk to her at the Rose Dance.

With a sigh, she tucked her note pad away and gathered her dishes. If she left now, she'd have a little extra time to set up in the lab before the students arrived.

***

"Do you have to go now?" Dani whined, leaning on Noah's shoulder. They'd enjoyed a simple dinner and a movie on the DVR. She'd almost forgotten what it was like to spend an evening with him, he'd been so busy.

"I'll be back before the dance on Sunday, I promise," he said, looking down at her with eyes that melted her soul. "I really want to get a look at Atkinson's place for myself."

After dinner, he'd filled her in on the research he was doing on Dr. Atkinson, but mentioned that he'd yet to speak to the man personally. When he left here six years ago, Dr. Atkinson had opened his own laboratory facility in Atlanta. Apparently he'd been there ever since and was reasonably successful and well respected in his work.

"You promise?" she asked. "The lab probably won't even be open tomorrow."

"I promise, and yes, it will. I talked to the secretary," he assured her. "But I better get to the house. I haven't even washed my clothes yet and I still have to pack. My plane leaves at the crack of dawn."

Reluctantly, she got up from the couch and walked him to the door. "I don't know why it's so important that you go there tomorrow," she said, still pouting.

"So I can spend some time off with you next week, silly," he touched her nose. "Besides," he looked down at Bandit wiggling at his feet and Charlie watching them suspiciously from her place on the couch, "you've got plenty of company."

"I'll miss you," she said as he kissed her good night.

"I'll call you tomorrow night, and you have my cell number if you need me," he said.

She closed the door with a sigh after she watched him go, then headed for bed determined to keep the time between now and Sunday's dance as full as she possibly could.

***

In keeping with her plan to keep the day full so time would pass quickly, Dani decided on an early morning shopping spree. She hadn't splurged on a new formal in years, and she'd sold most of what she used to wear before she left Austin. With a sense of purpose, she headed for a nearby mall and fully expected to spend most of the day shopping for something special to wear tomorrow.

The annual Rose Dance was a black tie affair, one of the biggest events of the season. As luck would have it, she found the perfect dress in the first store, an ice blue satin off the shoulder number with a tight fitting bodice and swirling full skirt that fit like it had been made for her. An hour later, she had new shoes and accessories and a whole day to kill. She wandered the mall aimlessly for a while, but was still home before noon.

The day was mild, so she spent some time in the garden, but the ground cover had pretty much taken care of the weeds and it didn't take long to have it in shape. With the day and the night stretching interminably before her, she decided to tackle something more challenging. The one thing she'd been meaning to do, but always found a way to avoid, was cleaning out the cellar.

Before she could talk herself out of it yet again, she gathered a pail, a sponge, a broom, and an armful of trash bags and headed for the back yard. She'd forgotten the padlock, and had to set her things down on the ground to retrieve the key, but a few moments later she was on her way. Two steps down, the fresh, crisp autumn air was replaced by a cold, damp, musty smell that tickled her nose. The lone light bulb, stuck to the ceiling like an afterthought, had an opposite effect than its intended use. Instead of the warm glow of a reassuring beacon shining light into the darkness, it revealed shapes and shadows in all the crevices and corners that screamed for illumination.

After the initial chill and sense of foreboding, she gradually became accustomed to the dim light and worked hard at emptying and scrubbing the shelves, humming to herself to chase away the silence. The shelves were wide and deep along one wall, sturdy enough to hold the weight of filled canning jars to last throughout the year. She had to go back up to refill the water bucket several times, but, little by little, she saw progress.

Once she finished all the shelves and carried the trash up to the street, she went back into the cellar determined to clean the floor. She might never use the place again, she didn't have that much to store and the thought of canning fruits and vegetables far exceeded her culinary skills, but at least she could lock the door and know it was done.

With a scrub brush in hand and a fresh pail of Lysol water, she attacked the floor with a mixture of annoyance and enthusiasm. The knees of her jeans were wet and muddy, so she worked backward, cleaning as far in front of her as she could reach, then scooting back, grateful that at least there was a visible difference between what she'd done and what she hadn't.

As she rocked back on her heels to give her back some relief, Dani felt the boards move beneath her. Shifting her weight, she felt them move again. Curious, she turned around and pressed down on the board with the palms of her hands, surprised to see the boards come up on the other end. There was a whole section of floor in the corner that wasn't fastened down.

Unwilling to leave a job half done, she scurried up the stairs again for a tool box from the garage and a flashlight to help the dim bulb with illumination. When she returned, she set to work, using the biggest screwdriver she had to pry up the first board, hoping to locate the joist so she'd know exactly where to place the new nails. Buoyed by the fact that she'd seen few spiders or bugs all day, she flipped the board over as soon as it was loose, then fell back as a rank, decaying odor hit her in the face. Something was under the floor!

Squinting the same way she did when trying to shield herself from a scary scene in a movie, she crept back up on her knees and shone the flashlight beam down into the hole. What the hell was that?

The board was about four feet long, but only six inches across. She couldn't make it out, but whatever it was, it was big, covered with cloth that was covered with mud. A little leery, she pulled up on the next board, which came right off in her hands. She still couldn't quite identify the stench, but she knew what the cloth was - it was a sleeve, and that was a hand coming out of it!

It took a minute to realize the screaming she heard was her own voice!

In her haste to get out of the cellar, she slipped and fell three times going up the stairs. When she reached daylight, she had to stop for a moment and get her bearings. Rubbing a trembling hand over her eyes, she ran to the back door and grabbed up the phone in the kitchen.

The message on his answering machine reminded her that Noah was out of town. Damn him! He wouldn't be much help from Atlanta. Still shaking, she dialed 911 and tried to keep her voice from quivering as she explained the situation to the operator. That done, she grabbed her purse and sank down on the couch and dialed Noah's cell phone number.

"Russell," he barked into the phone.

"Noah," even to her, it sounded like a wail.

"What's wrong?" the bark turned tender.

"Noah, there's a dead body in my cellar!"

"What?" he thundered. "Dani where are you?"

"I was cleaning the cellar and the floor was…"

"Are you still in the house? Have you called the police?" he sounded frantic.

"Yes, I'm still here and they're on their way," she said, taking slow, deliberate breaths.

"Jesus H. Christ!"

A wave of reality washed over her as she closed her eyes, hearing the frustration in his voice.

"I'm sorry," his voice took on a more controlled tone. "Tell me what happened."

"I was cleaning the cellar and some of the floor boards were loose," she said, wishing she could see him while she told him. "I was just going to nail them…"

"You couldn't have waited until I was there?" he interrupted, volume increasing with every syllable.

"Noah!" she yelled back at him. She didn't call him to do this. "Why can't I clean my own damn cellar?"

Dani walked a fine line between enjoying the feeling of being protected by him and being annoyed that he acted like she was helpless. Bandit followed her to the door as she heard sirens coming closer.

"They're here, I'll talk to you later," she peeked out the curtains.

"No! Hold on," he said. "I want to talk to them."

"Just a minute," she carried the phone out on the porch as the first squad car drove in and parked behind her car. Was she imagining it, or had the sunlight ducked behind an ominous bank of clouds? Was she seeing everything through a dingy, brown filter of death?

"Ms. Jones?" the officer asked as he approached. Tall and stern, he reminded her of a State Trooper she'd once tried unsuccessfully to talk out of a speeding ticket.

She nodded. "Noah Russell wants to talk to you," she handed the phone to him.

"Russell?" he spoke into the phone as Dani rubbed her arms to fight the chill that came from inside. "Yeah, I just got here...............okay ....okay.........no," he looked up at her. "Roger that," he handed the phone back to her.

"What?" she asked into the phone, wishing like hell Noah was here.

"I'll be there as soon as I can. You know where the key to my house is. Why don't you wait for me there?"

"They're not running me out of my house," she said, aware that the officer was waiting. "Noah, I'll talk to you later."

After answering a few basic questions for Officer Wylie, she led him through the back door and out to the door of the cellar. He motioned for another officer to join him from the driveway and soberly instructed her to wait as they proceeded down the stairs. As if she could be coerced to go back in there.

"They're in there," she pointed to the cellar door as yet another officer rounded the corner of the house. Bet they didn't have this kind of fun every day.

Rubbing her arms against the cold, she wandered to the back door and turned on the outside light. It was getting darker by the minute. Moments later, the three officers resurfaced, exchanging grim, two and three word sentences in subdued tones.

CHAPTER TWELVE

At Officer Wylie's instruction, Dani went back into the house to wait as the physical evidence squad moved in to unearth the body. She started a pot of coffee, then browsed through the refrigerator and cupboards, knowing it was time for dinner even though she was far from hungry. When the phone rang and she discovered Beth on the other end, pouting over a broken dinner date, she gladly agreed to meet her for a bite to eat and a late movie. Officer Wylie hardly seemed to notice her when she asked if it was all right for her to leave and she was soon on her way.

El Chico's was fast becoming her most frequented restaurant. Beth met her in the parking lot and regaled her with familiar nonsense as they were seated and proceeded with their meals. Although Dani knew she'd tell Beth the gory details of her afternoon, she enjoyed the normalcy of Beth's chatter and was in no hurry to change the subject.

"Too much," Beth groaned, pushing away a plate of half eaten enchiladas. "Why do I always order this when I know I can't eat it all?"

"Because it makes nice leftovers?" Dani guessed, smiling. That was the fate of her own dinner. It smelled good when the waiter delivered it, but her stomach reacted to the first bite of her taco by sending out a warning gurgle and she'd only managed to finish a few bites of her rice.

"Are you going to tell me what's bothering you or do I have to start guessing?" Beth asked.

"You'll never believe it," Dani warned, then launched reluctantly into an abridged account of the day's activities. When she got to the part of her discovery in the cellar, Beth's eyes were like saucers and she gasped audibly.

"Oh my God," she said in hushed tones when she could speak.

"I'm sayin'," Dani sighed, subdued by the new onslaught of confusion and anxiety that came with telling the tale. Beth's bubbly, non-stop conversation during their meal had helped her forget, but talking about it again threw it right back up in her face.

"I *told* you that house is haunted!" Beth hissed. "What are you going to do?"

"What can I do?" Dani shrugged. "Besides, the house didn't bury that dead body."

"I wonder who it is?" Beth said with a sparkle in her eye. "Ooh! I bet it's one of those students that disappeared!"

"Beats me," Dani had to smile at her perverted enthusiasm. She could just imagine Beth reenacting the whole story with a healthy dose of literary license to anyone who would listen tomorrow. Encouraged by a smattering of oohs and ahs, it would no doubt grow more menacing and exaggerated with each telling.

"Oh you know it is!" she insisted. "Girl! You've gotta get out of that house!"

"Oh, yeah, right," Dani scoffed. "And live where? I bought the house, remember?"

"Well, I don't know, but how can you sleep there? Sell it!"

Dani laughed out loud at that. "You want to buy it?"

"Ooh," Beth's face fell. "Good point."

"I'm not moving," Dani said. "It pisses me off that somebody wants me out of there. There's nothing wrong with the house."

Beth looked stumped. "Well, at least get a bigger dog."

Anxious to change the subject, Dani mentioned the upcoming Rose Dance and Beth launched off into another direction allowing Dani to end the evening on a more upbeat note. The conversation ranged from who'd be wearing what to who'd be dating who and the two were giggling by the time they crossed the parking lot in search of their cars.

Dani's apprehension returned in full force as she turned her car toward home though. Her foot eased off the accelerator little by little as she approached the house, fearful of what she'd find. All sign of the squad cars had vanished and it looked like it did any other day. Purposefully avoiding so much as a glance toward the back yard, she let herself in the front door and carefully locked it behind her. Greeted by Bandit dancing around her feet and Charlie, who jumped up on the couch and assumed her customary accusing position for having been abandoned, Dani breathed a sigh of relief. In spite of all the unnerving experiences, she'd come to love her new home.

After tossing and turning most of the night, Dani slept nearly till noon on Sunday. With concentrated effort, she kept her mind on schoolwork until time to dress for the dance. A quick call from Noah assured her he was on schedule and she finished her preparations feeling a little like a teenager getting ready for the prom. She was just putting the finishing touches on her hair when the doorbell announced Noah's arrival.

Dani hurried down the stairs, a little awkward in the heels she'd shunned for so long. His appearance at the front door took her breath away. Clad in a tuxedo that had to be tailored to fit, his eyes twinkled in the light of the porch and his hair was tamed into shoulder caressing waves that looked better than her own.

"Ready?" he smiled down at her, amused by her stair.

She nodded. "Do I need a coat?" The wind blew right through the crocheted shawl draped around her bare shoulders.

"I'll keep you warm," he promised, sliding an arm around her shoulders as they walked toward the truck. "Sorry, the limo's in the shop," he teased, holding her arm as she stepped gingerly up on the running board to get in.

"Right," she mumbled, relaxing a little.

A moment later, he was behind the wheel. He started the truck and adjusted the heater, then turned toward her. "You look marvelous."

Dani smiled, not knowing how much he was teasing.

The country club was literally covered in roses. From the moment they'd entered the front door, chic fabric ribbons of royal blue dusted with rose petals led the way to the dining room and to the ballroom. Antique baskets filled with fragrant petals lined every available countertop and shelf in the rest room and every shade and variety of rose was represented there somewhere. The theme for the dance was Midnight in the Garden, and the decorating committee had done a lovely job of recreating the motif. Elegant latticework supported climbing vines of roses and the buffet table was generously appointed with containers of tea roses. Even the ceiling in the ballroom, darkened to a midnight blue, had tiny twinkling lights arranged in constellations of rose shapes.

The band, reportedly a group from the college, did a fine imitation of the big band sounds and dancers enthusiastically embraced the swing dance craze. The whole atmosphere provided a welcome antidote to the dreary and cold gray skies that heralded the arrival of an east Texas winter.

Dani breathed in the festive mood as she watched the dancers impatiently from a wrought iron bench along the side wall, one foot kicking softly to the beat of the music. She and Noah were just finishing a wonderful buffet meal when his pager went off. As he assured her he'd be right back, she offered to wait in the ballroom, drawn magnetically by the candlelit ambiance and music that wafted through the doorway.

At one point, she thought she spotted Caroline Crane across the room, but she'd lost all sense of the urgency she'd felt earlier. There'd be time enough to track her down for questioning another day. All thoughts of pursuing the mystery of the missing students vanished as she drew in a breath of sheer pleasure at Noah's approach from across the room. Reality would creep in soon enough. This was a chance for fantasies to come true.

She'd seen his dress clothes in his closet once, but a quick glance at fabric on hangers did nothing to prepare her for the vision of his muscular form draped in a carefully tailored black tux. His every day appearance was so far removed from the country club society Mark insisted they frequent that she'd wondered more than once if that was why she was attracted to him. But seeing him now, she knew he'd put those doctors to shame on their best nights.

"Sorry," his voice warmed her like brandy as he extended his hand. "I didn't mean to be so long."

Dani smiled up at him, taking his hand and suppressing a quick shiver of anticipation. "You don't have to go, do you?"

"I'm all yours," he said with a hint of a smile as he led her to the dance floor. Maybe it was the caress of the music, or the feel of his hand warming the small of her back, but Dani felt like she was in heaven. As the music slowed and the evening drew to a close, she rested her head on his shoulder, wondering if there was a way for this to go on forever.

*** *

The morning went by in a blur. It was nearing the end of the semester and everyone seemed anxious for the Thanksgiving holiday to begin. Dani's last class was dismissed early with warnings to complete their semester projects by the time they returned next Monday. She'd spent so much time worrying about her microbiology project, the other classes had been neglected a little.

With a sigh, Dani set her lunch tray down on an empty table in the corner and retrieved her spiral from the book bag. The course in question was Ethology, the biological basis of animal behavior. Topics to be studied include fixed action patterns, dominance, conflict behavior, and phylogeny and ontogeny of behavior, genetics and ecology of behavior. Fortunately, a lab research project wasn't assigned for this semester. All she had to do was pick a topic and design a potential research proposal.

Between bites of an overcooked hamburger, Dani referred to her class notes and jotted down the most interesting studies she could think of, wondering idly if she'd have time to get the bulk of this paper out of the way tonight. The last thing she wanted to do was spend her entire holiday in front of the computer screen.

"Mind if I join you?" Joe Abraham's voice interrupted her scribbling and she looked up in surprise.

"Not at all," she smiled. The cafeteria wasn't even half full, and he had nothing but a cup of coffee in his hands.

"Last minute research?" he quizzed, glancing at her notes.

"Nothing like waiting till the last minute," she smiled again, wondering why he'd sought her out. As she thought about it, she didn't remember seeing him in the cafeteria often.

"Those were the days," he offered, looking casually around the cafeteria. "So," he turned his attention back to her, leaning forward slightly, "how have you been?"

"Good," she nodded. "How have you been?" Shooting the breeze was never a comfortable thing for her. Why didn't people just get to the point? Decorum, she answered herself, finishing the last bite of her burger.

"Oh, I'm fine," he dismissed the question with a wave of his hand and leaned in, adopting a tone that was barely more than a whisper. "I heard about the body they found in your cellar last weekend."

"Yeah," she sighed. She should have known it would be big news in a town this size, but it had surprised her a little to find it on the front page of the local paper. Thankfully, they hadn't printed her name and up to now, no one had mentioned it to her.

"That must have been terrible for you," he continued. "Do they have any leads?"

"I really don't know," Dani shook her head. "They don't think I did it," she tried to smile. All Noah had said was that it was a male and probably Thad Gregory, but she hadn't pressed him for details. In fact, she didn't much want to talk about it at all.

"Do they know who it is?" Joe persisted.

"The body hasn't been identified yet, as far as I know," she answered vaguely. Something about his intensity made her uncomfortable.

"I see," he murmured, leaning back in his chair. "What are you going to do?"

"What do you mean?" she looked at him quizzically, trying to read the curious expression on his face.

"Well," he seemed discomfited, eyes darting around the room again, "I'd imagine it might be uncomfortable for you staying there after finding a snake in your house and now this…"

"How did you know about that?" she asked abruptly. She hadn't told anyone but Beth and Mike and hadn't heard anyone else talking about it.

He looked surprised. "Dr. Crane, I believe…"

"Oh," she said. Of course, Dr. Crane would know, since the snake was missing from the lab, but from the way he acted toward her, she doubted he even remembered her name. "Well, I don't really know what you mean. There's nothing for me to do."

"You're not selling the house, then?"

"No," she said shortly, annoyed that he seemed so interested.

Whether he picked up her cue or just got the information he came for, she didn't know, but he stood to his feet.

"Well, you take care. I better get back to work," he said.

Dani nodded, but didn't bother to answer since he was already striding away from the table. She turned back to her notes, but put them away a few moments later. Her concentration was shot.

CHAPTER THIRTEEN

Snuggled close to Noah on the couch, Dani sighed as she looked into the fireplace.

"What's the matter? You sound sad," Noah said softly, tugging a strand of her hair with the arm he had draped around her shoulder.

"Oh, I don't know. Holiday let-down I guess," she sighed again.

"I thought we had a pretty good time," he murmured, nuzzling her ear.

Dani smiled. "We did. That's the problem. Reality starts again in the morning." The past three days had been nearly perfect. Crisp, cold days and long, cozy nights. Noah had taken the weekend off from work and they'd spent the whole time together – laughing, reading, playing games, talking. Doing everything Dani wanted to do and loving every minute of it. Although she knew he was watchful, Noah had taken great pains to help her forget the skeleton in the cellar and everything else that had happened.

"Well, I'm real and I didn't think you had a problem with that," Noah suggested.

"You know what I mean," she nudged him in the side with an elbow.

"I know what you mean," he smiled. "There's always Christmas."

She smiled again. "Yeah. There's that. Assuming I get my students and my self through finals."

An odd expression flitted across his face as she glanced up at him.

"What?" she asked.

He made a face. "I want you to be careful on campus."

Dani leaned away from him to get a better look at his face. "Why?"

"Well…it's probably nothing," he seemed reluctant.

"Noah," she prompted.

He sighed. "I didn't know whether to say anything or not…"

Dani felt a twinge of alarm. "What?"

85

"Your boss."

"Dr. Abraham?"

He nodded. "I looked into the files about his wife's death."

"And?"

"There was some question that maybe it wasn't an accident," he admitted. "No proof, just questions."

Dani didn't know what to say about that. "But it was ruled an accident, right?"

He nodded again.

"So there's really nothing to worry about, right?"

This time, he didn't nod. "Maybe it was an accident," he conceded finally, "but it's better to be safe than sorry."

"Noah," she twisted around on the couch so she could face him. "So what am I supposed to do?"

"Just watch your back."

She looked at him blankly.

"You know, be careful. Don't be alone with him."

Dani frowned then dropped her head on his chest and he circled her with his arms.

"I'm not trying to scare you and I'm sure you're careful. I just don't want you to take any chances."

Dani raised her head and looked into his eyes with tears glistening in her own. "You really think he might have done that?" She thought of the expression on Joe's face as he told her about his wife's death. He looked genuinely distraught – she couldn't believe he would have killed his own wife.

"I don't know. Maybe someone else killed her. She worked at Ophidian."

Dani exhaled slowly. "You sure know how to take the festive out of a holiday, don't you?"

***

So much for the holiday, Dani thought, racing across campus as fast as she could with a twenty-pound book bag weighing her down. A cold front had moved in the day after Thanksgiving, making it all the more difficult to return to campus Monday morning. Trying in vain to hold her coat closed against the frigid wind, she wished she'd taken time to button up before venturing out of the warm lab. At least she'd taken heed to the howling of the north wind this morning, dressing in her heaviest jeans and tucking the tapered ends into thick slouch socks before buckling on her hiking boots. If this was a preview of weather to come, she might regret leaving Austin. The idea of a white Christmas was one thing, the reality might be something else altogether.

When the storm clouds rolled in late Thanksgiving night, it made for a cozy evening in front of the fireplace, snuggling with Noah, thinking about the holidays still to come. Today, with no fireplace and no Noah, it just felt cold. She tugged hard to open the door against the wind, then jumped out of the way as it hit her backpack slamming shut behind her.

Dropping her backpack beside the desk, Dani shook her head after removing her stocking cap and shrugged out of her coat. Just two more weeks until the semester ended, then a whole month of nothing but puttering around the house, getting ready for Christmas and Noah. A sigh escaped her lips as she sat down at the desk and wondered where to begin. She was older and wiser enough not to put off all her major projects until the end of the semester like so many of the students did. So, while they felt the panic of getting everything done on a two-week countdown, she just wished it was over.

The closeness she'd shared with Noah over the holiday stirred up a lot of things inside that needed some undivided attention. Maybe it was her naturally suspicious nature, coupled with the bizarre events of the last two months, but she'd always believed if something seemed too good to be true, it usually was. And, as much as she hated to admit it, Noah seemed too good to be true.

With another sigh and a glance at her watch, she reached for the files that needed typing and reluctantly got started. Tedious, but necessary work that did little to stop her mind from wandering. Everywhere she'd turned for answers about the missing students, she'd run into a brick wall. Even talking to Noah about it didn't help much anymore. If he'd learned anything from his end of the investigation, he wasn't talking and bringing the subject up with him caused a noticeable emotional distance. If there were answers to be found, he'd either find them on his own and let her in on it later, or she'd be the one to uncover them. A team effort seemed out of the question.

Dani jumped when the phone rang, piercing the silence. "Ophidian," she said.

"Whatcha doing?" Noah's warm voice caused her heart to flutter.

"Nothing that can't be interrupted," she smiled into the phone and spoke softly. "What are you doing?"

"Calling you, silly," he teased. She heard the smile. "What time do you get off?"

She glanced at her watch again. "In about an hour. Why?"

He sighed loudly. "I've gotta work tonight. I thought if you were off we might have time to grab some grub before I go. Guess not, though."

"Noah!" she whined. "Every night this week?"

"More shoppers, more shoplifters," he explained. "It'll be like this till Christmas, I'm afraid."

"But you're a detective!" she argued.

He laughed. "Investigator. And they think I blend into a crowd real well."

"Well that sucks," she chuckled despite the slight pang of disappointment. The idea that he could blend into anything was amusing.

"I'll call you when I get in tonight, okay?"

"I guess that'll have to do," she said, smiling even after she'd hung up the phone.

She'd finished the reports and sat wondering if she should look for something else to do or go ahead and sign out early when she heard a door slam down the hall. The sound of stomping footsteps preceded Mike into the office. The expression on his face was even more dark than usual.

"What's wrong?" she asked, watching him flip through the stack of reports she'd just placed in the file basket.

"I'm surrounded by idiots, that's what's wrong!" he snapped. When he got to the paper he was looking for, he slammed the others down on the basket and turned to stomp out of the office, then stopped at the door. "Where's the original of this?"

"Which one is it?" she asked, grateful his irritation wasn't directed solely at her.

"Copperhead," he waved it at her like she should be able to read it from across the room.

Dani fished the original notes out of the trashcan, hoping she hadn't made a typo and handed it to him. "What's wrong?" she asked again, studying his face as he compared the forms. "Did I type something wrong?"

"No," he shook his head, still reading, "and I didn't count anything wrong, either." With sudden determination, he strode purposefully from the room, his angry footsteps echoing down the hallway.

Deciding she'd had enough for one day, she shut down the computer and gathered her things, then pulled her coat on and buttoned it. She had a gloved hand on the doorknob and her cap snug on her head when she realized what he'd said. A chill ran down her spine. The brown snake they found in her house was from the lab. Now a copperhead was missing? Brown snakes were scary, copperheads were deadly.

Immediately she turned and headed for the hall and the copperhead lab. She'd never sleep unless she talked to Mike first. As she approached the lab, she was distracted by the sound of heated male voices coming from inside Dr. Crane's office. She stopped, not sure she wanted to walk in on that, when the door burst open and Mike stormed across the hall and into the copperhead lab. She was still standing there staring when the door opened again and Emil emerged. He shot her a glare without speaking, tossed a knit scarf over his shoulder and stomped down the hall, hitting the bar on the exit door without a backward glance.

Dani exhaled, wondering what kind of argument had prompted the scowl that contrasted so vividly with the red scarf. Somehow, Emil seemed the least likely person she knew to get caught up in holiday spirit to the point of wearing a cheery scarf with a snowman on the tail.

Bracing herself, she proceeded to the copperhead lab and eased open the door.

"Mike?" she hesitated just inside the door. Mike was in front of one of the nursery tanks, examining it closely.

He looked surprised to see her, but not annoyed. "Whatcha need?"

She shrugged. "I was just checking…" Suddenly, she was afraid to ask.

He raised himself from a crouching position and turned to face her with a strange expression on his face. "I'm missing a baby."

Dani's stomach sank. "Are you sure?" From the nursery tanks she'd observed, it was hard to tell how many of the little buggers were in there all piled and coiled together.

He nodded. "I thought I was missing one about a week ago, then I told myself I'd just miscounted. I didn't miscount again. It's the same tank and there's another one missing now."

A shudder caused her to cross her arms and squeeze. "What do you think happened to it? Could it have crawled out somehow?" Just in case, she cast a quick glance around the floor at her feet.

"No," he shook his head. "No way."

"Is there anything I can do?" she asked helplessly.

He looked completely discouraged and shook his head again. "Don't say anything about this, okay? I've gotta figure something out."

"All right," she agreed. "See you later."

He nodded but didn't speak again as she backed out of the room.

The thought of the missing copperhead haunted her all the way home. Just because it was small, didn't mean it was any less deadly. In fact, the opposite might be true, both from venom potency and the ability to hide in smaller places. Feeling a little foolish, but determined nonetheless, Dani examined every crack and crevice in the house with a flashlight as soon as she got home.

Convinced she'd done all she could, around eight she gave up the effort, parking the flashlight on the night stand beside her bed. With a bowl of hot soup and a grilled cheese sandwich, she sat down at the dining room table and doodled on a nearby notepad. How did everything get so complicated?

As she dabbled in her food, her mind wandered over the facts as she knew them. Even when she started jotting them down on the notepad they were sketchy, with too many gaps to tell a story. Try as she would, she just wasn't good at speculation and half-truth. When the subtle pulsing in her head turned into a persistent throb, she abandoned the dining room in favor of a seat on the couch in front of the television. Low lights and a cup of hot tea aided by a couple of Advils would surely bring relief. Unfortunately, the sitcom she watched only encouraged her to trade one line of thought for another. Watching the single working girl agonize over a potential boyfriend's commitment wasn't the best choice for TV viewing in her present state of mind.

Her head hurt too much to pursue any scholastic endeavors. Besides, she was pretty much done for the semester. A few quick flicks of the remote assured her there was nothing there to keep her, so she reluctantly shut everything off and moved upstairs for a long, hot bath and a good book.

When darkness wrapped around her as she climbed into bed, sleep was elusive even though she felt exhausted. Not from lack of sleep, but from lack of peace. Like she'd been running and hiding from someone or something for too long. Was it only a few months ago she'd moved here, satisfied that at last, her life was moving in the direction she'd been destined to go?

Rolling over on her side, she pulled the comforter up over her ears as if that would stop the relentless questions that pounded her psyche. She was just drifting off to sleep when she realized that Noah never called.

***

Bandit's loud bark propelled her out of the bed and she was half way to the bedroom door before she fully woke up. With her mouth open to call his name, she stopped. Bandit never barked at things outside the house, especially after bedtime. As usual, he'd been curled up on the foot of the bed when she went to sleep. What if he was barking at something *inside* the house? With her mind racing back to the missing copperhead at the lab, she quickly slipped on her shoes, then turned back to the bedside table to retrieve the gun Noah left her. Of course, hitting a coffee can target in the back yard might not be as difficult as shooting a slithering snake with the diameter of a number two pencil. Taking time to assure it was still loaded, a flash of light caught her eye as she passed the bedroom window on the way to the door. Bandit's barking had stopped, but her heartbeat took up the rhythm and sounded nearly as loud in her ears. Creeping to the edge of the window, she peered out, scanning the woods across the road from her house. Nothing was visible.

The clock on the bedside table said 4:39. She must have done a little more than drift off to sleep. What would cause Bandit to leave her room and start barking downstairs at this hour? Her eyes fell on the phone and she was tempted to call Noah, but didn't. She had to be able to stand on her own two feet.

Slowly, hugging the wall, she eased her way down the stairs in total darkness, expecting to feel something slither beneath her feet at every footfall. She made a mental note to move a flashlight upstairs. Moonlight shining through the front windows illuminated Bandit, wide-awake, wiggling and sniffing at the front door like he wanted to go outside.

Dani turned on the lights, scanned the floor for signs of movement, and sank down on the couch, staring at the door while Bandit danced around her feet. She really shouldn't open the door, she told herself. "What is it Bandit?" she asked softly, wishing like hell he could answer. Finally, curiosity got the best of her and she turned the deadbolt and eased the door open a crack then slammed it shut again. Shit! Well, at least she knew where the missing snake was.

With trembling hands, she dialed Noah's number. So much for independence.

"Russell!" his groggy voice barked.

"Noah?" her hesitancy was quite a contrast.

"Dani! What's wrong?" She imagined him sitting straight up in the bed, suddenly alert.

"I really hate to ask this, but could you come over?"

Silence. "Now?"

"Well, yeah…" The dial tone was his answer.

Dani was in the kitchen filling the coffee pot with water when she heard him on the porch. She crossed the living room and stood just inside the door, waiting.

"Can I open the door?" she called to him from the entry.

"Please," his voice sounded calm and sure. "I don't want to touch it out here."

Grimacing as she saw that the little snake still dangled from the doorknob, she moved aside to let him enter.

"What happened?" he asked, moving swiftly toward the phone, bringing a wave of cold air inside with him.

She waited as he notified dispatch to send a forensic team and wondered if she was their sole business these days. "I woke up when Bandit started barking then I came downstairs and he was sniffing at the door. So I opened it."

He sank down on the couch beside her and frowned. "You should have called me and not touched the front door."

"Sorry," she sighed. "I didn't want to wake you for nothing."

"Dani! What if whoever left that was still out there when you opened the door?"

That reminded her. "You know, I saw a flash of light across the road right before I came downstairs!"

His frown deepened.

"I stood there and watched but I never saw it again. I thought I must have imagined it," she tried to explain.

From the expression he wore, her explanation wasn't good enough and she got up to go make the coffee. A squad car arrived just as she emerged from the kitchen with cups in hand.

"I want to see that," Noah spoke in low tones as the officer removed the snake from the doorknob with some kind of tongs.

"Hold your horses," the man told him, slipping the snake into a bag.

Dani scooted closer to the door, curious to see what it was Noah was so interested in. There was a slip of paper, folded and wrapped around the doorknob with a rubber band. She hadn't seen it because the snake was draped over it.

With gloved hands, the officer gingerly removed the rubber band and caught the note before it fell to the ground. He unfolded it carefully, then held it out for Noah to read. Dani read around his shoulder. The paper was clean aside from one typewritten line. "This one is deadly. The next one won't be dead."

"I'd say that's a pretty clear threat," the officer said, carefully placing the note into another plastic bag. "Know what kind of snake this is?"

"It's a copperhead," Dani answered before Noah had the chance and both men looked at her in surprise. "It's missing from Ophidian just like the other one."

Noah murmured something unintelligible to the man, then escorted her back to the couch. "Tell me."

Dani raised her hands. "There's not much to tell. I found out before I left work today that the count was off by one in the copperhead lab."

"Who do I need to see?" his voice sounded as deadly as the snake's venom.

She sighed. Mike asked her not to mention it, but neither of them anticipated this. "Mike McKay," she admitted. "He didn't want me to tell anyone. I suspect he doesn't want Crane to know. At least not until he can figure out how it got away."

Noah sneered at that. "I don't think it just got away."

"You know what I mean. Mike's the only one who works in that lab."

"Well you sure won't be working there today," he said sternly, glancing at his watch.

"I beg your pardon?" She couldn't believe he'd say that.

"You heard me," he said, as if that settled it.

Dani stood, eyes blazing. "I most certainly will be working today! I'll be damned if I'll let someone scare me away from my only source of income!"

"And I'll be damned if I let them get close enough to kill you because you're too stubborn to be careful!" He stood up and faced her with smoldering eyes that softened as his words struck home. "What time do you go to work?"

She wasn't sure she wanted to answer him, but the concern in his face was real. "I have class at nine, labs at one and Ophidian at four," she admitted, looking wearily over at the early morning sun creeping through the window. "Maybe I'll skip class and just go in at one," she conceded.

"Good idea," he agreed. "Why don't you go on back to bed? I'll stay here until they finish up and come back for you at 12:30."

She nodded at that. At least she could sleep without worrying that something would crawl out from under her bed when she wasn't looking. Trudging back up the stairs, she pulled the blinds to keep the sun from streaming across her bed and set her alarm for 11:00, just in case she was still sleeping by then. In spite of the trauma, she was fast asleep in minutes. It didn't last long, though. Snakes crawled through her dreams. By 9:30 she gave up the attempt.

CHAPTER FOURTEEN

"Cold enough for you?" she greeted Beth, joining her at an empty table in the cafeteria. Apparently the university prioritized energy conservation. As a result, it was cold, inside and out. Expecting warmth in the cafeteria at least, Dani wouldn't have been surprised to see puffs of condensation emerge from her lips as she spoke.

"Oh, honey, just wait," Beth grinned, moving her bag to make room for Dani's tray.

"I asked for snow," Dani concurred, sliding out of her coat and hanging it on the back of the chair.

"Well, I sure wouldn't want to be snowed in at your house," Beth pretended to shudder.

Dani smiled, but didn't offer information about the latest event. Somehow, up to now, it had seemed more like a joke. It wasn't funny anymore.

As usual, Beth talked enough for both of them, bubbling away about her latest project woes and the best campus gossip. Dani only half listened, enough to nod at the appropriate times and offer an occasional "oh really?" It wasn't until she heard the word "Ophidian" that Beth grabbed her full attention.

"What?" she prompted.

"Yeah," Beth nodded. "Who'd have thought I'd ever date a creepy crawler?" she laughed. "But he's really sweet and I love that accent. Almost like going out with Antonio Banderas!"

Dani dropped the pretense that she knew what Beth was talking about. "Who did you say again?"

Beth rolled her eyes. "Dani, I swear, you never listen!"

"I'm sorry," she shook her head. "My mind wandered just for a second. Tell me!"

"Emil!" she said emphatically. "We've been out three times now and we're going out again tonight."

Dani's eyebrows shot up in surprise. Emil wasn't bad looking, she supposed. Especially if he got rid of the surly expression he usually wore when she was around. But Antonio Banderas? "You really like him, huh?" It was all she could think of to say.

"Oh yeah, he's great! You're not the only one with good taste in men, you know."

Dani tried to pay better attention as they finished up their lunch, but it wasn't easy. Labs weren't easy either, with students in a panic trying to catch up and get everything done before the holiday break. Busying herself with student questions and storing unneeded equipment in anticipation of the semester break, Dani hardly had time to think of Noah again until she saw him sneak in the back door and stand leaning against the wall with an insolent expression on his face.

She noticed more than one of the young coeds casting furtive glances his way. No wonder. With his tall, muscular physique and angel face with devil eyes, he'd be quite the catch to take home for Christmas. As if he read her thoughts, he looked up and met her eyes across the room. She offered a small smile and a wave but he didn't return them. Probably mad because she didn't wait for him to drive her to school. With a tiny twinge of guilt, she finished what she was working on and urged her students to do the same.

"I didn't expect to see you so soon," she offered once the room was cleared out.

"That's odd," he said, strolling toward her with his hands in his pockets. "I expected to see you at 12:30. And at home."

"I couldn't sleep," she hedged, pulling on her coat. "I didn't want to bother you at work so I just came on. No biggie."

He looked at her intently for a moment. Long enough to make her squirm. "We're going to talk about this, you know."

She nodded.

***

Working at Ophidian with Noah parked in a chair in the office was unnerving, and not just for Dani. It was impossible to miss the glares shot at him one or another stuck their heads in the door. Either she'd gotten used to their attitudes, or they liked him even less than they liked her. When Dani darted down the hall to retrieve a lost file and overheard a heated discussion coming from Crane's office, she'd had enough.

"Let's go," she told Noah, gathering her books and stuffing them in her bag before she pulled on her coat.

"Off early?" he asked, easing up out of his chair.

She glared at him. "This isn't going to work," she snapped, following him to the car. "Crane will fire me before he'll let you stay there and watch me work."

"Hey, I'm just doing my job," he shrugged.

"Don't I have a say in that?" she stopped beside the car and looked up at him angrily. Protection was one thing. A full time bodyguard was another. "Nobody's going to do anything to me here on campus with thousands of people!" She unlocked her car and got in.

Noah gave her a tight-lipped expression that said he didn't agree but wasn't going to argue about it. Wordlessly, he got in the passenger side. The ride home was tense and without comment. When she pulled up in the drive and parked the car, she was surprised to see him head for the path to his house instead of following her inside.

"Where are you going?" she called, wishing she didn't have to ask, but feeling a little intimidated about going back in the house alone.

He answered without turning around, "I'll be back later."

Stunned, she stood on the porch and watched him disappear into the trees, then hurried to get her key in the door, locking it tightly behind her. She didn't feel much better inside, peeking around every corner and jumping at every sound. Once she'd changed her clothes, she went back downstairs and turned the music on. Maybe it would drown out the noises she was afraid she'd hear. But nothing held her interest long enough to keep her occupied and she found herself sitting on the couch staring blankly at the front door, wishing it was all a bad dream.

Bandit's persistent whining and sniffing reminded her that she hadn't let him out, so she grabbed her jacket again, tucking the .38 Noah left for her in her pocket before pulling on her knit gloves.

"Come on boy," she told him, desperate to hear the sound of a human voice, even if it was only her own.

Bandit spent a few minutes busily sniffing around the porch, then proceeded to the yard while she watched from the swing. Even though it was windy, cold, and gray, she had to admit it was beautiful out there. Peaceful, even with the undercurrents of danger. She'd given up on the gardens after the second freeze, but the withered plant life would have to be removed and made ready for hard winter.

As she scanned the horizon while Bandit playfully chased leaves, her thoughts inevitably settled on Noah. Somehow, she had to work things out with him. Or maybe with herself. He was the best thing to happen in her life in a long time. Maybe ever. She didn't want to risk spoiling it. He might be overprotective, but he wasn't Mark and he was only concerned about her safety. They should be in agreement there. Would be if she'd come out of denial long enough to face facts. But the idea that she was the target of some madman's obsession was too overwhelming to face, especially when she was out here all alone.

A yip from across the road caught her attention and she squinted, trying to locate Bandit in the dusk of early evening.

"Bandit!" He'd gone off across the road again, no doubt chasing a bunny.

With a sigh, Dani got to her feet and took off after him, calling his name.

"Bandit!"

Once she'd entered the cover of trees, she suppressed a shiver and stopped to listen. Usually, he wasn't too hard to spot. Not with his white and gray coat in a world that had largely turned brown. Ducking to miss low hanging branches, she examined the ground in front of her carefully before each step. Anything might be lurking beneath the mat of fallen leaves and pine needles. Despite the isolation and threat of danger, there was something comforting about the silence punctuated only by the crackle of dead leaves beneath her feet. It was a world that seemed far removed from the hectic pace of the campus. When a glance over her shoulder showed trees that nearly obliterated her view of the road that ran in front of her house, she knew she'd gone far enough. Reluctantly, she turned around, calling Bandit one more time and willing him to come back. She didn't need one more thing to worry about.

She hadn't gone far when a splash of color caught her eye and she changed direction. There, on the branches of a low-lying bramble bush, a piece of red yarn fringe was hung on the thorns. It looked like something that would be found on a winter scarf. Odd. It was large enough for her to notice twenty feet away in fading light. Surely she hadn't overlooked it the last time she came out this way. Dani scanned the ground around it for anything else, then removed her glove and carefully pried the yarn from the grip of the thorns and slid it in her pocket. Her mind wandered back to that flash of light she'd thought she'd seen early this morning. But would the person who left the snake on her door escape through the woods? Escape to where?

She turned once again and looked into the trees. As far as she could tell, there was nowhere to go. Unless they knew something she didn't. Still, with darkness falling fast, now was not the time to explore the woods facing her house. Strolling slowly back to the house, Dani called for Bandit periodically but couldn't even hear him crashing through the underbrush anymore. Wearily, she settled into the porch swing, pulling her coat up around her neck to stave off the wind.

She had no idea how long she sat there, but it was dark enough for approaching headlights to signal what she hoped was Noah's return. Lights flickered through the trees as he turned into his driveway and she watched expectantly for him to emerge from the canopy over the well-worn path between the houses. Despite their difficulties, her heart skipped a beat at the sight of his form, draped in a black denim coat that nearly reached the ground and the mane of dark hair blowing in the wind. His head was downcast, intent on the ground at his feet. His hands were firmly tucked in his pockets.

He didn't look up until he'd nearly reached the porch steps. "What are you doing out here?"

"Bandit ran off," she explained. As if on cue, a bark floated across the road, followed closely by the sound of Bandit racing through the leaves.

Noah glanced over his shoulder. "The prodigal returns."

"Bandit! You naughty dog!" Dani got up to greet him. Wagging his whole body with his tail, Bandit bounded up the steps and danced around her feet.

"Put him inside and let's go get some dinner," Noah suggested.

Obviously, he wanted to talk on neutral ground. Dani opened the door to let Bandit inside, then remembered the gun in her pocket. "Just a sec," she told Noah who stayed on the porch. She went into the dining room and traded the gun for her purse, then met him back out on the porch.

Noah accepted the keys she handed to him after she locked the door and they made their way to the car.

CHAPTER FIFTEEN

"Feel like a steak?" he asked once they were in the car. The Taurus seemed so roomy when she was alone was now filled with his presence. His head nearly brushed the roof and his coat spread over the console that separated the seats.

"Sure," she agreed, looking at him closely. His eyes were guarded and his face looked tired. Suddenly, she felt like a selfish brat. He was only trying to look out for her and she had to throw a tantrum and drive off by herself just to show him who was in charge.

"Noah," she put a gloved hand on his arm, "I'm sorry I went to school without you this morning and I'm sorry I've been such a pain."

The tiny grin he offered in return didn't reach his eyes. "It's not easy, is it?"

Dani followed his lead and kept quiet until they were seated in the restaurant. Once the waitress took their orders, Dani sucked up what bravado she had left and asked, "So, what's the verdict, doc? Am I worth saving?"

He studied her face for a moment, then a small smile tugged at the corners of his mouth. "You can be a pain, you know that?"

She smiled. "Yeah. But it's not like I've got a monopoly on that trait, you know."

His grin turned sheepish and he raised his hands in mock surrender. "Point taken. So what do you want to do about it?"

That sobered her up. "Why don't you tell me?"

He waited a long time before he answered. "I'm in a really awkward position, here."

Dani didn't like the way that sounded. "Why?"

99

Frustration was evident on his face as he groped for the right words. "It's hard to explain. As a cop, I know exactly what I should do. As a man," he acted like he was at a loss for the correct term, "I let my heart rule my head sometimes."

"What were you going to say?"

"What do you mean?"

"As a what?"

"Man will do nicely, thanks."

"Friend? Lover?" she teased, enjoying his discomfort just a little.

He grinned, reluctantly, then turned the tables on her. "Exactly what would you call me? What do you want from me, Dani?"

Suddenly, she was inordinately interested in her salad.

"Well?" he waited.

How could she answer him when she couldn't even answer the question for herself?

"And there, my dear, is the root of the problem," he said softly. "I thought you were a woman who knew what she wanted."

So did I, she thought. "What do you want?" she asked.

"You mean besides wanting this all to be over?" He watched her steadily, tracing a pattern in the condensation on his glass.

She chuckled. "Yeah."

"Are you ready to lay all the cards on the table?" He took her silence for consent. "You probably have no idea what it means, but my relationship with you was personal long before it was professional. Had it been the other way around, personal would never have entered into it."

"So, you're saying if you'd met me giving me a ticket or something we'd have never gone out?" Somehow, she found that hard to believe. The connection she'd felt with him was immediate and she didn't think his line of work would have altered it in any way. After all, he'd looked like some kind of criminal with that big gun strapped to his leg and she'd gone out with him anyway, hadn't she?

"Well, I don't like to say 'never' but that certainly would have been the plan," he said.

"I don't see what difference it makes," she shrugged, pushing her salad plate away.

"It makes a difference because I care too much what happens to you."

"That's ridiculous," she scoffed. "Are you saying you don't care what happens to other people when you work on their cases?"

"No," he raised his hands, "I'm saying I don't care to the point that it keeps me from being objective. With you, I get to a point where what you want and what you think clouds my judgment about what's best in the situation."

Dani rolled her eyes. "So what do you do? Stop seeing me?" Maybe it would hurt less if she said it first.

"That's kind of impossible since I live next door and someone's stalking you, isn't it?"

"The police would assign someone else, wouldn't they?" she countered.

That struck a chord and his nostrils flared while the muscle in his jaw clenched. "Is that what you want?"

"I didn't say that," she snapped, frustrated. "I just don't know why you can't do both. If we were dating and you weren't a cop, wouldn't you still look out for me?"

"Of course I would. But the lines have to be drawn somewhere. I need to know what you want so I can know where those lines are. One minute you're totally dependent and the next you act like I'm intruding on your personal life. What am I supposed to do?"

Dani sighed. That was a fair question. "I'm sorry about that."

The waitress arrived with their meals and they both picked at their food in silence for a while.

"I guess it would be better if we both knew exactly where this was going," she offered, finally.

"That's what I'm saying," he agreed. "Where do you want it to go?"

"Noah, that's not fair!" she protested. "You tell me first."

The muscle in his jaw started working again. "All right," his voice was curt. "I care about you more than I've cared about anyone for as long as I can remember. I was willing to give it time… to wait and see if you felt the same way. But all this shit has forced us to get close in a hurry and I don't like it when I feel you pushing me away. I'd rather be alone the rest of my life than feel like I'm straddling a fence and ready to be knocked off at any moment."

His words were weighted, pummeling her like stones. Dani chose her response carefully. "I know I do that. I'm sorry. But my marriage was a total sham. I believed him; I trusted him and he was lying to me the whole time. And I know you're not him. You're nothing like him. I love," she caught herself just in time. "I love having you close and feeling protected but I'm afraid."

"Afraid of what?" he asked softly.

"Afraid to be wrong when I trust you," she said. What she really meant was she was afraid she wouldn't live through it again.

He nodded like he thought that was fair.

"If it helps at all, I trust you more than I trust anyone," she added miserably.

"Dani," he reached across the table and touched her hand. She met his eyes. "I understand. Just tell me one thing…"

She nodded.

"Would you still want me around if I wasn't a cop?"

"Uh!" That took her completely by surprise. "Of course! Why would you ask that?"

"Just checking," he smiled. From the way he visibly relaxed, her answer must have satisfied something lurking in there.

"Noah," she leaned forward and whispered. "I have an idea. Let's go back to my house and pretend all this isn't happening and you can pretend you're not a cop if you want to."

"Ya think?" he grinned at her.

"I think," she smiled. "Now eat so we can go home."

***

The first sight to greet Dani in the morning was Noah emerging from the bathroom wearing low-slung jeans and a towel draped around his neck. "I've got to tell you, I miss the shower when I stay over here," he said, taking a seat on the edge of the bed.

"Me too," she said, rolling over so she could reach his back, unable to resist the temptation to give it a rub. "Maybe you should build me one."

He laughed. "Oh, sure. No problem. I'll trade in my badge for a plumbing license."

"Gee," she pretended to pout. "I thought last night you said you'd do anything for me." Dani ducked when he tossed the damp towel at her.

"A plumber, I'm not," he assured her, getting up and crossing to the door. "Better get up, you'll be late to class."

She made a face at his back as it vanished out the door, then rolled off the bed and headed for the closet. A quick glance out the window affirmed that it was still December so she dressed accordingly.

The feeling of contentment that came from having an understanding with Noah followed her all through class and into the lab. Attendance was down as more and more students completed their semester's work and she found herself alone in the lab with almost an hour to spare before heading over to Ophidian. With any luck, she'd have time to finish cleaning and storing the dissection tools that had been turned in. At this rate, all her work would be done long before next Friday's deadline.

"No class?" Joe Abraham poked his head in the door and looked around.

Dani smiled and shrugged. "Most of them have turned in their finals. The others don't stay long."

"Yeah," he nodded his agreement. "Everyone's anxious for the holidays." He wandered in and perched on the corner of her desk. "How've you been?"

"So, so," she answered. "How've you been?" She knew what he was wondering but felt reluctant to discuss it with him for some reason. Maybe it was the glare of the fluorescent lights, but his face looked even more pale and drawn than usual.

"I'm tired," he admitted, but the look in his eyes told her it was more than that. "Of course, I'm always tired this close to finals."

She smiled. "Yeah. I only have two more to take next week, but I'll be glad when they're done."

"Well," Dr. Abraham got up and nervously shuffled his feet, looking around the room. "Dr. Crane treating you all right?" His creased forehead contradicted the assumed casualness of his tone.

Dani wiggled uncomfortably in her chair, then got up and started gathering her things. "Let's just say it's not the same as working for you," she flashed him a smile she hoped would put an end to his questions.

"He can be a little blunt at times," he concurred. "You're doing okay, though? No more snakes hiding at your house?"

Dani's head jerked up as if she'd been slapped. "Why would you ask that?"

"Oh, no reason, just my pitiful attempt at humor," he answered quickly and tried to laugh it off. "I better get back to work!"

He scurried from the room as fast as he could without running, leaving Dani staring after him and shaking her head. As much as she hated to talk to Noah about Joe Abraham, it looked like she had no choice. His behavior was becoming too unsettling.

When she reached Ophidian, she found a note taped to the door saying the lab closed early and work would resume Monday. Last night's compromise with Noah included meeting him at the PD at six so she wouldn't arrive home alone, but now she had an extra two hours to kill. Dani walked slowly to her car, then turned on the heat and sat idling, wondering what to do.

Finally, she put the car in gear and started rolling toward the exit. Why not do what everyone else was doing? Noah promised to cut down a Christmas tree for her this weekend, but she could still go shopping for decorations and maybe some groceries for making cookies and candy. It was about time for a little holiday cheer in the log cabin, wasn't it? With her mind made up, she pressed on the accelerator and tried to forget the problems that had plagued her of late.

With festive decorations and jovial holiday shoppers, Dani caught a little of the holiday spirit and found herself enjoying the effort. Long checkout lines caused her to pull in to the police parking lot exactly twenty minutes late and just in time to catch Noah getting into his truck. Maneuvering her car to block the truck, she rolled down the passenger window and leaned over. "Hey! Bet you thought I gave you the slip again, didn't you?"

Noah frowned as he walked toward the car but it wasn't convincing. He was obviously glad to see her. Leaning on the open passenger window, he looked at the collection of bags in the back seat. "Shopping?"

She smiled. "I got off early and I knew I couldn't go home."

He returned her smile. "You'll probably want me to carry it all in, too, won't you?"

"Nah," she teased. "We'll let the elves get it."

"Right," he chuckled. "Follow me."

Back at the house, Dani made a quick supper of soup and sandwiches while Noah carried in the bags then went next door to check his mail and pick up some clean clothes. They'd agreed he should stay with her for the duration. At least until her stalker was identified and stopped. She bustled around the kitchen, excited about the idea of stringing tinsel and lights while Noah was gone to work, then greeting him with fresh baked cookies and hot eggnog when he came home. Home. Funny how he seemed to belong there.

She was surprised to see him come in the door with damp hair and clean clothes.

"I took a quick shower," he explained before she had a chance to ask. "Let me stow this then I've gotta hit the road!"

That put a frown on her face. He would have to work the first night after their new agreement.

"You can at least sit down long enough for a bowl of soup, can't you?" she asked when he came back down the stairs.

He looked at his watch. "Half hour, tops," he agreed.

"Fair enough," she smiled, pouring him a bowl then going back for another for herself.

"You seem chipper enough today," he observed when she sat down beside him.

"I'm glad it's Friday," she said. "It was a pretty easy day and next week should be even better."

"How's your boyfriend, the doctor?" he teased, putting a scowl on her face.

"That's not funny, Noah," she said. "I'm beginning to think you may be right."

His boyish grin was immediately replaced with a frown. "What happened?"

Without mincing words, she described the incident in the lab.

"He asked if you'd found any more snakes?"

"Something like that, yeah," she admitted. "Weird, huh? Or am I just paranoid? He said he was making a joke."

Noah shook his head. "It's not funny."

"No," she agreed. "I still don't think he has anything to do with it, though."

He shot her a knowing glance. "You don't think anyone you know had anything to do with it."

He had her there. They'd discussed it several times and she could see his logic, but still. The thought that she could talk to someone face to face and they'd pretend to be nice then turn around and leave snakes and threats at her house was more than she could comprehend.

"Hey!" she jumped up suddenly, remembering the yarn she'd forgotten to show him yesterday. "I forgot to tell you…" she retrieved the red scrap from her pocket and laid it triumphantly beside his bowl. "I found this across the road yesterday, right in the same area where I thought I saw a flash of light."

Noah picked it up and examined it, then looked up at her. "You *forgot?*"

She shrugged. "I don't think it was there the last time I went over there looking for Bandit. I'd have seen it."

"Exactly where was it?"

"Stuck on a bramble bush."

He looked closely at the scrap of fabric, rubbing it gently between his fingers. "So your stalker bundles up in the cold, huh? Does your boyfriend wear a red scarf?"

Dani's mouth dropped open. "No, but I know someone who does, or at least did a couple of days ago." She recounted the brief altercation between Emil and Mike at Ophidian the same day Mike discovered the copperhead missing.

"What was the fight about?" Noah asked.

"I don't know, the snake I guess. Emil's not a real friendly guy." It suddenly dawned on her that she was speaking of the man Beth compared to Antonio Banderas.

"What?" Noah must have seen the change in expression.

"Emil just started dating Beth," she said.

A strange expression flitted across his face. "Your best friend on campus."

She nodded.

"What's his whole name?" Noah pulled a spiral notebook out of his pocket.

"Emil Betancourt," Dani said, remembering the numerous reports she'd typed with his name on them.

"I'll check him out," he said as he finished writing and stuck the spiral back in his pocket. "I've got to go," he smiled softly, taking her hand and pulling her out of the chair. "Walk me to the door?"

Dani got up and slid an arm around his waist, then stopped and kissed him. "How late will you be?"

"Too late," he stroked the side of her face with one finger, then leaned down to kiss her again. "Do me a favor, be good while I'm gone, okay?"

CHAPTER SIXTEEN

With the last of her finals behind her, Dani was all too ready for school to be over. It hadn't been as difficult as she'd feared, going back to school after so many years. In fact, she'd enjoyed it for the most part. But she'd found, being older, she had far less tolerance for completing studies that had little relevance to her chosen career aside from the resultant diploma.

With the students all gone, Dani made quick work of cleaning the lab then sat down at her desk to finish grading the papers that had been collecting the last few days. It was her least favorite part of the job and, as such, the one she postponed until the last possible moment.

"God! I am so glad that's done!" Beth swooped dramatically into the lab and flung herself down in a chair adjacent to Dani's desk.

Dani looked up with a smile. "Finished?"

Beth rolled her eyes. "Finally! I swear I wish I didn't have to do this next semester!"

"Oh, come on, it's not that bad," Dani said. Everything for Beth was melodramatic.

"The hell it's not! These kids don't have a clue! They're just selfish and lazy and incompetent," she snapped.

Dani laughed. Beth seemed hardly more than a kid herself.

"So, give me the scoop," Beth leaned suggestively toward the desk, blue eyes wide. "How are things with Wonder Detective?"

Dani sighed. "Fine," she offered a small smile.

"Fine!" Beth scoffed. "Details, I want details! Are you engaged yet? Is he buying you a ring for Christmas?"

"Whoa!" Dani laughed. "Who said anything about getting engaged?"

"Come on, Dano," Beth shot her a knowing look. "You're obviously crazy about the guy and you're not getting any younger."

"Geez, Louise!" Dani laughed again. "You're more obsessed with him than I am!"

"In your dreams, Dano," Beth chuckled. "I've seen how he looks at you. You're in denial."

Dani thought about that. Beth probably had a point. She was aware that Noah seemed to be waiting for a commitment she just couldn't give and the idea troubled her. What if she waited around for too long and he moved on? What would she do without him? She sat up and started gathering the stack of papers she'd already graded, separating them from the rest of the stack. She didn't want to think about that.

"I'm right, aren't I?" Beth asked.

"It's too soon," Dani tried to blow it off.

"For him or for you?"

"Damn, Beth! Give it a rest, will you?"

Beth smiled. "Don't wait too long. You don't want this one to get away."

Dani looked up and locked eyes with her, ready to do battle, but Beth's expression discouraged that and she sighed. "I just don't want to get burned again."

Beth's expression softened. "Honey, we'll all get burned again, sometime, somehow," she said knowingly. "The point is, who better to be burned by?"

Dani smiled and shook her head. "There's logic."

"I mean it!" Beth insisted. "What if he's the real thing and you never know because you're afraid to try? What a loser."

"Great," Dani chuckled. "Now I'm a loser. You're a good friend, Beth."

"You know what I mean," she rolled her eyes.

"I get your point and I'll consider it," Dani said, reaching for the drawer that contained her grade book. "Now get out of here and let me post these grades so I can go, too."

With an exaggerated sigh, Beth got up and started for the door but Dani's shriek stopped her in her tracks.

Dani's hands shook as she sat staring at the drawer she'd just opened and slammed shut.

"What?" Beth asked, approaching the desk.

Dani didn't take her eyes off the drawer. "There's a snake in that drawer."

"Oh, God," Beth sounded disgusted. "I told you, these kids are so juvenile." She moved around the desk and reached for the drawer.

"No!" Dani yelled, stopping her. "It's alive. I think it's a copperhead!"

"Dano, you've lost it. Nobody would put..." her voice trailed off as she examined Dani's face. "Who would put a copperhead in your drawer?"

"Just watch the drawer," Dani instructed, reaching for the phone to dial Ophidian.

"Let me talk to Mike," she instructed the girl who answered. She must have sounded important enough or urgent enough. The girl dropped the receiver on the desk and Dani heard her from a distance calling Mike's name. After what seemed an eternity, she heard heavy steps approaching the phone.

"What?" Mike's voice was sharp.

"Mike, it's Dani. I need you to come to Biology Lab 4 right now."

"What the hell for?"

"Are you missing another copperhead?" she asked.

There was a long silence. "Why?"

"Because there's one in my desk. Could you come here now, please?"

He hung up the phone.

"Is he coming?" Beth asked as Dani hung up the phone.

Dani nodded, scooting her chair away from the desk but keeping her eye on the drawer. "You don't think it can crawl out of there, do you?"

"Shit!" Beth jumped back at the thought.

Dani reached for the phone again, dialing Noah's cell number.

"Russell," his voice was a welcome relief.

"Noah, there's a snake in my drawer at the lab," the words rushed out.

"What? Are you okay?"

"Ye-es," her voice started to quiver. "I'm waiting for Mike to come."

"Which lab?" he was all business.

"Four."

"I'll be right there."

Dani and Beth waited in silence, jumping when Mike burst through the door.

"Where is it?" he barked, looking mad as hell.

Dani pointed, then got up and moved away as he approached the drawer. Gloved to the elbows, he carried a cloth bag and a stick with a noose on one end and a Y on the other.

"I'll just wait over here," Beth said, moving toward the door, her freckles standing out in stark contrast to her ashen face.

"One of you has got to hold the bag," he snapped, looking first at Beth, then at Dani.

"Hey, it's your lab," Beth told Dani.

Great. Dani tentatively reached for the bag Mike held out, then spied the trashcan beside the desk. "How about if I put the bag in there?" she asked, dumping the trash on the floor then lining it with the bag Mike gave her and scooting it over beside him.

Mike shot her a withering glance, but didn't argue. Slipping the end of his stick through the drawer handle, he slowly opened the drawer to reveal a small copperhead, coiled atop the grade book, watching them with tongue flicking.

"Beth," Dani spoke softly to avoid startling the snake any further, "watch for Noah so he doesn't storm in here and scare it."

"Don't let anyone else in here," Mike added.

Beth nodded and slowly opened the door, stepping back into the hall while keeping her eyes on the desk. Mike moved slowly, trying to catch the snake's riveting head in the noose, but it eluded him, hissing and striking with a force that caused Dani to jump. Patiently, he tried again, finally pinning the snake in a corner of the drawer with the Y end of the stick.

"You're not going to touch it, are you?" Dani asked, horrified, as he reached for it with his free hand.

"Would you rather I left it here?" he asked sarcastically.

Dani's blood ran cold as he moved swiftly, grasping the snake securely just behind the head and lifting it from the drawer.

"Get the bag," he said through clenched teeth.

Out of the corner of her eye, she saw Noah come through the door, approaching slowly. "I've got it." Swiftly and silently, he moved around the desk and grabbed the bag from the trashcan, holding it open for Mike to lower the snake. A moment later, the bag was closed, undulating silently on the floor beside the desk.

"What the fuck happened here?" Noah asked sharply, looking first at Dani, then at Mike.

"I was just going to get my grade book and I found it there in my drawer," she pointed to the open drawer.

"Is it one of yours?" Noah asked Mike who nodded grimly. "Who touched the drawer?"

"No one but me," Dani said, remembering that Mike used the stick to open it.

"Copperhead, right?" he asked Mike who nodded again. "Where's your boss?" he turned to Dani.

"I don't know. I haven't seen him today," she said, looking over at Beth.

"Me either," Beth spoke from the doorway. "Listen, can I go now?"

Noah looked over at her. "Were you here when she found it?"

Beth nodded.

"Then you'll need to stay." He reached for the phone and called for a squad car. "Stay here, all of you," he instructed, then strode from the room. When he returned, he had a pale-faced Joe Abraham and a campus security officer in tow. Two uniformed police officers appeared a moment or two later.

"All right," Noah said sternly. "Let's get some answers."

The inquisition, as Dani referred to it, lasted the better part of two hours. When it was over, against Noah's advice, Dani insisted on going back to Ophidian to help Mike close up the lab for the holidays. She was sure she'd hear about it later, but she was numb right now. She wanted to finish her work then never go back there again.

When she left with Mike, Noah was still questioning Joe and Beth about who had access to a locked lab.

"Well, that was festive, wasn't it?" she said to Mike, wearily dropping her book bag on the table in the file room.

He grunted in response but didn't answer as he headed off down the hall with the snake bag in hand. The place was eerily quiet, with most of the employees already gone for the holiday. Dani was finishing the last of her reports when she looked up to find him in the doorway.

"Can I see those?" he nodded at the report file. Dani handed it to him and he scanned the pages, his expression growing darker with each one.

"What?" she asked.

"Something's not right," he handed it back to her, then reached for another. "Count how many Madagascar Hognose we should have."

"Sure," she opened the file and pulled out her notepad, making little stick marks to tabulate each group. They worked in silence for a few minutes, with Mike doing the same thing on another file.

"Shit!" he said, causing her to look up.

"What?"

"How many do you have?" he looked at her.

"Um…" she tallied it up in her head, "looks like eight mature and twenty-seven in nursery," she said.

"No way!" he jumped up from the floor and took off down the hall. Ignoring her instincts to avoid the labs whenever possible, she followed him and found him in lab seven counting out loud.

"What's wrong, Mike?" she asked, hovering just inside the door. He motioned for her to be quiet and continued counting, turning toward her as he finished the last tank.

"Is that the file?" he came toward her with his hand outstretched.

Nodding, she handed it to him, watching as he checked each tank again. "No fucking way," he turned to her with a stricken look on his face, then snatched up a file laying on the table beside him and brushed past her through the door. Reluctantly, she followed him again, pausing momentarily as she realized that he'd entered lab twelve, the only one where they kept venomous reptiles. Ophidian housed and bred a large variety of snakes, but the Southern copperhead (Agkistrodon contortrix), was the only venomous one.

"Mike, what's wrong?" she asked again, noting that a ghostly pallor had replaced his usually ruddy complexion.

"We've gotta check every lab," he said, brushing past her on his way back out the door.

Dani caught up with him again in the file room, where he was busily removing folders from the bottom drawer. "Here," he placed a stack on the table in front of her. "You tally them up, I'll go count them," he said.

"Are you going to tell me what we're doing?" she asked, beginning to feel alarmed by his sense of urgency.

He looked at her steadily through narrowed eyes for a moment, then hissed, "The numbers are all wrong, every single one I've checked."

"Well, maybe it's the files," she suggested, remembering the disarray in the file room before she cleaned it up.

"That's what I thought too, at first," he said, still whispering. "But I'm the only one who takes care of the hognose Madagascar and the Copperheads. I just did an update last week. We're missing more snakes," he said.

"Maybe they're on the dead list?" she offered, referring to the running page they kept of casualties in each lab.

"Dani," he took on the tone of a parent reasoning with a child who refused to understand, "I've lost one baby Copperhead in the last month. We're missing twelve! Thirteen if you count the one I just brought back from your lab."

"Oh," she said meekly, swallowing a lump of dread that was forming in her throat. Mike waited for her to add up the first file, then headed off to verify the count while she moved to the next one. One by one, they went through each species, growing more concerned when he came back with a short count every time.

With a look of utter defeat on his face, Mike slapped the last folder down on the table and slumped into the chair beside it. "Brown snake is the only one not missing any," he said with a groan.

"Except the one that showed up at my house before," she reminded him.

Grabbing a pencil off the table, he started adding a column of numbers on the outside of the file. "Jesus!" he exclaimed, throwing the pencil at the wall. "We're missing over a hundred snakes!"

Dani pulled the pencil from behind her ear and started her own line of numbers, looking up at him when she was through. "We should have 1012," she said. "How could we be missing a tenth of them and nobody notice?"

"I noticed," he snapped. "Why the hell do you think I'm doing this?"

"You know what I mean," she frowned. "I sure as hell didn't take them. Don't snap at me!"

"Crane's gonna have my ass," he moaned, covering his face with his hands.

"What do you think it is?" she asked with all sorts of scenarios running through her mind.

He shook his head, speechless for a moment. "Somebody took 'em," he shrugged.

"But who? And why?" she asked. "And how?" There was no way she could imagine anyone making off with more than a hundred snakes and not attracting attention.

"I don't know!"

"Well, think about it," she insisted. "Did somebody come in here and get them all at once, or have they been sneaking them out a little at a time?"

He frowned, but looked like he was considering the question. "I know I wasn't missing thirteen in the Copperhead lab on Friday," he said. "The others, I can't be sure. But some are pythons and boas. There's no way anyone could get out of here with all of these in one trip, that's for sure."

"So it must have happened over the weekend," she said, stating the obvious. "What are you going to do?"

Mike sank to the floor, dropping his head into his hands. "He'll fucking fire me."

"Mike, it's not you," she reasoned.

"Tell that to Crane!" he looked up at her with panic in his eyes.

Noah chose that moment to join them, entering the hall from the office door. Dani looked up at him, squatting on the floor in front of Mike.

"What's going on?" he asked suspiciously.

Dani looked back at Mike. "You've got to tell him."

"Tell me what?" he asked ominously.

When Mike didn't answer, Dani did. "We're missing over a hundred snakes."

"You're kidding," he said, but his voice was deadly serious.

"Do we have to make this an official report?" Mike asked, looking up at Noah.

Noah's eyes narrowed. "Come talk to me." With that, he turned and headed back to the office. Dani and Mike joined him there.

CHAPTER SEVENTEEN

Mike looked more discouraged than Dani had ever seen him and, despite their differences, her heart went out to him. He wasn't very friendly to her, but he worked hard and she knew Crane would blame him for the loss, even though he had nothing to do with it.

Noah looked skeptical as he took notes from the information Mike gave him and surprised her by telling Mike he wouldn't file the report just yet. She waited until they got back to the house to ask him why.

"I guess I need to update you about a few things," he sighed, getting up from the couch to stoke the fire.

Dani felt a little thrill as she watched him, muscles working in his broad back as he leaned into the fireplace. She couldn't help but compare him to Mark sometimes. Mark felt like any kind of household activity was beneath him. Since Noah had been staying with her, even with an incredibly long work schedule, it seemed like he was always doing something. Cleaning the fireplace, running a load of laundry, helping with dishes. She even found him mopping the bathroom floor once. Hard to imagine. She rubbed his arm as he sat back down beside her. Oddly enough, she had mixed feelings about him finding out who her stalker was. Once he did, she'd have no reason for him to stay here. At least none that she was willing to consider.

"You have an idea who's doing all this?" she asked.

"I have some suspicions," he nodded. "First of all, your Dr. Abraham seems a little shady to me."

"No he's not," she said. "Is he?"

He looked at her in amusement. "Still defending the boyfriend?"

Dani nudged him with her elbow.

"Did you know he was fired from his last job?" he asked.

114

Dani was shocked. "What for?" As far as she could tell, he was an excellent instructor, very diligent about his work.

"Suspicion of misappropriation of funds."

"Shit! I'd never have dreamed......" her voice trailed off.

"Yeah. And, although I don't have all the info yet, his bank accounts seem a little heavy for a professor's salary. His net worth is in excess of $500,000."

Dani didn't have an answer for that either. "Maybe he inherited it."

"Maybe."

"Is that why you agreed not to make an official report about the missing snakes?"

He shook his head. "It seems that Dr. Atkinson and Dr. Crane both have some questionable backgrounds. I'm looking into that too. Besides, I don't think McKay had anything to do with it and I don't want to tip my hand to Crane until I know more."

Dani nodded. "I'm glad of that. Mike's a little different, but I don't think he's doing all this."

"You're just soft on him because he gave you that cat," Noah smiled, nodding at the purring feline that occupied the corner of the couch.

She smiled and snuggled up next to him as he raised his arm and draped it around her shoulders.

"Did I tell you I like the way you've decorated the house?" he asked softly.

"I love Christmas," she smiled.

"Guess I'll have to get shopping and fill up that space under the tree," he nodded to the corner where the graceful fir reached to the ceiling. Dani already had gifts wrapped under the tree for Beth and Mike and a couple for the local foster children's program.

"You don't have to do that," she shook her head. She'd been wracking her brain trying to decide on a gift for him, but as yet she had no ideas.

"Darlin'," he stroked her cheek, "I rarely do anything because I have to. Except go to work, which I have to get ready for about now."

Dani groaned. His working evenings was no fun. She missed their dinner and movie nights. With decorating done and no more papers to write or grade, the evenings seemed far too long. "Want something to eat before you go?"

"Nah," he shook his head. "I'll grab something later."

Locking eyes with him, she felt herself falling into the chocolate brown orbs. Warmth started in the pit of her stomach and radiated throughout her body until she shivered. I love you, Noah. The words pounded inside her head, but there was no way she dared voice them out loud. He answered the unspoken invitation with a kiss. Lips soft as velvet against her own, contrasting with the scratchy feel of his beard. Dani didn't remember ever feeling safer and more secure in all of her life. Beth was right. She'd be a fool to let him walk away.

Noah winked at her, then moved to get up. Dani watched as he tugged on his coat and headed out the door to work, then turned her attention back to the blaze in the fireplace. Thinking about a future with Noah was disconcerting, but not nearly as disturbing as the thought of one without him. Hoping to avoid that train of thought, Dani got up and decided to get busy.

With Noah off to work, she started the evening by making a casserole that would be easy to warm if he was hungry when he came in, then after cleaning up, she spread a collection of Christmas cards out on the table and addressed them to old friends in Austin. There weren't many she cared to correspond with after the divorce, but a few still held a warm place in her heart. Once that was done, she decided to go upstairs for a long, hot soak in the tub.

She'd just climbed in the tub with a good book when she heard Bandit barking downstairs. Great. Even though he stopped as suddenly as he'd started, a tiny quiver of fear kept her from enjoying the bath, so she climbed out a few minutes later and dressed warmly in a pair of flannel pjs and wrapped her terry cloth robe tightly around her before going back downstairs. Noah rarely returned from work before midnight, but she'd been waiting up for him, ready to fix him a bite to eat if he was hungry. Maybe she was more domestic than she thought.

When she positioned herself on the couch with a stack of magazines and catalogs to peruse, she noticed Bandit seemed unusually interested in the front door. With visions of the snake that dangled from her doorknob just last week, and the more recent visitor to her desk drawer, she ignored his interest and determined to catalog shop until she had an idea of the perfect gift for Noah. But Bandit's incessant whining got the best of her and she finally got up and peeked out the window beside the door. With the porch light on, she saw that there was no one around, but she couldn't see the doorknob from the window. Knowing she shouldn't, she unlocked the door and carefully eased it open. No snake on the doorknob, but there was a huge manila envelope propped on the door that fell as she opened it wider.

Dani bent and retrieved it, then quickly shut the door and locked it again. It was an interdepartmental envelope like they used at the college with her name sprawled across the front in magic marker. She wasn't sure, but it looked a little like Mike's handwriting. Reluctantly, she unwound the string that held the clasp closed and let the files slide out on the couch cushion beside her. It took awhile, but she finally deduced that the papers contained proof, or at least indication, that Dr. Atkinson had been using Ophidian to obtain grant money under false pretenses. If what she was reading was right, it looked like he was also selling off some of the snakes for his own personal gain, and at phenomenal prices!

Dani's mind went into overdrive. It must have been Mike who dug up this information for her, but why did he give it to her? Why not give it to Crane, or even to Noah? Someone who could do something about it, at least. Nervously, she bundled all the papers back up in the envelope, then put it beside her computer with the rest of her Ophidian paperwork, then paced restlessly in front of the fire, wondering what to do about it.

Obviously, Mike trusted her to do the right thing, but what was it? She knew his job was important to him. He just started the PhD program so he was a few years away from managing his own lab, but if Crane fired him, it would be a big blow to his record. No one would want to hire a lab manager who lost over a hundred snakes. He was trying to help her and save his own job at the same time. She'd have to be very careful.

Maybe the best thing to do was to approach Crane on her own. Tell him everything. If he knew she'd been the target of a stalker who was using snakes from Ophidian to scare her, maybe he'd go easier on Mike. According to the paperwork in the envelope, Atkinson was the one she needed to worry about, not Crane. The longer she considered that option, the better it felt. Finally, with eyes growing tired as the fire died out, she sank back onto the couch and drifted off to sleep waiting for Noah. Her last thought was that she'd probably wait and tell Noah after she'd had a chance to talk to Crane. Noah wouldn't be nearly as concerned about protecting Mike's job as she was. He'd never worked for a PhD. He didn't know how complicated it could be.

She must have slept soundly because she woke in her bed with sunlight streaming through the window and went downstairs to find Noah already gone to work. The damp towel in the bathroom and fresh pot of coffee told her he'd been there. He probably assumed she wouldn't be going anywhere since her classes and lab work were finished, but she hadn't promised not to. With a sense of determination, she dressed quickly and hurried from the house before he could call and tell her not to go.

The campus was nearly deserted. There were a few straggling students, undergrad mostly, in the throes of finals, and professors finishing up their grading for the term. Dani was relieved to see Dr. Crane's car parked in its usual space outside Ophidian, although it didn't appear anyone else was there. She wavered for a moment, wondering again if she was doing the right thing. Steeling herself for his harshness, she mustered a modicum of courage and entered the office.

As she'd expected, the offices were deserted. Her footsteps echoed down the hallway, accentuating her isolation and increasing her anxiety. Dani paused to take a deep breath and steady herself before entering Dr.

Crane's outer office. Dark and vacant, it made approaching the ribbon of light shining through his partially open door all the more intimidating.

"Dr. Crane?" she knocked on the door frame of his open office.

"Yes?" his voice was rich and deep, and reasonably pleasant, for him at least.

"Could I talk to you for a minute?" she peered nervously into the room.

Dr. Crane was seated behind his desk, as usual, but dressed in a pullover sweater without his customary lab coat. A parka was draped across the arm of the couch that lined the wall adjacent to the desk. A shock of white hair fell loosely across his forehead and he seemed a little less foreboding than normal. His eyes narrowed and she suspected he was trying to remember who she was.

"Certainly. Come on in."

"Dr. Crane," she perched skittishly on the edge of a chair facing his desk and decided not to mince words, "there's a problem I think you should be aware of." The walls were decorated with a variety of prints and photos, all containing snakes of one variety or another. All making her skin crawl.

"Problem?" He didn't look much like a man who tolerated problems.

"Yes sir," she swallowed, trying to contain her nervousness. "It's a long story, but..." she groped for the right words, kicking herself for not rehearsing exactly what she'd say in advance. "Someone has been stalking me since I moved here. Twice, there have been snakes left at my house and they both came from here. Then, yesterday, there was a copperhead in one of my desk drawers in the Biology lab. It was from here, too." Dani swallowed again. None of it was coming out the way she'd intended and his stare grew more intense with each word.

"You're sure of this?" he asked, a frown darkening his countenance.

"Yes, sir," she answered.

"Why would someone want to do that to you?" When he leaned forward and focused his stare, Dani felt the hair on the back of her neck rise. No wonder Mike didn't want to tell him.

"Well," she cleared her throat, "I think it's because I bought Dr. Atkinson's old house."

Dr. Crane raised his eyebrows and rocked back in his chair, understanding dawning on his expression. "I see. Is that all you came to tell me?"

"No, sir," she said, determined to finish. "I've been doing a little investigating and I've discovered that Dr. Atkinson may have been misappropriating grant money when he was here." For now, she'd rather leave Noah out of it.

Dani watched him closely for a reaction, but didn't see one.

"And you think this is why someone is stalking you?"

Dani couldn't put her finger on it, but something wasn't going the way she'd expected. Dr. Crane didn't seem surprised or even concerned that the snakes were from his lab.

"It's the only reason I can think of. You know, they did discover a skeleton buried in my cellar."

"I heard that," he nodded, "although I didn't realize it was yours, of course. The house, I mean," he almost smiled. "I guess this is a problem, isn't it?"

Dani didn't know what to say and shifted nervously in her seat.

"What would you like me to do?" he asked, suddenly solicitous.

Dani sighed. "I… well……… I…………"

"Just say it child," he encouraged in a voice he no doubt intended to sound comforting. Instead, it sent a chill down her back.

"I don't want you to blame Mike McKay for the snakes that were used," she blurted it out. "I know he didn't take them and I don't want him to get fired because someone else was trying to scare me."

Crane's eyes narrowed slightly as he considered that. "McKay?" He nodded. "Of course not. I'm sure he's not to blame." He looked at her expectantly.

Dani got up. "Thank you, Dr. Crane," she said, anxious to get out of there. "I appreciate that."

"You're very welcome, young lady," he offered a cheesy smile. He didn't even know her name. "I'll be sure and look into this. You have a good holiday, now."

"Yes, sir. You too," she fairly ran from the room. Her effort might have failed miserably, but at least she'd tried. She also managed to escape without revealing that there were still a hundred more snakes missing.

Dani paused to button her coat before leaving the office and was surprised when the knob was pulled from her hand as she reached for it. A tall, stately woman she recognized as Mrs. Crane entered the room, filling it with expensive perfume and a disdainful attitude.

"Pardon me," she said crisply, looking Dani over carefully.

"Excuse me, Mrs. Crane," Dani tried to smile, hoping the woman wouldn't wonder what she was doing here alone with her husband.

"Don't I know you?" she asked, looking down her patrician nose with a critical expression on her face.

"We've not met, but I've seen you around," Dani offered. "I'm Dani Jones, I work here part time."

"Danielle Jones," she said the name slowly. "Of course. My husband's mentioned you often."

That was news to her. Dani would have sworn he didn't even know who she was. Besides, weren't they divorced now?

"Well," Mrs. Crane moved past her toward the hall.

With the feeling she'd been dismissed, Dani reached for the doorknob again.

"Danielle," Mrs. Crane turned back at the hall door, "Give my best to Noah, won't you?"

"Noah?" That caught her completely off guard and she turned back in surprise.

"Yes, Noah Russell," Mrs. Crane offered a cynical smile. "I understand you're seeing him now." The emphasis on 'seeing' would be hard to miss.

"Okay. Do you know him?" Stupid question but she had to ask.

Mrs. Crane gave a throaty laugh. "Of course, Noah and I go back for years, dear. I'd suggest you watch him. He's a sly one."

With that, she disappeared into the hall, leaving Dani with her mouth open. Exactly what was Mrs. Crane insinuating? And how could she have known him for years if he'd only moved here a few months before?

The thoughts plagued her all the way home. When she put the key in the lock of the front door, she heard the phone ringing and considered not answering. She wasn't ready to talk to Noah just yet. Its persistence unnerved her though.

"Hello," she barked.

"Hey, don't bite my head off!" Fortunately, it was Beth's voice.

"Sorry," Dani grudged. "What's up?"

"I'm pissed, that's what's up," Beth said. "Emil is such an ass!"

Dani rolled her eyes and sank into a nearby chair, shrugging her coat off her shoulders and leaving it hanging on the chair back. "What happened now?"

"Ugh! He stood me up last night, then, when I called him while ago, he said he doesn't want to see me anymore! Can you believe that?"

Dani was tempted to chuckle but stifled it. With all that had happened lately, the last thing Beth needed was to date someone from Ophidian. "I'm sorry. Men are beasts, aren't they?"

There must have been an edge in her voice because Beth waited a moment to answer. "You have a fight with the Wonder Detective?"

"Not yet," Dani said ominously. "Hey, do you know anything about Caroline Crane?" If anyone knew the dirt on the woman, it would be Beth.

"The Ice Bitchess?" Beth had a title for everyone.

"That bad, huh?"

"Worse," she said. "Why?"

"Oh, just something she said."

"All right, time for a confab. Meet me for dinner," Beth said.

Dani looked at her watch. It was only half past three. "Now?"

"No, silly. But, hey – I have some shopping to do. Go with me to the mall then we'll have dinner!" her voice took on a surge of excitement.

"Deal!" Dani said, glad for an excuse to get out. "Where shall we meet?"

"Ummmmm let's say.........JC Penney's at the mall. Jewelry department in half an hour."

Dani smiled. "I'll see you there."

Dani sighed as she locked the house up behind her. Once again, for reasons she couldn't even state, the warm, cozy, inviting atmosphere had been replaced by a chilling suspicion. Would she ever be able to fully trust anyone again?

Even a spontaneous shopping spree didn't offer the enjoyment it would have even a few hours earlier. The only one she desperately wanted to get a gift for was Noah and now she wasn't even sure of that. Fortunately, Beth had enough holiday cheer for both of them, in spite of her recent breakup. Soon, Dani found herself laughing and picking up odds and ends for the house. By the time they were done she had a bagful of items, including gifts for Bandit and Charlie.

Once they were tucked away at a corner table in the mall cafeteria, Beth turned inquiring eyes toward her.

"All right, now spill it!"

Dani didn't have to wonder what she was talking about. She'd already brought it up once but Dani talked her into waiting until dinner.

"It's probably nothing," she demurred.

Beth waited expectantly.

"I ran into Mrs. Crane today. She told me to give her best to Noah."

"No shit?"

Dani grimaced. "She said they'd known each other for years. But that doesn't make sense since he just moved here."

"Just moved here?" Beth looked confused.

"Yeah. In March. Why?" The response in Beth's eyes hit Dani like a punch in the gut. The way her eyes darted away when Dani spoke confirmed the hit.

"You mean a year ago in March, don't you?"

"No. I mean this year. Why?" Dani knew she didn't want to hear the answer but she had to ask.

"Because I remember seeing him last year. He was at the Rose Parade."

"Maybe it was someone who looked like him," Dani suggested, grasping at straws.

"Right. Like there's all kinds of guys walking around that look like that," Beth scoffed. She stopped when she looked at Dani again. "It's possible, I guess."

Dani felt her world spinning.

"Hey, why don't you just ask him?"

"I already did," she said grimly. "He said he moved here in March."

"Men!" Beth muttered. "Let's talk about something else."

Dani only paid half attention to Beth's chatter. Her mind was already at work sorting and deciding how to do what she knew she had to do. By the time she left Beth in the parking lot her mind was made up. She had to distance herself from Noah, and fast. Before she lost her nerve, or even her sanity!

CHAPTER EIGHTEEN

With all the determination she could muster, Dani stopped at Home Depot and bought some new locks then headed home. Tears streamed down her face as she gathered Noah's things and stuffed them into his duffel bag. She nearly lost it when she found a note Noah had left on the dining room table. It read : "No peeking at your surprise! See you soon. Noah." With the note clenched tightly in her hand, she sank into the nearest chair and sobbed until she was dry. Why did he have to lie to her? She could forgive a lot of things, but the wound from all of Mark's lies was still too painful. There was no way she could tolerate any more. Playing on that determination, she grabbed a pen and a notepad and started writing.

"Noah. I can't do this. You haven't been honest with me and that's the one thing I can't tolerate. If you care about me at all, you'll accept this. I can't bear to argue with you right now. Your things are packed in the duffel bag on the swing. Please, just take them and go. I promise, if there's another problem I'll contact the police right away. Have a good life. Dani."

With a sigh that ripped out her soul, she got up and carried the duffel bag out to the porch, then she went back inside to get the locks and screwdrivers. With a little effort, she had the deadbolt replaced in half an hour. She didn't bother with the doorknob, knowing the new deadbolt would prevent his key from working. Feeling like she was locking the door on her future, she turned resolutely away and headed for the back door.

She tried to smile at the sight of Bandit romping in the leaves while she worked, but failed miserably. Somehow, she'd get on with her life. It occurred to her that it might be easier if she sold this place and moved to another school, but that thought was followed immediately with the realization that nobody was likely to buy the place. Without the money from the house, she'd never make it. Maybe Noah would get disgusted and move.

But Noah was everywhere she looked. In front of the fireplace, snuggled in the couch, perched on a chair at the dining room table. Mopping the bathroom floor. Worse, he was in her bed. She'd never rid herself of his presence in this house. Tears blocked her vision yet again, even though she'd been sure earlier that she'd cried all the tears she had in her. With a trembling hand, she wiped them away and secured the door, then called for Bandit. Shit. While she was fumbling with the lock, he must have wandered off in the back yard. Why did he always do that just before dark?

Too weary to search for him, she closed the door and locked it, hoping he'd come scratching before it got too late. She tried to get interested in television to occupy her mind, but kept the sound low in case Bandit came scratching at the door. Apparently, advertisers were convinced that all programming should have a happy, holiday theme these days. With her heart breaking, she was hardly inclined to celebrate. As it drew closer to midnight and she knew Noah would come back soon and find the note fastened to the front door, she shut everything off downstairs, scooped up Charlie, and made her way upstairs. Turning on the radio to drown out the sounds in her head, she reluctantly climbed in bed with the best book she could find. It was challenging to pick something exciting enough to keep her interested without scaring her half to death.

In spite of the music, shortly after midnight she heard the creaking of Noah's weight on the front porch, followed by what sounded like his fist against the wall. Dani closed her eyes tightly and waited, but there were no more sounds. Unable to concentrate, Dani put up the book and turned off the lamp but there was no sleep to be had. At a quarter to two, Dani got up and snuck down the stairs. She just had to see if Noah's things were gone from the porch. Maybe that would give her some closure. She despised herself for not being able to confront him in person, but she knew she'd have never been able to do it. Those doe eyes could melt her in a single glance and she'd have been trapped until he turned on her. Then she'd have been helpless to escape.

A quick peek out the window showed the swing swaying in the breeze. Empty. Noah was gone. Dani trudged back up the stairs and climbed into bed, pulling the comforter up around her ears and ignoring the tears that trailed down her cheeks once again. She'd never felt more alone, even with Charlie curled snugly at her feet.

***

The morning sun assaulted her harshly and she squinted eyes that were swollen from crying. Slowly, feeling like she'd aged fifty years overnight, she made her way to the bathroom. Cold water did little to ease the swelling and the sight that greeted her in the mirror was frightening. Good thing she had no plans to go out today.

Determined to get on with her life, she headed downstairs and made herself a pot of coffee and a bowl of oatmeal, fending off the relentless bombardment of memories that haunted her. You'd think she'd known Noah for years instead of a few short months. Telling herself that it would get easier with each passing hour, she kept herself busy, scrubbing, rearranging, mopping. Her plan fell apart when she vacuumed the living room and spied the surprise Noah's note must have referred to.

There, beneath the Christmas tree, was a tiny package, wrapped in glossy blue paper and sporting a curly gold cascade of ribbon. Drawn to it against her better judgment, she knelt in front of the tree and picked it up with trembling hands. The tag read simply: To Dani From Noah. She dropped it like she'd been stung while tears filled her eyes yet again. She didn't even want to know what was in the package. It was too small and reminded her far too much of a jewelry box.

Near panic, she got up and left the vacuum in the middle of the floor. Grabbing her jacket, she headed for the back door. She'd seen how many leaves had collected in the back yard when she changed the lock. Maybe raking would be a good idea. If that didn't work, she'd go traipsing through the woods in search of Bandit. Anything to get out of that house. It was too full of Noah.

Who was she kidding? she asked herself as she paused to look over what she'd accomplished. With every move, she strained to see through the trees to determine whether Noah was home. Every sound caused her heart to skip a beat as she wondered if it was his truck pulling up in the drive. Walking away from the pile of leaves she'd accumulated, she abandoned the effort and sank down on the back porch. Somehow, she had to get through this.

After a few minutes, she headed back inside to fix something for lunch, going through the motions by rote. She couldn't even tell what kind of soup she'd eaten if she hadn't seen it on the can label. After lunch, she sorted through her dvd collection for a movie that wouldn't be too painful to watch. It was more challenging than she anticipated, though, since everything she had was something she'd either watched with Noah, or reminded her of him.

Finally, she selected 'Outbreak' and sat down on the couch, determined that she wouldn't develop a fear of being reminded of him that would dictate how she lived.

Although the movie was an old favorite, she hardly enjoyed it, but stuck it out to the end. When it was over and she caught sight of the tiny gift nestled beneath the tree, she got up and grabbed her coat again. Maybe she'd go out for dinner.

Choosing a restaurant she felt sure Noah would never frequent, she ate alone, surrounded by diners full of holiday cheer. She felt like she was enclosed in a plastic bubble, able to see and hear everything around her, yet nothing touched her. She was alone with a pain that was nearly unbearable and there seemed to be no relief. More than once, she considered calling Noah. Telling him she was sorry and asking him to pretend it never happened. But that wouldn't work. Sooner or later, she'd get to this place again.

Unwilling to go home yet, Dani headed back to the mall. Not that she wanted to do any shopping, but it was a good place to get lost in a crowd. She stayed until closing time, wandering from store to store, taking a break on one of the strategically placed benches when her legs grew too tired. On the drive home, she felt a prick of conscience. Noah had stressed to her how vulnerable she was traveling these isolated roads alone late at night. Whatever her situation, some things hadn't changed and that was one of them.

As she pulled into the drive, she scanned the yard for any sign of Bandit, but there was none. Charlie greeted her at the door, rubbing against her ankles and purring 'Naowwww' no doubt to remind her that she'd not yet been fed. Dani pulled off her coat and hung it on the rack, then proceeded to the kitchen to put out some food for Charlie and fix a hot drink for herself. With the two new novels she'd picked up at the mall tucked under one arm and the Suisse Mocha mug in the other hand, she headed upstairs. The bed was no more welcoming than it had been last night, but she climbed in anyway. The lack of sleep from the night before caught up with her and she dozed off with book in hand and the lamp still on.

Dani jerked straight up in the bed, not sure what woke her but certain that something had. A glance at the clock beside the bed showed her it was almost four AM. She held completely still, listening. When she heard nothing for a few minutes, she reached over and turned off the lamp, but sleep eluded her.

Until now, she'd been so caught up in worrying about her failed relationship with Noah that she hadn't given much thought to any impending danger to herself. Not smart. Before, she'd had Noah watching out for her. Now she was on her own. She wondered again about Bandit's absence. He'd run off before, sure, but he always came back. It wasn't like him to be gone two nights in a row.

Tossing and turning, she wrestled thoughts of Dr. Atkinson, Dr. Crane, and Mike, interspersed with slide shows of Noah's pervasive presence in her life and drifted off into a troubled sleep. Morning greeted her with a pounding headache and dark gray skies that promised snow.

With thoughts of Bandit uppermost in her mind for a change, Dani dressed warmly and took off into the woods, hoping to find him before a snow storm endangered his life. Play was one thing. Getting stranded in freezing temperatures was another and the weatherman was predicting heavy snow and ice.

Keeping her gloved hands tucked securely in her pockets and a stocking cap snug over her ears, she started her search across the road where he usually wound up, even though he'd disappeared in the back yard. Rustling wind and crackling branches encouraged her to keep her right hand around the handle of the .38 nestled in her pocket after taking it out to make sure the safety was still on.

Against her better judgment, and Noah's advice if he'd known, she proceeded deeper into the woods than she'd gone before, hoping that the cold weather ensured any snakes were hibernating deep in their nests. Although the sight of a reptile didn't alarm her as much as it used to, she was by no means comfortable with them.

There was no sign of Bandit, but her search revealed a small shed tucked way back among the trees. The door hung loosely on rusty hinges and the whole thing looked like it would collapse in a high wind. Dani scanned the area surrounding the shed, wondering if she was closer to another property than she knew, but there was nothing visible. Warily, Dani approached the shed and peeked through the door. The inside was clean and swept with nothing but a rickety chair propped against one wall and a battered Coleman lantern in the corner.

Dani was so excited with her discovery, she forgot at first that she and Noah were not on speaking terms and had run half way back to the road with the intent of calling him before that realization struck a discordant note in her psyche. Slowing her pace, she trudged back across the road, casting a furtive glance toward Noah's house as she passed her own and proceeded down the driveway to the back yard. Since this was the last place she saw Bandit, it was worth a look. She still wasn't ready to be in that empty house alone.

The wind had disrupted all of her previous leaf raking efforts, spreading a carpet of fallen leaves across the yard. Dani noted that the only place left uncovered was the area surrounding her cellar. Odd, when that was the place most densely covered when she first found it. The woods behind the house were much thicker and more difficult to navigate. It didn't help that she'd not been this way before, so everything looked unfamiliar. It took more than twenty minutes just to get far enough in that she couldn't see the house anymore.

When the trees closed in so close together that it was hard to squeeze between without getting scratched, Dani reluctantly turned back, calling Bandit's name every few minutes. The first snowflakes hit her cheeks as she emerged from the cover of the trees and she wondered what she'd done to cause the things she'd put such hope in to turn on her and leave her feeling so empty. She'd so looked forward to the first snow, almost childlike in her anticipation. Now all she could think of was that Bandit might be caught somewhere in it, freezing to death. Was nothing as it seemed?

CHAPTER NINETEEN

"Hello?" Dani answered the phone call that interrupted her dinner preparations. Determined to make the most of her holiday, Dani already had a pecan pie in the oven, a pot of chicken soup simmering on the stove and was preparing a couple of pork chops to stuff and grill.

"Hey, Dano, whatcha up to?" Beth's cheerful voice warmed her.

"Dinner. How about you?"

"Nah. I've given up eating until I lose eight pounds," Beth said, laughing.

"Right," Dani smiled.

"Just dinner," Beth added. "Not chocolate."

Dani laughed at that, an odd but welcome feeling. "You called to tell me this?" She held the phone between her shoulder and one ear, stirring the stuffing mix.

"No, duh!" Beth pretended annoyance. "I'm calling on request. Have you heard from Mike?"

"McKay?" Dani asked in surprise.

"Yeppers."

"No, why?"

"Because we can't find him, silly. He was supposed to meet Kathy at Cheddar's at six, but he hasn't shown. When she called, his roommate said he never came home last night."

Dani's chest tightened at the news but she tried to remain calm. "I haven't seen him since day before yesterday," she told Beth. "But, I rarely do and I don't think he's ever called here."

"All righty then!" Beth's chipper voice said she wasn't too concerned. "Talk to you laters!"

Dani couldn't shake a nagging feeling of growing dread as she finished cooking her dinner. Suspicious thoughts paraded through her mind as she chased bites of pork chop mindlessly around her plate with a fork. Had Mike been the one to deliver the envelope to her house three nights ago? Did he decide to turn in what he knew and vanish without a trace? Or did his disappearance have something to do with her little visit with Dr. Crane?

The thoughts plagued her as she finished her meal and cleaned up, then followed her into the living room. She started a fire to help the heater ward off the cold, then sat in front of it, wishing the warmth she felt on her hands would somehow permeate her heart. The longer she sat staring, the more she knew – Noah needed to know about the envelope and all that happened after. She'd promised to inform the police if anything else happened. She should at least keep her word.

With more than a little trepidation, she crossed to the phone in the dining room and called the police. After being transferred from one officer to another several times, she finally found one who was willing to take her statement. She kept it brief, but left nothing out. Satisfied that she'd done something to help, she turned everything off and curled up on the couch in front of the fire with one of the books she'd started reading last night. The antics and hi-jinx of a female private investigator were just what she needed to lighten her mood a little. The girl's complicated relationship with a cop didn't take up much space in the story so it only helped to assure Dani she wasn't the only one with a difficult relationship.

The ringing of the phone startled her out of a particularly tense chapter. Dani dashed to the dining room to pick it up then carried the cordless phone back to the couch.

"Hello?" she answered pleasantly, expecting to find Beth on the other end.

"I understand you have some information I need," Noah's curt voice cut through her like a knife.

Totally unprepared, she stammered, "Uh… I … uh… just what I told the officer…"

"Dani, cut the crap," he interrupted harshly. "What the fuck is going on?"

Switching her emotions to autopilot, she recited the story again, leaving nothing out. "I thought you should know," she finished.

"You found the envelope Wednesday?"

"Yes."

"And you decided to tell me tonight when you heard McKay was missing?"

"Yes." Dani felt miserable, but there was no other way to answer. No explanation would be good enough.

His silence spoke volumes and Dani shuddered to imagine what he must be feeling.

"Is there anything else I should know?" she heard an edge creep into his voice.

"No."

More silence.

"Noah…"

Dial tone.

Just as well, Dani thought. There was no point postponing the inevitable.

Determined to beat the rapidly developing pattern of fitful sleep, Dani took a dose of NyQuil before bed, hoping it would soothe her nerves as well as her headache and allow her to enjoy a night of dreamless sleep. Maybe then she'd feel equipped to face another day. Instead of the desired results, it only made her groggy enough to think, for an instant when she turned over and bumped into Charlie, that Noah was back in her bed and all was right with the world.

When she awoke again around two, her mouth was dry and she was wide awake. So much for sleep inducing drugs. Deciding she'd do a little more reading rather than lying in the dark thinking about things she'd rather avoid, she slipped on her house shoes and made her way downstairs. Using the light on the vent-a-hood to avoid too much glare, she fixed another cup of Suisse Mocha and wondered idly if it was her caffeine intake before bed that kept her from sleeping. Never bothered her before, she reminded herself.

With a sigh of acknowledgment, she dug in the pantry for some crackers and pulled a block of cheddar cheese from the refrigerator. She was stacking her stash on the table and searching for a sharp knife to cut the cheese when she thought she heard a faraway bark. Bandit!

Flinging open the back door and wincing from the shot of cold air that greeted her, she paused, listening.

"Bandit?" she called tentatively into the night.

There it was again. Muffled, but she was sure it was Bandit. Taking no thought for the cold, she rushed back into the house and hurried up the stairs. Struggling to get her Reeboks on over bulky socks, she didn't bother to change out of her sweats and just pulled a heavy sweater on over her t-shirt. She raced downstairs and jerked on her coat, pulling on the stocking cap as an afterthought. Bandit must be freezing! There hadn't been enough snow to really cover the ground, but the temperature was in the low thirties and ice crackled, weighing down the branches of nearby trees.

After she finished buttoning her coat, she slid her hands into her gloves and picked up the flashlight she'd left on the kitchen counter. There was no thought for her safety, just that of her faithful friend. Something that was in short supply these days.

A gust of frigid wind took her breath as she stepped out on the back porch and peered out into the darkness. The porch light cast an eerie semi circle of illumination that reached no more than ten feet out into the yard. Beyond that was total darkness. Clouds obliterated any light she might have gleaned from stars or moon.

Carefully pulling the door behind her, she tried to leave it open enough to add to the light, but the wind whipped it open again and she had to close it to avoid freezing temperatures inside as well as out. When she reached the perimeter of the porch light, she clicked on the flashlight and tried to walk softly. In the silence, the crunching of frozen grass underfoot seemed to echo as loudly as the target practice with her new gun.

Cautiously, she made her way to the edge of the yard, pausing every few steps to listen and call Bandit's name. In the few short minutes she'd been outside, her cheeks and lips went numb from the cold and she didn't even want to know what the wind chill factor was. When she started to shiver uncontrollably, she knew she had to give up and go back inside. If Bandit was well enough to bark, she had to believe he was well enough to find his way home.

Sorely disappointed, Dani turned and started back toward the house. As she passed the cellar doors, she thought she heard a faint whine. Closer inspection with the flashlight revealed the padlock was gone from the doors. With fear gripping her heart, she leaned closer and called Bandit again. This time, he answered with a sharp bark. Damn! He was in the cellar!

Refusing to even consider how he got there, Dani jerked open the doors and peered down into the darkness, surprised the air that met her was considerably warmer than what was outside. Must be well insulated, she thought.

"Bandit! Here boy!" she waited expectantly for him to come bounding up the stairs but he didn't. "Bandit?"

His answering bark was shrill, but not moving. Dani shined the flashlight into the hole, but its beam didn't even illuminate the bottom of the stairs. The batteries were getting weak. Maybe Bandit was hurt and not able to climb. Her desire to find Bandit and take him inside overrode her fear of the cellar and she started down the steps, wishing the flashlight did more than provide a tiny tunnel of a beam to pierce the darkness.

She nearly lost her footing, slipping on something on the steps, but when she shone her flashlight on her foot she didn't see anything out of place. Bandit's bark had given way to a persistent whine and all her thoughts were on reaching him.

The floor was so dark that even with the flashlight, she still saw more shadows than shapes. Shining the light along the wall as she reached the lower steps, fear gripped her heart as she located Bandit. He was in a doggie carrier perched precariously on one of the top shelves. Every time he barked, the whole thing shook. Obviously, his presence here was no accident.

"Be still Bandit!" she called, sweeping the floor with the flashlight before she took that last step.

It looked like the floor was covered with rope, but she couldn't be sure. The lamp on her flashlight was dimming, offering the promise of light without really delivering. If only she could reach the string that dangled from the overhead bulb. Swinging the flashlight up toward the ceiling, she spotted it and took a step, reaching out with her other hand. She wasn't surprised to feel a piece of the rope beneath her left foot, but she was shaken when it felt like it moved. Jerking the string in her hand, she froze in terror as the light flooded the room. The floor of the cellar was crawling with snakes!

Too terrified to move, or even scream, her mind raced. She was vaguely aware of the pieces of a jigsaw puzzle falling into place in her head, but couldn't do anything about it. When one of the smaller snakes slithered lazily across her instep, she forced herself to wait, then slowly stepped back up on the first step, prepared to turn and run like hell. As she did, she looked up just in time to see the cellar door slam shut in her face!

Knowing in her heart that it was no accident, she climbed frantically to the top, pushing against the door with her shoulder, but to no avail. Whoever was after her finally got her. She wouldn't be surprised to know the padlock was firmly back in place and now, she didn't even have the assurance that Noah would come looking for her. Not any time soon, anyway.

Willing herself to remain calm, she made herself look back down at the floor. If the lab was missing over a hundred snakes, she knew there were at least that many on the floor below. Fortunately, they didn't seem interested in the stairs. It was probably too cold near the door. What looked like a tiny space heater hummed away in the far corner and most of them were clustered around it. The few that weren't were coiled tightly in corners and on shelves, going into hibernation mode she hoped.

Think, Dani! she chided herself. The choices she'd made left her alone again, with only herself to depend on for rescue. She tucked her hands back into her pockets and sat huddled, hunchback, on the top step, keeping a guarded eye on the steps below. Although some of the snakes had found perches on the shelves, there didn't seem to be any movement near Bandit's cage. She could only hope that his barking would keep them at bay. The holes on the cage front were plenty big to allow one of them to slither inside. It wouldn't take long for a copperhead bite to kill her poor dog. Her, either, for that matter.

The feel of the gun in her right pocket was reassuring, although she knew a handful of bullets wouldn't help much in this situation. How long would it be before someone noticed she was missing? Too long, she thought, despairing. School was out. No classes, no work. Beth might call in the morning, but she was just as likely not to call again for days. Besides, even if she called and got no answer, she'd just assume Dani was out shopping or something. And the way Noah sounded on the phone earlier, it would be days before she'd hear from him too, if she ever did. As far as the rest of the world was concerned, Dani had no appointments or commitments with anyone. Ever.

Shuddering at the implications, Dani felt a tear escape and slide down her cheek. Noah wanted a commitment. All he'd wanted to know was whether she was willing to pursue a relationship. He hadn't asked for forever. He hadn't really asked anything she couldn't give. So what was she afraid of? Afraid he'd marry her, let her pay his way through medical school, then leave her? Dani closed her eyes with a sigh. She must have been crazy. Temporary insanity. There was no other logical explanation. Noah was exactly the kind of man she needed, the kind of man she'd hoped Mark was, but never would be. And he was hers for the asking. But, like a fool, she'd let a snide remark by a woman she didn't even know condemn the best relationship she'd ever had without even questioning it. Why didn't she just ask him about what Caroline Crane had said instead of jumping to conclusions and throwing him out of her life? If he'd acted suspicious when he answered, she could have decided then, but, the way her luck was running, he'd have had a perfectly logical explanation and she'd never given him a chance!

The way it looked right now, Dani figured she deserved whatever she got. She took her hand out of her pocket long enough to look at her watch then slipped it back inside. Was it possible only an hour had elapsed since she got up to make coffee? It seemed like years. Dani looked up at the cellar doors, examining them closely to see if there was any way out from the inside. They had to be fastened on somehow, but she didn't see it. Probably screwed into the wooden frame that supported the ceiling.

She glanced across the room at the shelves and shuddered as she saw one of the larger snakes slithering along the second shelf in search of a spot to coil, or in search of prey. She preferred the former thought. Any tools she had available to her would be located there, on those shelves. At this point, they didn't seem worth the risk.

CHAPTER TWENTY

Making his way home just after midnight, Noah drove far enough past his own driveway to get a good look at the front of Dani's house before turning in. Tired to the bone, both in body and in spirit, he still wanted to be sure she was safe. Except for the front porch light, the house was dark and the Taurus was parked in its usual place close to the walk. All was well.

He backed up the truck, then turned into his driveway, getting out to walk wearily to the door and into a cold, unwelcoming house. Although she'd only spent one night there, he couldn't help but remember how her smile lit up the place. Even worse was the contrast between his place and hers. Every room in her house was warm and inviting. Her personality screamed from the wildlife photographs she had hanging in the living room and hallway to the eclectic choice of mismatched stoneware she used for dishes. And especially in the contrast of the tropical print comforter she loved on the bed to the cozy flannel sheets.

Everything about Dani was a contradiction, but in her, it seemed perfectly logical. She didn't conform to the norm because she was like no other. Dani Jones was a living, breathing contradiction in terms.

Too wired to turn in yet, Noah fixed a cup of instant coffee and plopped down in the worn out easy chair facing the front window. He'd spent the better part of the last two nights in this chair. After sharing her bed, he'd had no interest in his. The scent of her perfume still lingered on the pillow she'd used when she stayed there. He'd really done it this time.

No matter how he prided himself on detachment and being able to be objective in any situation, somehow, she'd crept past all his defenses and rooted herself irrevocably in his heart. Scowling at the bitter, lukewarm mouthful of coffee he swigged, he got up and poured it out in the kitchen sink, then retrieved a beer from the refrigerator. Maybe he'd just drink

135

himself to sleep. He was off tomorrow. At this rate, it was the only way he'd get any rest.

With one cold beer in hand and another as a backup, he dropped back into the chair and stared out the window, tired of fighting to keep his mind from examining and re-examining the relationship. It was easier to just let it run its course. There was no argument, really. He'd settled the issues that concerned him weeks ago when he'd finally admitted to himself that he'd fallen hopelessly in love with her.

For years, he'd listened as colleagues lamented their foibles of love, secretly amused and maybe feeling even a little superior. He was above all that; it could never happen to him. He wouldn't allow it. A harsh laugh gurgled in his throat as he opened the second beer. Like he'd really had any choice in the matter. Hell, the only choice he was allowed was whether to admit it or not. The falling was something he had no control over.

To be fair, he did understand her reluctance. After what she'd been through, he'd worry if she trusted too soon. The passion was there, no doubt. And, he believed she loved him just like he loved her. She was just terrified at the thought. How could he blame her for that? In any case, he'd never let her go without a fight. She was too precious to him. In his heart, he knew he'd never love again. Not like this. He'd never let anyone get close enough. Now that it had happened once, he knew the signs. With another loud sigh, he let his head roll back against the chair and prayed that sleep would take him to a better place.

The persistent sound of an alarm dragged him from a deep sleep. Disoriented at first, he shook his head as if that would clear it, then realized it was his phone. Still dark out, he glanced at the window. His watch said 5:04. Who the hell would call at this hour? He wasn't on call.

"Russell," his voice sounded gravelly, even to him.

"Noah, it's Graham," a familiar voice woke him up. "I just got something for your desk, but I thought maybe it shouldn't wait."

"What is it?" Noah was on full alert now.

"You know that Atkinson guy you've been scoping?"

"Yeah."

"You just got a copy of a missing persons report from Atlanta PD. Says his secretary reported him missing day before yesterday but it waded through the usual 24 before it came out on the wire."

"Fuck me!" Noah barked. "They knew I was watching him. You'd think _"

"Yeah, I know," Graham interrupted. "I'll put it on your desk, but I knew you'd want to know. Your girl tucked in safe for the night?"

"Far as I know," Noah answered curtly. "Thanks Graham."

When he hung up the phone, he wandered back to the window, peering through the trees even though he knew he could see nothing. Or maybe he could, he thought. Without bothering to grab his coat, he walked out on the front porch to get a better look. A soft glow emanated from the kitchen window. Was she up at this hour? That light wasn't on when he came home. Maybe she wasn't sleeping well.

He thought back to the terse conversation they'd shared last night. She sounded fine when she answered the phone, but one word answers weren't like her. He'd assumed she was annoyed to hear his voice. Maybe it was more than that. It bothered him enough to go back inside for his coat. It would only take a few minutes to stroll over and scope out the house, just to be sure. If his hunch was right and Atkinson was in this up to his neck, he'd bet money he was in the area somewhere if he wasn't in Atlanta.

A few minutes later, he crossed the drive and peered through the blinds into the kitchen. The light over the stove was on and there was a coffee mug and a stack of crackers beside a block of cheese on the table but no sign of movement. Quietly, Noah moved toward the front of the house. It looked like she'd gotten up for a snack, but then where was she? Why did she leave it in the kitchen?

As soon as he came around the front corner, he saw another soft glow from her bedroom window upstairs. He tried to peer in one of the front windows but it was too dark to see anything. Something didn't feel right. Maybe he was overly protective, but he didn't want to take the chance.

He wandered slowly out into the center of the yard to get a better view. It didn't look like there was any movement in the bedroom, either. He knew where the lamp was. If she passed between it and the window, it would cast a shadow. He knew she liked to read in bed, too, but she wouldn't fix a snack then leave it downstairs. She'd either take it with her or put it up.

In spite of his unease, he really didn't want to wake her and endure her wrath. She'd made it pretty plain she'd be happy if she never saw him again. He was prepared to work through that, but the thought still hurt. Bad. Quietly, trying to avoid the creaking boards, he approached the front door and tried the knob. Locked. Nothing to do but knock. He did. Once. Again, louder this time. There was no sound, no answering bark from Bandit, although that didn't mean much.

Troubled, but not ready to call for reinforcements, he made his way around to the back of the house. This time, when he tried the door, it opened easily in his hand, setting off an alarm system deep inside.

"Dani?" he called out, entering slowly and closing the door behind him. His fears deepened as he moved through the dining room. She wouldn't go to bed and leave the door unlocked. The coffee mug was full but untouched and cold. "Dani?" Silence.

He proceeded rapidly through the living room then pulled his gun as he started up the stairs. Ears tuned to any noise, there was nothing but the sound of his boots on the stairs. The bedroom door was wide open and she'd obviously been in bed at one time, but her book was propped open on the comforter and Charlie was curled in a ball where Dani's feet should have been. A quick glance in the bathroom revealed nothing. His heart rate seemed to increase with each step he took as he moved rapidly down the hall, throwing open the bedroom and bathroom doors. All empty.

He descended the stairs two and three at a time then stopped cold when his eyes fell on the coat rack. It was empty. Surely she wouldn't have been foolish enough to go outside in the middle of the night. In his heart, he suspected she would. Since the back door was open, he headed that way, still wondering what could have possessed her to do such a thing. He stopped in the kitchen to pick up the flashlight but it was nowhere to be found. God, please don't let her be out wandering through the woods at this hour!

Dani was shivering uncontrollably now and had been for longer than she could think. She'd tried warming her hands over the flame from a cigarette lighter she saw on a nearby shelf, but only succeeded in burning her finger. She'd dozed off for a little while, amazingly enough. Probably a delayed NyQuil reaction. But the cold woke her up again and this time she was grateful. A quick scan of her surroundings showed that two of the larger snakes had decided to perch on the lower two steps but they were well below her feet. She didn't know what she'd have done had she woken with one crawling on her. Her head told her she should be safe as long as she didn't panic, but her heart told her that panic was inevitable if one should actually dare to climb on her.

At one point, she'd stirred and thought she heard Noah's voice calling her name, but she never heard it again and figured it was just a dream. Or maybe wishful thinking. He'd rescued her from the cellar once before. Twice wasn't likely. Or was it? If she strained her ears, she could make out the sound of grass crunching, just like when she'd walked out here. She opened her mouth to call out, then stopped suddenly. What if it was her captor, returning to see if she was dead yet?

Heat flashed through her body as her adrenaline went into high gear. The footsteps were coming closer. She was definitely in danger. Carefully, she wrestled the gun out of her pocket and clicked the safety off. There was no way in hell she'd scoot down the stairs to mingle with the reptiles. She'd have to take her chances with the human kind of threat. He'd get a good surprise when he opened those doors this time. She'd have a gun pointed right at his face.

As she sat poised, waiting, she tried frantically to recall all Noah had taught her about facing a potential threat. He'd said never pull a weapon unless she fully intended to use it and don't wait and give them a chance to get it away from you.

Best she could tell, she had two things going for her. One, he wouldn't be expecting it, and two, he'd have at least one hand busy trying to open the door. She'd have to move fast. Her heart hammered as she heard the padlock clank against the door. She had to fight to keep from closing her eyes in fright, but she was ready. It clanked again. Any moment now.

Her life wasn't passing before her eyes, maybe that was a good sign. But what was taking him so long? Confusion crept in and her arm was getting tired but she didn't dare lower the weapon. She heard a man's voice. Was it Noah? Or was it the one who put her in here? All of a sudden she didn't know what to do. If it was the man who put her in here, she'd want to be quiet, let him think she was dead so she could surprise him. But if it was Noah, looking for her, he might see the lock and think there was no use looking in here. Suddenly, it came to her. What had drawn her here in the first place?

"Bandit!" she hissed, hoping she couldn't be heard from the outside. "Bark Bandit!"

Bandit heard her. He pressed his nose against the cage and whimpered.

"Louder, boy!" she encouraged with another whisper. "Bark! Roof!"

He wiggled and whined, but no barking.

"Roof, roo roo!" she tried to imitate his sound the best she could, but her whispers just weren't exciting enough. She heard footsteps again, but this time they seemed to be moving away. It was now or never.

"Roof! Roof!" she barked louder, hoping like hell it sounded like a dog from outside. "Roof, roo roo, roof!"

Catching the idea, Bandit joined in at full voice, bringing tears to her eyes. She tried to focus on outside sounds between barks. Was it soon enough, or had he already gone too far away to hear it? No. There it was again, another step.

"Roof!" she encouraged Bandit again and was rewarded by a voice outside calling "Bandit!"

It was Noah! Thank God! Summoning her voice, she was unable to speak around the sob that choked her. "No…Noah!"

"Dani?" Sharp and clear, it was like an angelic message. Noah came for her!

"Noah! Noah!"

"Hold on, I'll be right there!"

As long as she lived, Dani knew she'd never hear anything sweeter. A moment later, there was pounding then the doors flung open wide and Noah's strong arms reached out to pull her to him.

"Whoa!" he said, spying the gun still clinched tightly in her hand. She sobbed as he pried it from her fingers, put the safety back on and shoved it in his pocket. "Where's Bandit?"

"Oh, God, Noah," she clung to his jacket and peered fearfully back down in the hole.

"Holy shit," Noah said, looking over her shoulder.

"It's crawling with snakes," she offered in a trembling voice. "Bandit is in a dog carrier up on the top shelf." Her apparently inexhaustible supply of tears flowed freely down cheeks that were rapidly numbing again from the cold wind.

"Is he alright?" he asked softly.

"So far, but Noah..."

"Baby," he took her chin in his hand, "we'll work it out and we'll get him down. Right now, you need to go inside where it's warm."

"Noah, please......... don't leave me," she wailed. All the reserves of strength she'd depended on the last few hours vanished like a whiff of smoke in a high wind when she was in his arms again.

"Inside," he said, firmly pointing her toward the back door.

She sank gratefully into a dining room chair, never letting her eyes off his magnificent form as he strode to the phone and punched in the numbers. Once he'd summoned the troops, he put on a pot of coffee, then pulled up a chair beside her and rubbed her cold hands between his own.

"Whatever were you thinking?"

Dani examined his face, meeting his eyes without reservation. "I couldn't sleep then I thought I heard Bandit barking. I was afraid he'd freeze to death."

"He ran off again?"

"Two days ago."

"How'd you get in to the cellar? I tried the key. It didn't work, or did you change that too?"

"No," she said miserably. "There was no lock on it when I heard him. And my flashlight wasn't working very well so I had to go all the way to the bottom to turn on the light in the cellar. When I did and saw the snakes, I tried to get back up the stairs but someone was up there and they closed the door. I guess they locked it."

"You didn't see them?"

She shook her head. The lights of a squad car caught her attention through the dining room window. Noah got up to meet them and left through the back door. Dani followed him and stood watching inside the screen, not wanting him out of her sight. If nothing else, the experience she'd just endured showed her how wrong she'd been. What if Noah hadn't come looking? Sooner or later she'd have fallen asleep. Just one copperhead visitor and a twitch in her sleep, she'd have been dead.

Noah heeded her request and came back in the house once he'd explained the situation to the officers. Dani was vaguely aware of halogen lights being set up behind the house and a flurry of officers and technicians busy about their tasks.

"Don't worry, animal control is here. They'll bring Bandit in once they get to him," he assured her, pulling her to her feet and leading her to the couch. As gently as if she were a child, he unbuttoned her coat and slid it from her arms, then knelt and removed her shoes, rubbing her cold, stocking - covered feet between his hands. "Snuggle up," he ordered, pulling the afghan off the back of the couch and covering her with it. "I'll get a fire started."

Fearing she might be hallucinating, she followed him with her eyes, not daring to utter a word lest she break the spell. Exhausted, she let her head fall back on the cushion and closed her eyes, comfortable as long as she could hear him moving around. The sound of muted voices got her attention and she struggled to raise her head and open her eyes but it took too much effort.

"Hey, I'm off duty and she's in shock. I've told you all you need to know. You can question her in the morning. She's not going anywhere," Noah's voice carried from somewhere behind her.

With a soft sigh, she shifted positions so her head rested easily against the arm of the couch and a small smile flitted across her lips as Noah lifted her feet and sat down on the other end with her feet tucked inside the afghan and resting on his lap.

CHAPTER TWENTY ONE

When she woke, sunlight streamed through the windows and the fire was nothing but glowing embers. Noah was fast asleep on the other end of the couch and Bandit was curled in a furry ball on the rug in front of the fire. Dani shifted, trying to stretch stiff muscles without waking anyone else. If not for Noah's comforting presence, she'd be tempted to believe last night was just a bad dream.

Easing her feet gently off his lap, she struggled to sit up, then scooted off the couch and walked stiffly into the kitchen to start some coffee. Her mind was in a fog, not fully awake, but she knew she needed coffee. When she emerged from the kitchen, mug in hand, Noah was still sleeping, or so she thought until she tried to sneak past him to the stairs.

His long, lean arm shot out and his hand clamped a vise-grip on her forearm.

"Hey!" she yelled. "You nearly made me spill my coffee!"

He loosened his grip. "Where you going?"

"Upstairs to get out of these filthy clothes," she told him, reaching out to touch his tousled hair.

"Put that down," he ordered, nodding at her coffee mug. She set it on the table beside the couch. That done, he took her hand again and pulled her down into his lap, wrapping strong arms around her and holding her close. "I am so grateful that you're safe," he whispered, nuzzling her hair.

Dani wrapped her arms around his neck and inhaled the scent of him. "I'm so grateful you came looking. I was afraid you wouldn't."

Noah pulled back enough to look deep into her eyes. "I'll always come looking," he assured her seriously.

"Noah…" she touched his face, eyes filling with tears. There were no words for the regret she felt. "I'm sooooo sorry. I should have trusted you…"

He stopped her by placing a finger to her lips. "We're still new at this. We'll learn how to work it out."

"I was so stupid," she said, stroking his hair. "I was afraid you'd never want to speak to me again."

He smiled softly. "I'll admit, you had me pissed. But I finally figured out you were worth fighting through it."

"Noah, you're too good to me," she meant every word. Maybe that was the problem. She knew how to react when a man treated her badly. It made her suspicious when she met one who didn't.

"Let's make a deal," he said seriously.

She waited.

"Let's promise each other when something goes wrong, we'll sit down and at least try to hash it out. All right?"

Dani nodded, lost in brown eyes that were miles deep and filled with promise.

"I have another idea," he said, eyes beginning to twinkle.

"What?"

"Why don't we see if that big clanky tub you love so much is big enough for the both of us?"

"Ya think?" she smiled.

"I think," he winked and scooped her up in his arms to carry her upstairs.

After visiting the police station to give official statements about last night's incident, Dani and Noah had the rest of the day free. With Christmas only days away, and the promise of more snow in the interim, the streets were filled with last minute shoppers, creating an atmosphere that was crisp, clean, and festive. Christmas carols blared from every available speaker and Salvation Army Santas rang their bells on the street corners.

With Noah at her side, Dani felt like a giddy school girl. Separating only long enough to make purchases not seen by the other, they ended the day in a mile long checkout line at the grocery store, stocking up in case the snow left them housebound for a day or two.

Dani thoroughly enjoyed the day, even the ordeal of unloading a car full of groceries and rearranging cabinets to be able to fit it all in. While she started a pot of chili, Noah trekked next door to retrieve clothes and toiletries. He returned, suitcase and duffel bag in hand and an odd expression on his face.

"What's wrong?" Dani joined him in the living room, drying her hands on a dishtowel.

He dropped the bags beside his feet. "I just want you to know I'm staying here to make sure you're safe until we catch this guy," he said awkwardly. "I don't want you to misunderstand......... to think I'm expecting anything more permanent than that."

Dani cocked her head to the side and tried to interpret the troubled expression he wore. The longer she looked, the more he seemed like a little boy lost, confused and expectant at the same time. Dani smiled. "What if I want something more permanent than that?"

The shades dropped on his eyes and his face took on a guarded expression. "Then you'll have to tell me that."

"Deal," she smiled again. "Now get that upstairs and stop cluttering up the room I just cleaned."

Under the tree looked barren since they'd delivered the gifts Dani had for Beth and the foster children. All that remained was the one tiny package from Noah and the one Dani had for Mike. With Noah busily starting a fire and the chili simmering away on the stove, Dani ducked into one of the extra bedrooms and spent the better part of an hour wrapping the gifts she'd bought for Noah today. She'd found a couple of sweaters she knew he'd like, and a few books she hoped he'd like.

Two felt stockings with appliqués of Santa and his reindeer nearly jumped in her shopping cart, so she'd set to work looking for smaller items to stuff Noah's with. Happily, she wrapped a bottle of his favorite cologne and a CD of ZZ Top's greatest hits for his truck. The last two items had her stumped, though. Caught up in the holiday mood, it seemed like a good idea at the time. Now she wasn't so sure.

Dani opened the first box and looked at a gold pinky ring. He didn't wear much jewelry, aside from an earring, but it seemed appropriate. It was a gold snake that coiled around the finger. A fitting gift for the man who seemed destined to save her from the creatures. The second box held an earring – a small hoop with a tiny dangling heart. She'd wondered at the store if it was too feminine, although a man like Noah could wear anything without fearing ridicule. It seemed symbolic of her giving him her heart to wear. She might as well give it to him. In reality, she'd already done that.

When she was finished, she carried them all downstairs and positioned them under the tree, stepping back to admire the results. Then, she went in search of a hammer to hang the stockings.

"You have been busy, haven't you?" Noah smiled from his customary seat on the couch, lowering the newspaper to watch her in action. "Oh, man, you should have told me about the stocking," he frowned. "I didn't get anything for that."

"Well, it's not Christmas yet, either," she grinned, then headed off to the kitchen to check on dinner. When she came back into the room bearing a tray with steaming bowls of chili and a package of saltines, she found him sitting in front of the tree looking at the gifts.

"You're worse than a child," she laughed, setting the tray down on the coffee table.

"These are all for me," he said soberly.

"Yeah," she nodded, "except for the ones for Bandit and Charlie." She didn't get his point.

"I have to go back to town," he said.

"Noah," she chided. "Come eat your chili."

He joined her on the couch and started eating, but didn't say much. When she'd finished hers, he looked over at her. "I'm serious. I have to go back into town, but I can't leave you here."

"Noah," she argued, beginning to feel a little embarrassed, "if it's just the gifts…"

"Dani, will you go back into town with me before it snows?" he looked at her earnestly.

She couldn't resist. "Yeah. But you don't have to do this."

His face broke into a smile. "I want to."

"Let's take the truck," he said when they'd bundled up and got outside. "I've got chains on it."

She looked at him in surprise, but didn't argue. He held her hand and led her through the trees to his driveway, then helped her up in the truck. Although her Taurus was plenty powerful to her, his F150 had a lot more get up and go, especially on tiny country roads. The clicking of the chains was an interesting sound, but oddly comforting as the snow flurries started not long after they left. She'd hate to see the storm that could stop this truck.

Noah drove straight to the mall and towed her along like an eager boy hurrying to get to the toy store. He left her parked in the electronics department to shop for videos and CDs while he roamed the rest of the store. When he still hadn't returned almost an hour later, she began to wonder. The thought of his anticipation warmed her heart and put a smile on her lips. He really could be like a little boy sometimes. The thought appealed to her.

As she paced back and forth near the entrance, waiting for him, her eyes lighted on a display of Nintendo games and she wandered over for a closer look. The system itself was marked down to an incredibly low price and the games weren't too expensive either. Suddenly, she imagined the two of them, snowbound, sitting on the floor in front of a roaring fire playing video games. It might be fun.

She'd just finished paying for it and the clerk was bagging her selections when he joined her, shopping bags filled with boxes on both arms.

"What have you done?" he asked, eyes wide as he watched the clerk stuffing bags.

"See what happens when you leave me alone too long with a credit card?" she teased.

"Oh, my God," he rolled his eyes. "Let's get out of here before you do something I can't beat."

Dani laughed and collected her parcels. Swirling snow greeted them as they left the store, and they ran like children through the parking lot to the truck. It was a tight squeeze, getting all the packages in the cab with them, but they didn't dare leave them in the truck bed to get all wet. The wipers stayed busy brushing the snow from the windshield and the appearance of smoke curling from her chimney promised cozy and comfy just inside the door.

As soon as they had the packages inside, Noah left Dani to sort out her games while he disappeared upstairs with his bounty. When he came back down, arms full of packages, Dani had the game and accessories spread on the floor all around her and a look of utter confusion on her face.

"Problems?" he asked cheerfully, stuffing tiny items in her stocking after leaving the larger ones beneath the tree.

"These instructions might as well be in a foreign language," she grumbled. "I can't figure it out."

"Let the master have a go at it," he dropped down beside her on the floor, brushing her cheek with his lips before reaching for the instruction sheet.

Dani gladly scooted all the pieces closer so he could reach them and got up, stretching. She noticed that he'd taken time to change his clothes and wanted to do the same.

"I'm going to go change," she informed him and headed up the stairs.

When she returned, he was so engrossed in his project she headed straight for the kitchen. Eggnog. Mechanical shooting sounds coming from the living room told her he'd been successful. She joined him on the floor, much more comfortable in flannel pjs and fluffy slippers.

"Wanna play?" he asked, gratefully accepting the steaming mug she offered.

"Of course, silly," she smiled. "Tell me how."

They spent the next hour racing Mario Kart, shooting it out with Star Wars and helping Banjo Kazooie in a never ending search for his kidnapped sister, Tooty.

"I'm done," she groused, throwing the controller down when her Banjo died the death for the third time, falling off the narrow crosswalk into a boiling pit of lava. "I think I'm too old to sit in the floor this long." She stood and stretched then padded into the kitchen for a refill. "Want some more?" she called.

A moment later, he came around the corner and set his mug on the counter, then stepped up behind her and slid a strong arm around her waist. "More what?" he murmured suggestively, nibbling her ear.

"Mmmm," she smiled, wiggling around so she could face him and wrap her arms around his neck. "You spoil me."

He kissed her softly. "I love it."

"You wicked man," she teased, kissing him back, melting at the feel of his hard body next to hers.

"Only with you," he murmured between kisses that grew more urgent each time.

"You promised to watch a movie with me," she reminded him.

"How about if I watch you watching a movie?" he backed up a little to allow her room to refill her cup, then refilled his own and followed her back to the couch.

Dani set down her mug, then popped The Horse Whisperer into the DVR while he turned off the lamp and made room for her on the couch. "Can we make out during the previews?" he asked, pulling her close.

She turned to face him, taking his face into her hands and kissing him soundly. "You're the best thing that's ever happened to me, Noah Russell," she whispered, close enough to feel his warm breath on her cheek. The intimacy of the fire and the comfort of his arms had all her defenses down. It was true, and at this point she couldn't think of any reason to hide it from him.

He looked as though he might speak, then cupped her chin in his hand and pulled her closer, dusting her eyes with kisses then seeking her mouth with his own. As his warm, soft lips caressed hers, everything else receded, leaving her aware only of his touch, his taste, the musky aroma of his cologne and his hair. It seemed all she would ever need in this life was wrapped up in him.

With the movie forgotten, Dani abandoned her soul to his lovemaking in front of the fire. For the second night in a row, the two slept soundly on the couch, this time, entangled safely in each other's arms.

Dani woke when Noah stirred, reaching up to brush back the hair that covered his cheek.

"Penny for your thoughts," he whispered, startling her. When she didn't answer, he opened his eyes, examining her face only inches from his own.

"I wish it could be like this forever," she answered softly.

In response, he pulled her close, embracing her in a bear hug that allowed her to feel the beating of his heart next to her own. "I wish I could promise it would," he answered, as if holding her tight could make it happen.

"Back to reality, I guess, huh?" she smiled, warm in the circle of his arms.

"Mmmmmm, I guess," he moaned softly.

"Hungry?"

He smiled.

"Breakfast? Food?" she prompted, teasing.

He groaned louder this time. "I suppose you want me to cook?"

Dani smiled. "You're the breakfast chef."

"You make a mean omelet," he countered.

Dani struggled to get up. "Fried eggs, over medium, with bacon and toast," she flung the words over her shoulder, dodging his hand as she passed behind the couch on the way up the stairs.

Upstairs, she bathed quickly and dressed warmly, layering long johns under her sweats. There was too much snow outside. Sooner or later, she'd have to build a snowman. If the chill in the air inside was any indication, it was literally freezing cold outside. Bounding down the stairs, she was greeted by the smell of bacon frying and fresh coffee brewing. Maybe this afternoon she'd have time to bake a batch of tollhouse cookies. As far as she knew, Noah wasn't due back at work until tomorrow evening and she'd have him all to herself until then.

"What? It's not done yet?" she teased, slipping into the kitchen behind him to fill her coffee mug.

"No griping at the chef," he answered good-naturedly. "Sit down and get out of my way."

"Grouchy," she observed, but did as he asked. A few minutes later, he joined her, with two steaming plates and a stack of toast.

"Do you have a plan for the day?" she asked between bites.

"You mean besides gathering more firewood?" he smiled.

"Yeah," she smiled back.

"Hmm," he pretended to consider it. "I suspect, at some point, I'll have to assist a certain lady in building a snow man."

"How'd you know?" she punched his arm, amazed at his intuition.

"Lucky guess," he grinned. "And, less fun but more importantly, you and I need to go over the facts of this case as we know them."

Her face screwed into a frown. "Ewww. I don't even want to think about it."

His expression was compassionate, but determined. "I know, but we really need to."

She was silent for a while as her mind wandered over territory she'd rather avoid. "Can I ask you something?" she said hesitantly.

"Of course," he said, pushing his plate aside and getting up for more coffee.

She waited until he sat back down, gratefully accepting a refill from the pot he'd brought with him.

He looked over at her curiously as he took his seat again.

"When did you say you moved here?" Even as she said it, Dani hated herself for asking.

"March, why?"

Dani tried to shrug it off. "Beth says she saw you here last year."

"Really? When?" he looked genuinely confused.

"I think she said the Rose Parade last fall."

"Oh. I came down for about a week, checking out the department…you know, kinda looking around to see if I'd really want to move here."

Dani sighed. As she'd suspected, it made perfect sense. He wouldn't have moved here without doing just that. Nobody would. But there was still the other issue.

"How do you know Caroline Crane?" she asked.

Noah's eyes narrowed and he leaned back a little as if to scrutinize her motivation for asking. He didn't look pleased, but answered anyway. "I believe she'd be the wife of your esteemed Dr. Crane."

Dani nodded, aware of a feeling of dread growing in the pit of her stomach.

"I first met her in Austin several years ago," he continued. "She was there attending some kind of society conference I was assigned to guard."

"Oh." It never occurred to Dani that he might have known her somewhere else. Still, meeting someone once at a conference would hardly constitute a relationship or even a remembrance years later. "Did you know her well?"

Lines of tension furrowed his brow and Dani knew he was exercising great control. "Not as well as she'd have liked, I'm afraid."

"I'm sorry, Noah. I had to ask," she said.

"You want to tell me why?" his eyes were guarded.

Dani sighed, wishing she hadn't brought it up. She felt like a fool already for jumping to conclusions that resulted in her throwing Noah out of the house. "I ran into her the other day and she made a point of telling me to give you her best. She intimated that you two knew each other well, and had for years."

"And you assumed…" he was careful to keep his expression neutral, but she saw the muscle working in his jaw.

"I'm sorry," she said again.

He nodded and took a drink of his coffee, then got up from the table. "I never slept with her, in case you're afraid to ask," he told her as he walked away.

"Where are you going?" she called after him, hating the feeling that she'd hurt him again.

"Out to get some wood," he said sharply.

Dani scooted her chair around and watched him pulling on his gloves and coat.

"Don't worry, I'm fine," he assured her without a smile just before he walked out the door.

Dani sighed again, then got up to clear away the dishes. Picturing Caroline Crane and Noah together, she knew she'd been way too hasty. There was no way he'd have ever been interested in someone like that. She should have known better.

CHAPTER TWENTY TWO

When Noah returned, carrying piles of wood to stack beside the fireplace, his expression was more relaxed, though hardly as joyful and open as it had been last night. Still, it relieved Dani's heart to know he was trying to understand. She warmed some coffee for him and met him with it as he stacked the last of the logs and removed his outerwear.

"Your face is cold," she smiled, brushing his cheek with her hand.

"It's cold outside," he agreed stiffly.

"Are you mad at me?" she asked sadly.

His expression softened at that. "No," he shook his head. "I'm not mad. I just wonder why she'd say something like that to you. She doesn't even know you, does she?"

"No," Dani shrugged. "Let's don't talk about her anymore."

Noah smiled. "Deal."

He did insist on talking about the case, though. Dani felt a little twinge of alarm, learning that Atkinson had disappeared. "Do you think he's the one doing this?" she asked.

"It kind of looks that way," he said, reluctant to give a yes or no answer. "It seems he was guilty of a lot of things. The thing I don't understand is why sell you the house if he didn't want you to have it and why would you be more of a threat to him than the guys he used to work with?"

Dani pondered that. "Well," she said, finally, "as for selling me the house, I bought it through a realtor who seemed incredibly glad to sell it and didn't ask many questions. I'm sure he had no idea that I was a student or that I'd be working out there."

Noah nodded. "That makes sense. And your problems here didn't really start until after you started asking questions around campus, did they?"

Dani tried to remember. "I'm not sure anymore. It seemed to start right away, but I was a little spooked living out here all alone. I could have imagined some of it."

"I guess it's possible that he got wind of your questions and that's what started it. But then who alerted him? Atlanta's pretty far away."

"Who do you think?" she asked, suspecting he had several theories and knowing she didn't have any. She avoided thinking about it at all if she could.

"I'd have to guess Crane, Abraham, or McKay," he said.

"Mike? No way," Dani shook her head emphatically. "Why would you think that?"

"Honestly, I didn't until you got that envelope and he disappeared. That makes me think he was involved somehow and got in over his head. That's why he gave you the shit and bailed."

"No," she was still shaking her head. "I think he stumbled onto something and ran because he was afraid they'd kill him."

"Interesting choice of words," he raised his eyebrows.

"What?"

"You said 'they'," he explained.

She shrugged, "I guess it seems like anything this horrible would need more than one."

"And preferably one you don't know, right?"

"Well, of course," she frowned at that. "Nobody wants to think someone they work with every day would lock her in a cellar full of snakes."

"Granted," he nodded. "But I don't want you thinking you can trust someone just because you know them."

The irony of the statement wasn't lost on her but she suppressed a smile. "How about if I promise right now to trust no one but you?"

The smile that played around his lips didn't reach his eyes. "Dani, we can't lose sight of the fact that somebody, whether you know them or not, wants you seriously dead. He's gotten more and more bold, and is probably getting pretty desperate about now."

She inhaled a deep breath, then let it out slowly. "You know what?" she met his eyes squarely. "Whether I know him or not, I'm not ready to die. He better write that down."

Noah smiled. He'd already learned that, with her, looks could definitely be deceiving. Underneath the frosted blonde hair and girlish figure was a woman with a backbone of steel. Stubborn as the proverbial mule.

After lunch, Dani coaxed Noah outside to build a snowman, then they indulged in a rough and tumble snowball fight that left them both breathless and covered with wet snow. Dani raced around the side of the house, dodging revenge after landing a particularly painful blow. As she ducked behind an evergreen tree, she spotted a bough of mistletoe hanging just out of her reach.

"Noah!" she called, all thoughts of the snowball fight temporarily suspended. "Come here!"

"Oh no you don't," he yelled back at her. "You're not suckering me!"

"Noah!" she laughed. "Allee, allee outs in free!" She paused, waiting to see what he'd do. "Noah, I'm serious. I found some mistletoe and I can't reach it!" When he still didn't answer, she peeked back out around the tree and was greeted with a snowball that knocked off her cap.

"Hey!" she yowled, scrambling for her hat. "I'm unloaded!"

"Unarmed," he laughed, striding toward her. "You okay?" he smiled down at her as she rearranged her cap.

"You owe me one," she said.

"The way I see it, you owe *me* one," he countered.

"All in good time, my dear," she smiled. "There," she turned and pointed at the mistletoe. "See? I can't reach it."

"And you think I can?" Noah looked up at it.

"Can you knock it down?" she squinted against the glare of the sun off the snow and tried to gauge the distance.

Noah looked around for a stick long enough, but didn't find one. Dani handed him a firmly packed snowball. "Your aim's pretty good," she told him.

He took it and tried. It was a direct hit, but the bough swung like a pendulum and stayed firmly attached to the tree. Another effort dislodged a few leaves, but the bough was still intact. After a third try missed completely, Noah turned to her.

"You realize, of course, that you don't need a twig of mistletoe to get me to kiss you," he smiled.

"I do," she smiled back at him, "but I still want it."

Noah looked up at the mistletoe, then back at her. He dropped to a crouching position and said, "Climb on."

"Huh?"

"Climb up on my shoulders and you reach it," he instructed. When she didn't move, he added, "How bad do you want it?"

"Are you sure you can do this?" she asked, gingerly swinging one leg and then another over his shoulders.

He laughed, grunting as he rose slowly to a standing position, gripping her thighs firmly in each hand. "Just don't make any sudden moves or we'll go down like the mighty oak." Carefully, he shuffled his feet until they were under the prize. "Can you reach it?" he asked, unable to see it.

"Step up about six more inches," she said, reaching out with one hand and holding tightly to the collar of his jacket with the other.

"Geez, your hands are cold!" he muttered, doing as she instructed.

"Got it!" she triumphed as the whole bough came off in her hands.

"Hand it to me," he held his right hand up beside his shoulder.

Gingerly, she lowered it into his waiting hand, then glanced around. "You know, I can see a lot better from..." she stopped suddenly, spotting movement between the trees on her far left. "Noah," she whispered and felt his hand tense on her left thigh. "Turn left a little," she said, still speaking softly.

"What is it?" his voice dropped to an answering whisper.

"There's somebody over there," she said, feeling her heart rate increase as she strained to keep her eye on the figure moving slowly through the trees. "Are you looking straight ahead?"

"Are you sure it's not a deer?" he asked quietly.

"Not unless it's walking upright." It was too far away to recognize a face, but there was definitely a person in the woods.

Noah lowered her gently to the ground.

"Do you see them?" she asked, straining to locate the person from her new perspective. "They were straight through there," she pointed. The trees were too dense, but she knew what she saw.

"Go back to the porch and get my gun," he told her, taking a few steps into the brush.

"Noah," she started.

"Go!" he hissed. She did. When she returned with his Glock, he took it and told her, "Go in the house and lock the door. Stay there."

Dani desperately wanted to argue, but his expression told her it would be futile.

"I'm not moving until you go. We're wasting time," he warned. She did as he asked.

Back inside the house, Dani kept her coat on and paced just inside the front door. Ten minutes turned into twenty. She'd give him five more, then she was going out after him. It would be dark soon and she'd never rest wondering if he was lost or hurt out there in the freezing weather. She wouldn't even consider a more fatal possibility. The only thing offering comfort at this point was the knowledge that a gunshot echoed through the woods and she'd certainly have heard it if there was one.

A few moments later, she saw Noah emerge from the woods just a few feet east of where he went in. She met him on the porch.

"What?"

He shook his head, stomping the snow off his boots before he went inside. "I lost him."

Relieved to have him back in one piece, and unsettled to think there was someone lurking in the woods near the house, Dani changed out of her wet things and cooked dinner in relative silence. Although they shared another pleasant evening in front of the fire, the atmosphere was considerably more subdued than it had been the last few days.

Dani awoke more rested, since they hit the bed early last night, but as soon as she pushed the comforter aside to get out of bed, she pulled it quickly back over her. It was colder than it had ever been since she'd lived in the house. Deciding maybe she could afford a few more minutes in bed, she snuggled up close to Noah, nudging him until he moved and draped an arm over her. Turning her face toward his chest, she wondered how he managed to stay so warm without even a shirt on.

"Hey," he mumbled through the comforter. "Why's your nose so cold?"

"It's winter," she quipped.

"In the house?" he peeked at her out of one eye.

"Maybe the heater's broke," she suggested, hoping it wasn't true.

Noah turned and looked over at the clock beside the bed. "Uh oh," he said, throwing back the covers and swinging his legs over the side of the bed.

"What?" she asked, pulling the comforter close to stop the draft left by his absence.

He flipped the light switch beside the door. "Power's out."

She moaned, watching as he dug through a drawer and pulled a sweatshirt on over his head, then ducked into the closet in search of house shoes. Dani stayed where she was, listening to the comforting sound of him moving around downstairs and cringing when she heard him muttering curses and slamming doors.

"All the power's out," he announced when he reached the bedroom door again. I suggest you get up and dress warm. I'll start a fire and see what I can find out."

She groaned again, watching him go, then reluctantly getting out of the bed. The long johns she'd worn yesterday were still downstairs in the clothes dryer, so she rustled through her drawers in search of another pair. When she didn't find them immediately, she settled for layering one pair of sweats on top of another, shivering as she removed her pjs and slid into a cold tank top, then a t-shirt, then a sweat shirt on top of those. With two pairs of socks and her warm fuzzy slippers, she considered how ridiculous she'd look wearing a stocking cap in the house. Deciding that would be extreme, she darted downstairs, glad to see Noah stoking the fire.

She chose a perch on the hearth once he had it going good and watched as he moved back into the dining room to pick up the phone. His expression caused a spark of fear to rise in her chest.

"What?"

"Phone's dead too." He crossed to the window and stood looking out. "There *is* ice on the lines," he added, mostly to himself. "Maybe it's the storm."

Dani didn't have to ask what else it might be. She was remembering the lurker in the woods and Noah's comment about how desperate her stalker must be getting. "But, Noah, if it was him here during the night, why didn't he just come in and kill us or something." She shuddered as she spoke, but she had to ask the question.

Noah crossed the room quickly to be at her side. "I never said I thought it was him," he took her hand. "It's probably nothing."

She smiled a little, grateful for his reassurance, but not buying it. "What do we do now? We can't even make coffee."

He chuckled. "I guess the first step would be to go to my house and see if the power's off there. And if the phone's out, I can use my cell."

Dani shot a doubtful glance through the window. As bright as the sun was glistening on the new fall of snow, she knew it was far colder out there than it was inside. The fire was just now beginning to ease the chill on her aching fingers and toes and she was sitting right beside it. Noah's words over by the window were carried on wisps of smoke. She didn't want to go outside.

"Sit tight," he squeezed her arm, then went up the stairs, returning momentarily with his shoes on and hers in his hand. "Here. Put these on," he said, dropping them on the hearth beside her.

"I have to go?" she asked, looking up as he walked over to the coat rack.

"No," he shook his head. "But I'd feel better if you had those on."

His unspoken fears shot through her like a jolt of lightening and she did as he asked. When he was all buttoned up with a scarf wrapped tightly around his neck and one of her stocking caps covering his head, he pulled the Glock out of his pocket and checked it before gloving his hands.

"Noah…"

He winked. "It's all right, baby. I'll be right back."

She was surprised to see him head for the back door, and even more surprised when she followed him and watched through the window as he headed straight for the woods behind the house. At first, she thought he was after someone, but then she saw him cut over and skirt the trail that joined the two yards. He must be afraid someone was watching. The thought chilled her even more and she stood stoically at the window, waiting for his return.

CHAPTER TWENTY THREE

It seemed like years, but in reality, according to her watch, was only about ten minutes. When he returned, he came back the same way he went, dragging a big branch behind him and swinging it in wide arcs to obliterate his footprints. He was seriously concerned.

The dark expression he wore when he re-entered the house confirmed her fears. "We've got a problem," he said, stomping his feet just inside the door.

Dani followed him back to the living room, not speaking. Knowing he'd tell her when he was ready and knowing she probably didn't want to hear it anyway. He shed his shoes in the kitchen to avoid soiling the carpet, then crossed immediately to the windows to close the blinds.

"Come on," he nodded toward the couch. "Sit with me."

She followed him mutely, snuggling into the corner of the couch beside him, touched that he'd saved the place closest to the fire for her.

"There's no power or phone at my house, either," he began slowly. "My lines have been cut."

Dani gasped at the thought and he tightened his already firm grip on her hand.

"I suspect yours have too, but I didn't look." He paused and she waited. "The tires have been slashed on my truck and on the passenger side of your car."

Dani exhaled slowly. "So it's not the storm."

"No, it's not the storm," he agreed. "The radio in my truck is smashed and I guess the cold killed the battery on my cell phone. There's no sign of a break-in at the house, but it's dead."

She let it all sink in for a minute. "So, basically, we're sitting ducks here."

"I'm sure that's what he'd like to think."

157

"What do we do now?" she turned to him, eyes wide.

"That's what we need to figure out. I'm not due in to work until six. No one will miss me before then," he said, thinking out loud. "Either the guy is smart and has something planned for the next few hours, or he cut the wires while it was still dark because he was afraid he wouldn't be able to once it was daylight."

Dani tried, but she wasn't following his train of thought. None of it seemed logical to her. "Talk English, Noah. I have no idea what you think."

He looked at her sadly. "I really don't know. It wouldn't be hard to find out I'm scheduled to work tonight. If he wanted to take another run at you, I'd think he'd have waited until I left, then cut the power and..."

"I get it," she shuddered. "But he didn't. What does that mean?"

"My best guess is, it means he wants us both."

"But... we were outside half the day yesterday. Why didn't he just shoot us?" They both knew he could have if that's what he wanted to do.

Noah shook his head. "Maybe he still thinks he can make it look accidental, I don't know. Why didn't he just conk you in the head instead of going to all the trouble of stealing snakes and locking you in the cellar?"

She nodded in agreement. It's true. He was obviously lurking nearby. He could easily have slipped up behind her without her knowing. "Because he wanted to put the blame on someone else?"

"Hey, that's pretty good," he smiled briefly. "You've been hanging around me too much. You're starting to think like a cop."

"Then whatever he does, he wants to make it look like it was someone associated with Ophidian."

"It's only a guess, but it's logical. There've been too many chances to kill us both."

"Then, does that mean it's *not* someone associated with Ophidian?"

Noah shook his head. "Not necessarily, but I'll bet Atkinson would like us to think it was someone who's still there so we won't look too hard at him."

"God, I'm tired of this," she shuddered again.

"You and me both, baby."

Dani sat, staring into the fire, then announced, "I'm not going to just sit here and wait for someone to come and try to kill me. What do we do?"

He smiled at that and tugged a strand of her hair. "Sometimes, waiting is all we can do, but you're right. We need a plan. Let's hypothesize. Assume you were planning to kill a school teacher and her cop boyfriend..."

Dani smiled, but appreciated his attempt to distance her from the danger.

"... you've eliminated their means of escape and contact with the outside world. Now they're sitting ducks. What would you do?"

Thinking like a killer was hardly something she'd done much, but she'd read enough mysteries that the idea wasn't totally foreign. "How did he kill the guy they found in the cellar?" she asked.

"Don't know," he answered. "Too decomposed to tell. And we can't be sure it was the same guy doing the killing, although I suspect it was."

"Well," she said after a minute or two, "I don't think he'll try the snake thing again… and if he was going to shoot us, I think he'd have already done that…"

He nodded.

"I don't know," she said finally, drawing a blank. "There's just too much I don't know."

"What I know is, we don't want to panic and make it easy for him. He may be thinking we'll try to walk out. That would give him a distinct advantage. We won't fall for that."

"That doesn't leave many options," she offered.

"No, it narrows it down some. But think of this. How many ways can he kill us when we're in here and he's out there? Especially when we're armed."

She thought about that for a minute, but he didn't wait.

"As long as we keep the windows covered, he won't try to shoot through them. He can't know where we are."

"But won't he assume we're close to the fireplace?" she reasoned.

"Maybe," he conceded. "So I'll board up this window. If he tried to break in, we'd hear him. If he tried to set fire to the house, we should know that before it ever got started good."

"Even if he poured gas all around the foundation?" she asked. Fire hadn't occurred to her.

"I think we'd hear him, but we probably should make a regular check of all the windows. Gas, I don't think he could pull off either, unless he snuck in while we were sleeping and we won't let that happen. Anything else, he'd either have to get in or get us out."

"Ho, ho, ho," she teased, feeling a little better about the whole situation. "Will they come when you don't show up at work?"

"Yep," he said with certainty. "So basically, we've just got to maintain for another…" he glanced at his watch, "…eight hours."

"I guess going back to bed is out of the question," she joked.

"I promise you," he looked her straight in the eye, "it won't happen in the next eight hours, but it will definitely happen." He got up and headed for the kitchen. "Come help me find something to block that window.

Their search revealed nothing of value for the purpose at hand, so they finally pooled their efforts and propped the dining room table in front of the window and stacked video cabinets behind it to add depth and hold the table in place. It still wouldn't stop a bullet at close range, but it would certainly slow the trajectory. With that done, they conducted a room-by-room search, making sure the blinds were closed and leaving the doors ajar to help them hear any noises from that area of the house.

Back downstairs, Noah secured all the windows, then pulled two guns and a box of ammunition out of his coat pocket. "I brought my spare," he explained, seeing the question in her eyes. "Get me yours," he added.

She retrieved it for him out of her coat pocket. He checked it and handed it back to her.

"Keep it with you, just in case." He stood up and tucked his Glock in the shoulder holster he strapped on, then put the other one in the back waistband of his jeans. Noah smiled when he saw her expression. "Welcome to the wonderful world of armed and dangerous."

"I guess it's better than the alternative today," she said.

"All right," he rubbed his hands together. "Now to more primitive issues." He disappeared into the kitchen and returned with a tray and a variety of kitchen utensils. "Get me a couple of wire coat hangers," he instructed. "Hungry, much?" he smiled when she returned.

"What are you doing?" she asked, nodding.

"We're going to have a good old fashioned wiener roast," he smiled. "If you collect a few more things from the kitchen, that is."

When she returned with a tray full of hot dog fixings, he was happily spearing foil-covered potatoes with hangers and arranging them around the embers beneath the grate. The glass coffee decanter was filled with water and sat on the hearth in front of the fire. He carefully threaded three wieners on a hanger and held them out over the flame.

Dani smiled, wondering if she'd have thought of any of this, or just been hungry until help arrived. It produced an odd brunch of hot dogs and chips with warm, weak tea, but she had to admit, it was good. The baked potatoes would take awhile, but they'd be good, too. With any luck, maybe they could go out to dinner.

After they'd cleared away the mess, Noah took a tour around the house, making sure all was secure, then dropped back down on the couch. "Only one problem I see," he mused.

"No," she shook her head. "We're already up to our quota in problems."

"Well, at the rate we're going, we'll have one more in a couple of hours," he said, nodding at the rapidly dwindling stack of firewood.

Dani looked at the few remaining logs then at the fire that needed a few more. "Oh, no," she said, "you're not going outside."

He raised his eyebrows. "It's going to get mighty cold in here if I don't."

"Shit. I'll put on my coat."

"I went out this morning without incident, didn't I?"

She frowned.

"I don't have to go right now," he said, conceding, at least temporarily, to her fears. "Got a deck of cards?"

She nodded and went to the closet to fetch them. They played Gin for awhile but Dani's mind wasn't really on the game. At Noah's suggestion, she retrieved one of her mysteries to read and he played solitaire. As the afternoon wore on, Dani noticed Noah beginning to fidget more, casting furtive glances at the windows and making more frequent trips upstairs.

The gray, overcast skies had totally blocked the sun and even though it was only approaching four o'clock, it was much darker in the house than it had been even half an hour earlier.

The last of the logs had been added to the fire over an hour ago and it had dwindled to a collection of glowing coals in the bottom with an occasional burst of flame that sputtered out almost as soon as it started. The wood had been pretty wet when he brought it in yesterday and obviously hadn't dried out fully. Consequently, the logs hadn't been completely consumed, but they weren't burning good either. From the look on his face, she knew what he was going to say before he spoke.

"Come upstairs with me for a minute," he said. "No, wait." He hurried into the kitchen and came back with a handful of cocoa mix envelopes. He took her empty mug and filled it with water from the coffee pot, then stirred in one of the envelope's contents. "Now. Ready?"

No, she thought, but followed him up the stairs anyway. At the landing, she was shocked to see a ladder extended downward from the ceiling. She'd never even thought of exploring the attic.

"You first, or me?" he asked. When she wavered, he smiled. "You first, I'll hold the ladder." When she still didn't move, he chuckled. "Don't tell me you're afraid of heights."

Dani knew she'd been uncharacteristically quiet all day, but she just couldn't seem to find the words when she needed them.

"Heat rises," he prodded.

She smiled and took a step, climbing the ladder slowly. When she reached the top, she was amazed. There was no way to tell how much room there was up there. The attic spanned the width of the house and had large windows on each end, making it surprisingly light in there. On both sides of both windows, Noah had hung large, black trash bags.

"Let me show you," he said, setting her mug down on a beat up coffee table in the center of the room. Without making a sound, he glided across the room and slid behind one of the hanging trash bags. "I doubt if anyone can see this far in with no light on, but just in case, I hung these to hide behind. Come here, try it."

Dani slipped in beside him and he backed around her. "See? You're already wearing a dark sweatshirt. If you pull this stocking cap down over your face, you could even stand in front of this and he'd never see you." He handed her a ski mask with cutouts for the eyes and mouth.

Dani was pretty impressed. From this angle, it looked like she could see for miles into the trees on three sides. If she needed to see the other side of the house, she just had to go to the other window. The only things she couldn't see from either location were the areas directly in front of and behind the house.

"Come look over here," he prompted, moving to the other window. "See my house? my truck?"

"Yes," she nodded. In fact, she could see the whole trail that led between the two better than she could from the ground. "But why are you showing me this now?"

He smiled softly. "Can't fool you, can I?"

She looked at him steadily, not returning the smile.

"I have to go for wood. We have no guarantee that this guy will move before dark, or that someone from the PD will come looking before dark. But when it gets dark, it's going to get damn cold. Your thermostat stops registering at 50 and we're there now."

Dani felt tears beginning to well up in her eyes, despite the fact that she knew he was right.

"Don't cry," he whispered, his voice breaking for the first time. "I don't have to cut down a tree. I already have a cord of wood beside the house. I just have to run over and get some. Ten minutes, tops."

"Can I see the wood pile from here?" she asked.

"No," he said apologetically, "but I swear, I'll hurry."

"And you want me to stay up here while you're gone?"

"Dani, it'll be over before you know it. Remember, this is what I do everyday?"

That wasn't entirely true, but close enough. Still, she couldn't stop the tears from flowing once he'd gone back down the steps. She wished she could turn up the volume and be certain that her ears recorded every sound. Dani sighed and checked her watch, then focused her eyes on the window.

True to his word, she soon saw Noah making his way through the trees from the back side. Forcing herself to take her eyes off him long enough to scan the area, she quickly located him again, moving ever closer to his house. She kept her gaze on him until his back disappeared into the trees next to the driveway.

Holding her breath, she raised her wrist so she could check the time, then concentrated on her watch for a moment fearing the second hand wasn't moving anymore. It was. And it continued to move, but nothing moved in the trees below. At eight minutes, Dani knew Noah should have been on his way back. At ten, she started to cry. At twelve minutes, with no sign of him, she thought she saw a movement nearer the front of the driveway. Frozen to the spot, she waited until her heartbeat pounded in her ears. Noah wasn't coming back.

CHAPTER TWENTY FOUR

With feet of lead, Dani tore herself away from the window and moved toward the stairs. Her mind was in chaos and she shook her head, silently begging for help from somewhere, anywhere. Warily, with shaking legs, she navigated her way down the ladder, then hit the stairs two at a time. Trembling so bad she fumbled the buttons, she pulled on her coat and tried to fasten it, then slid her shaking hands into her gloves. The last glance at her watch showed that Noah had now been gone for almost twenty minutes. Far too long. She wished they'd taken time to make a contingency plan, even though at the time she wouldn't have wanted to hear it.

Terrified that the movement she saw near the front of his driveway was the killer, she sucked up every ounce of courage she could find and headed out the back door. With ears finely tuned, she followed the path that Noah had taken, running in a crouched position, not realizing that she should have brought a flashlight until the cover of trees blocked out what little daylight was left in the sky. With her black sweats and jacket, the killer would have a hard time seeing her in here. Trouble was, she'd have a hard time seeing anything before long.

Walking more slowly, dodging the grasping arms of the trees that crackled and crunched as she nudged against them, she made her way across the ravine. The crunch of each footstep echoed in her ears and she wished she knew how to walk more quietly. Although the wind was bitterly cold, sucking the very breath from her nostrils when it hit her face, Dani was aware of only one thing. She had to find Noah.

At the edge of the woods, she stopped and surveyed the visible area. Not a sign of life anywhere. Taking a chance, since she'd never really noticed the woodpile that was his destination, Dani headed left toward the back of the house. Sure enough, there it was, just around the back corner.

But there was no sign that it had been touched recently. Actually, since the entire stack was covered with a three-inch blanket of snow, it was a safe bet that Noah never made it to the woodpile. Then where did he go?

Dani turned and retraced her steps, examining the ground as she went, fully aware that she was little more than a moving target. There, next to the house, she saw fresh footprints heading toward the back, but they stopped suddenly and it looked like he'd backtracked. The footprints disappeared at the driveway, but the wind had blown most of the snow clear from that area, leaving a thin sheet of ice over the frozen ground. Noah's driveway, like her own, wasn't paved, it was firmly packed dirt with a smattering of impacted gravel. Since the ground had been frozen hard before the snow fell, the snow didn't stick much in the high wind.

Worried about a lot more than leaving footprints in the snow, Dani skirted the driveway with her gun in hand, fully cognizant that she might just have to use it this time and praying that she did so wisely. She was almost to the road when she spied something that threatened to stop her heart. Pausing just long enough to scan the trees that lined the other side of the road for a sign of movement, she ran across the road, nearly losing her footing twice on the way. Skidding to a stop, she stared at the ground.

A bright red splotch that could only be blood glistened in the snow it melted when it touched. Fresh.

Heart pounding and short of breath, Dani edged her way into the trees, not sure at first which way to go. Footprints, she reminded herself. Look for footprints. Shivering uncontrollably as much from fear as from cold, she scanned the ground and located what might have been footprints. A few steps further in she saw another spot of blood, not much more than a few drops this time, but enough to assure her that something was very wrong and she was moving in the right direction. Fortunately, she'd been in this part of the woods often enough searching for a truant Bandit to make it seem quasi-familiar.

Pausing long enough to pull the ski mask down over her face and let the safety off her gun, she proceeded cautiously with a death grip on the .38. The snow was too sparse and scattered beneath the trees to make out any consistent trail of footprints, so she just followed her instincts. When she'd lost sight of the road and any sign of footprints or blood spots, she stopped, breathing deeply, grateful that the stocking mask filtered some of the bitter cold from the air she breathed. It did nothing for the pounding of her heart, however, or the vise-grip of fear that encased her soul like concrete.

Her watch was hopelessly concealed by the bulk of her coat over the sleeve of her sweatshirt, but the encroaching darkness told her she was rapidly running out of time. She doubted she'd survive the night alone out here with no power and no phone. Especially with no Noah and an unknown assailant intent on her demise.

As the shadows covered more and more ground, Dani covered less and less. She felt she'd make as much progress by crawling and could only hope she was still moving in the right direction. The road was no longer visible. When she could go no further, she stopped, leaning against the nearest tree and trying to breathe deeply while suppressing the sobs that threatened to rise up and overtake her. She didn't dare call out for Noah, but his name slammed relentlessly around inside her head, echoing through the canyons of her mind.

Knowing she had to move, she changed direction slightly. The opening between the trees spread just a few inches and she was able to see a little further. Following it around curves and corners, she finally caught sight of the shed dead ahead. Stopping again to make sure there wasn't someone waiting and watching, she gasped audibly when she spotted a man's body, crumpled in a heap about fifteen feet ahead through the trees that circled the back side of the shed.

Fighting the instinct to turn and run, she crouched low and put one foot in front of the other. Close enough to see that it wasn't Noah, she heaved a sigh of relief, but it didn't still the pounding of her heart. Wriggling the fingers that clenched her gun, hoping to restore some of the feeling, she wished like hell someone would wake her up from this nightmare. The fear that gripped her kept her more aware of her surroundings than the tingling pain that signified loss of feeling in her extremities.

A few steps further and she recognized the man on the ground. It was Dr. Crane. Noah's prime suspect after Dr. Atkinson. But if Crane was her stalker, and Noah took him down, where was Noah?

Suddenly, it occurred to her that maybe Noah had followed him here and got the drop on him, then headed straight back across the road to let her know. But if he found her gone, then he was bound to be out here searching for her. They'd not likely cross paths because she came across from his driveway when hers was directly across the street. She contemplated that for a moment. She probably should leave here now and make her way back across the street. But if Noah wasn't there, or if Crane wasn't the stalker, she was still in danger and it would be dark soon.

It will be dark soon, anyway, another voice inside argued back with her. What then? Maybe she should go back now and at least get her flashlight. It would be another hour or more before she could even hope for reinforcements. If something had happened to Noah out here, he could die from exposure in that amount of time. Wait a minute!

Someone was bleeding, enough to leave a trail. From this distance, she saw no sign of blood on Dr. Crane. Maybe if she got close enough to determine how he came to be lying there, she'd have at least one answer.

Praying she'd made the right choice, Dani crept closer, then stooped to a squatting position. There, in the middle of his chest, was a bullet hole with a round circle of blood on his shirt that dripped down over his left pocket and disappeared beneath his coat. No way he was shot all the way back by the road. The blood would have drained down toward his belt. He was shot right here. Someone else was bleeding.

Closing her eyes and taking deep breaths didn't do much to calm her, or to tell her what to do next. Weary beyond words and entering a chronic state of numbness, Dani got slowly to her feet, looking around the clearing. She wanted to scream Noah's name at the top of her voice, but doubted she could summon the strength. There was nothing for her but to keep searching. She had no doubt that was what she'd do until she simply couldn't search any more.

The shed was the logical place to start. She hadn't heard a sound except the crackling of ice-laden branches in the wind and the crunch of frozen weeds beneath her feet. All emotion was frozen, she wasn't even moved by the sight of a dead body less than five feet away, or the thought that he might have been coming for her. This must be what autopilot was like. No feeling, no thinking, just reacting according to how you've been programmed to react.

With another glance around the clearing, she closed the distance between herself and the shed, nudging the door open with her shoulder. The sight of Noah sprawled out in the floor of the shed brought a wave of panic. In an instant, she was by his side, dropping her gun on the ground beside him and fumbling to remove her gloves with fingers that were numb from the cold.

"Noah!" inside, it sounded like a hoarse scream, but to her ears it was a barely audible hiss. "Noah, please!" Blindly, she groped his neck for a pulse and amazingly enough she found one. Too nervous to tell if it was weak, fast, or slow, it was enough just to know he was still alive.

Quickly, she looked him over the best she could, trying to see why he was out cold. There was no sign of blood, but it was obvious he wasn't just sleeping. She'd never be able to move him. At least in here he was protected from the wind. Somehow, she had to get help.

Getting to her feet, she reached for her gun and turned toward the door. "Please hold on, Noah," she said, as much for her own benefit as his. Without pausing to look, she burst through the door and started back toward the road.

"Took you long enough," an oddly familiar voice stopped her in her tracks and she turned slowly to see a tall figure leaning against the shed. "I was beginning to think you weren't coming."

Dani was painfully aware of the gun in her hand pointing at the ground, but her attention was focused on the rifle cradled in the arms of the hooded figure that spoke.

"I'm sorry it has to be like this, but it does. Drop the gun and kick it over here."

Dani squinted at the figure she faced. Tall and lean, the voice sounded almost like a woman, but with a stocking mask much like her own, it was impossible to tell. Her mind raced, considering her options. It was almost completely dark now and she was only a few feet from the trees. She might be able to make it and get lost in there, but there was no help for miles. How far could she run?

As if reading her mind, the figure let loose a throaty laugh and revelation dawned. Caroline Crane. Unbelievable. "You can run, but if you do, I'll kill Noah. Is that what you want?"

"Why?" she asked feebly, unable to comprehend how this high society doctor's wife could possibly be behind all this.

She laughed again. "You'd never understand. Besides, it's not important. It's enough that you know I'll do it. Now drop the gun and kick it over here." The voice had an edge that wasn't there before and Dani feared she did, indeed, mean what she said.

She weighed her options and tried desperately to remember all Noah had taught her about using the gun he'd given her. Never pull it unless you intend to use it. Never let someone take it away from you.

But what about the TV shows where police have to surrender their weapons to protect someone? Not real, Noah's voice echoed from within. No officer would ever surrender his weapon. He'd die fighting before he'd do that.

Dani's shoulders slumped and she hoped she gave off an air of defeat. This woman didn't fool her. She'd shoot Noah if Dani tried to run, but she'd shoot him if Dani surrendered her weapon too. No way she'd let him walk out of here alive.

Hoping a straight shot was faster than swiveling a rifle, Dani raised the gun and fired straight at the form that was Caroline Crane. The shot did more than startle her attacker; it knocked her up against the wall of the shed and dropped her on the ground. The rifle discharged into the air as she fell, but once she hit the ground, there was no movement.

Cautiously, Dani approached the body keeping her eyes glued on the rifle still clasped within the motionless hands. When she got closer, she saw why Caroline carried the rifle the way she did. Blood covered her right shoulder and soaked most of the sleeve. It wasn't visible from a distance because of the fading light, but up close, the contrast with the royal blue sleeve was easy to make out. Dani's bullet hit her square in the chest and another stain was rapidly forming. Leaning over, she pulled the rifle out of her hands and carried it with her into the shed. If the woman was still alive, she wouldn't be armed and she wouldn't get far.

Not knowing what else to do, Dani dropped to the ground and sat beside Noah. Maybe she'd hear when help arrived. Right now, she'd done all she could do. She didn't know how long she sat staring, or what she thought during that time. It was like her mind was on hold. Numb like the rest of her. It occurred to her at one point that she really should go for help, but there was no way she'd leave Noah. She'd die here with him in the dark if she had to but she wasn't leaving. Besides, after all that had happened, she doubted if her legs would hold her up anymore.

She didn't know how long she'd sat there. Time had lost all meaning. Even the chaos of her thoughts trying to make sense of everything slowly tapered off until Dani just stared at the fading light through the crack in the door. Realizing that daylight would soon be gone, Dani propped the door open a little wider and went looking for anything that might help. She found a firestick right away and was thrilled to see that it had lighter fluid in it. Still, she'd need something to burn. It was hard to tell in encroaching darkness, but that might be a lantern across the room on a shelf.

Memories of her own snake-filled shed not so long ago made it hard for her search the shelves in near dark but she didn't want to risk using whatever amount of lighter fluid was in the stick. A low moan captured her attention and she turned.

"Noah!"

She flicked the lighter on again and held it where she could see his face. His eyelids were fluttering. "Noah! Noah, wake up!" she demanded in a voice louder than she thought possible. "Noah!" she prodded when he moaned again. Apparently he was coming around but still hadn't opened his eyes.

Sweeping the lighter toward the corner, she looked for the lantern. It was there! Now, if only it had fuel in it! She could only hope that Caroline, if she was the stalker, had stashed it here to help her navigate the woods in the night.

With more energy than she thought she had, Dani scrambled over Noah's legs and located the lantern, bringing it back to the spot she had staked out. She'd have to be careful of the flame, but she couldn't even see well enough to light the thing without it. Holding the lighter what she assumed was a safe distance away, she located the wick and tried to free it with her other hand. Miraculously, it lit and Dani choked back a grateful sob.

Adjusting the flame, she was thrilled to see it illuminated the entire room. Positioning it so she wouldn't accidentally kick it over, she turned her attention back to Noah and was shocked to find his eyes open, watching her every move.

"Noah," she sighed. "You're alive."

"Dani," his voice was weak, but lucid.

"Can you move?" she asked, fearing the worst since he lay so still.

"Head...hurts ...like hell."

"It's okay," she lied. She wasn't sure anything would ever be okay again.

"I heard... shot..." he sounded like each word required supreme effort. "Did...you... get him?"

"Him?"

"Atkinsssss..."

Dani's heart plummeted like a crashing plane. "I found Crane out back," she told him in a trembling voice, "and I shot Caroline Crane. I haven't seen Atkinson."

"Shit," he mumbled, struggling to rise up on one elbow. "We've... got to get out of here... he's......... out there."

Dani grabbed the gun she had laying on the ground beside her leg and looked fearfully at the darkness beyond the door. "Should I shut off the lantern?" she whispered.

"Turn it...down...not off..." he said.

"It must be after six by now," Dani said, hoping. "Your friends should be here soon, right?"

Noah groaned. "Atkinson......... called...told them... I won't be there..."

"He told you that?" she couldn't believe it.

He nodded. Even in the weak light, his face looked pale.

"Tell me what to do, Noah," she was out of ideas. Out of answers. Almost out of hope.

"Can you... make it...to the road?" he croaked.

"What's the point?" she asked wearily. "There's no help for miles. I'll freeze to death before I get there if Atkinson doesn't shoot me first."

"Take the lantern......... and... set my house...on fire..."

Dani looked at him incredulously. "You can't seriously mean that."

"Yes......... Dani...I'm not okay......... and you'll freeze... in here...we have to get......help..."

Dani considered what he said. Maybe he was concussed and not thinking rationally. There had to be a better way.

"But Noah, if I take the lantern, I'll be a moving target for Atkinson. If he shoots me out there, they'll never find you in time."

"Turn it off......... light it...again...when you get there..."

As bad as she hated to admit it, if he was right and Atkinson called and told them Noah wouldn't be in today, they might not come looking for him tonight. Meanwhile, Atkinson was still out there and ready to kill them both. And, she had no idea what Noah's wounds were but it wasn't hard to tell that he wasn't doing very well. He might not survive the night out here, even if she did.

"All right," she agreed. "Here," she placed the rifle on his chest. "Can you use it?"

"Damn straight," he tried to smile.

"Noah… I love you," she said, hoping it wasn't the last chance she had to tell him.

"Dani, I can……… beat that," he managed a crooked grin. "I… love you…too."

With great apprehension, Dani extinguished the lantern and held it in her left hand, wrapping her right firmly around the handle of the .38. She waited a moment for her eyes to adjust, then ventured to the doorway.

"Dani…"

She looked back over her shoulder, unable to see his face anymore in the darkness. "Yeah, Noah."

"I mean it."

CHAPTER TWENTY FIVE

Dani slipped out under the cover of night, ignoring the glimpse of Caroline's splayed legs still lying where they fell. Ready to shoot anything that moved, Dani picked her way carefully through the trees with nothing to guide her besides an image in her mind and an occasional glimpse of the moon peeking between the clouds. She hardly noticed the cold anymore and wondered if the beginnings of hypothermia had already set in.

The weight of the lantern was cumbersome, but the warmth it emitted when it brushed up against her leg was her only assurance that she wasn't totally numb. Her body was certain it was well after midnight by now, but her intellect reminded her it was probably around seven. Stumbling and bouncing off trees she didn't see until she ran into them, she made her way back toward the road, hoping and praying she was moving in the right direction. Pausing once in awhile to get her bearings and listen to the stillness that surrounded her, she was rewarded finally, with the sound of a car motor.

Holding her breath, although it wasn't really necessary, she waited, wondering if it was help or the enemy patrolling the edge of the woods. A glimpse of headlights through the trees told her she'd gone off course and she redirected, aware for the first time that she had no idea what Atkinson looked like.

Driven by the hope of help, she hurried through the trees toward the road, knowing somehow she'd just have to figure it out when she got there. She might have a nervous breakdown for shooting Caroline Crane later, but right now it was pure survival instinct. If she had to do it again, she didn't doubt that she could.

There was no sign of light as she approached the road, so she stopped at the edge of the trees and waited, hearing only the sound of her heart in her ears and the whish of her own exhale through the knit fabric of the mask she'd adjusted to cover her mouth. She could just make out the shape of her dark house in the hollow, so she turned right and followed the tree line toward Noah's. She couldn't picture herself actually setting fire to the house, but she had to figure out something. She wondered if she could blow up the truck and cause enough of a blaze to be seen by someone who'd care enough to call it in. On the heels of that thought came a mild chuckle that she was even considering such a thing seriously. Funny how priorities change and what seemed reasonable in a time of panic.

She stopped suddenly at the sight of a red glow near Noah's house. Moving more cautiously, she soon saw that it was brake lights on a car in his driveway parked right behind the truck. She hesitated to cross the road, not knowing who might be in the car, but didn't see any other option. Hoping she wouldn't slip and go skidding across, she stepped tentatively out in the open and moved as quickly as she dared to the trees on the other side. Once there, she disappeared into their welcoming branches, making surprisingly little noise in the process.

Hiding inside the branches of an evergreen that lined his drive, she caught a glimpse of a flashlight shining around the front porch area. Was it Atkinson looking for her? She waited, relaxing a little as the flashlight edged toward the other side of the house. The car lights were still on. Could she make it to the car and get away, leaving him there? That would be a much better idea than blowing something up.

Silently, she crept toward the back of the car, still hugging the trees until she got closer. When she reached the back end of the car, she held her breath, prayed she'd make it and lunged for the driver's door, jerking it open in one swift move, realizing too late that the passenger seat was occupied!

The man that stared back at her looked as startled as she felt, but there was no time for discussion.

"Out!" she ordered, waving her .38 at him and nearly choking on the blast of warm air in her face. "Get out now!" The car was already running. If he'd just get out, she could leave him standing and get to town for help. It really didn't matter who he was.

But he didn't budge, he just stared at her with his mouth open.

"I swear I'll shoot you where you sit if you don't get out of this car!" Dani was so intent on ousting the man in the front seat, she never heard the other man come up behind her.

"Drop the gun!" a heavy voice pierced her consciousness.

"No way," she argued without looking back. She saw the man cast a nervous glance at his unseen partner behind her. "Just tell him to get out and I won't hurt either one of you." She was running purely on desperation and instinct now.

"Lady, I'm with the Tyler PD and I'm telling you again, drop the gun!"

Tyler PD. It took a moment, but it registered. Still, even if she wanted to, and she wasn't at all sure she did, she was powerless to lower her weapon. "Show me ID," she said, looking the frightened man dead in the eye. "Really slow, get your ID. I promise, if you shoot me, you'll be sorry."

A look that might have been recognition played across his face, but he reached slowly into his jacket. "I'm just getting my wallet, lady," he assured her.

She wanted to believe him, knowing his partner most likely already had a gun aimed at her head. When she saw the familiar leather folder that housed his ID and badge, she didn't even have to look at it. "Oh, thank God!" she sobbed, lowering her gun. "You came to find Noah, didn't you?"

Vaguely aware of the other man drawing her slowly back out of the car while the one inside removed the .38 from her grasp, she sobbed relentlessly, not hearing a word they said. He propped her up against the car and frisked her for other weapons but she didn't care.

"Lady! You mentioned Noah. Where is he?"

The name brought her back to the present. "Noah! Oh my God. You've got to help me. I can't carry him! Oh! It's you!" she grabbed the front of the man's coat, recognizing him as one of the officers who'd come to the house when she found the skeleton in the cellar.

"Please, lady. Miss Jones, is it?"

She nodded mutely.

"I'm Officer Wylie. Try to calm down and tell me what happened."

The words tumbled out in seemingly random order, but Wylie seemed to get the gist of it. "Get some backup and an ambulance out here," he told the other man, still sitting in the front seat. "Miss Jones, can you take me to him?"

"Yes," she nodded. "But Atkinson is still out there somewhere. If we light the lantern, he might see us and it's hard to find in the dark."

"Why don't you let me worry about that?" he asked, moving to the back of the car and opening the trunk. Methodically, he removed his coat and pulled on a black vest, then pulled his coat back on over it and handed one to her. "I think this will fit over your coat."

"What is it?" she asked, taking it from him.

"Kevlar vest," he explained matter-of-factly. "Just in case. Ready?"

Dani nodded, anxious to get back to Noah, but Wylie was talking to the other guy who'd gotten out of the car and buttoning his coat. He joined them a moment later.

"This is Officer Huckabee," Wylie offered. "Did you tell dispatch what we're doing?"

"Yes sir," Huckabee nodded, flashlight in hand.

"I'll take lead," Wylie said. "You follow."

The three set off into the woods with Dani giving directions from behind Wylie's broad back. They made it to the shed without incident.

"Wait here," Wylie told Dani when they reached the clearing.

"I've got your back," Huckabee said over her shoulder.

A moment later, she heard a muffled, "Clear," from inside the shed, and raced toward the door before Huckabee had a chance to stop her.

"What took you so long?" Noah asked in a weak voice with that same crooked smile that kept her moving through the dark less than an hour before.

"Oh, Noah," Dani ran to his side and sank weakly to her knees, caressing his face in the dim light that finally seemed less threatening.

"I'm going back to the road to direct them in," Huckabee said behind her back. Dani was vaguely aware of the two men talking but only had eyes and ears for Noah.

"How are you feeling?" she whispered, leaning as close as she could get without collapsing on top of him.

"Mad as hell and too beat to do anything about it," he said. Maybe it was wishful thinking, but she thought he sounded stronger than when she'd left him earlier. "Did you find Atkinson?"

"No," she shook her head. "I'd have shot him too." Now that the immediate danger was past, some of her fear was giving way to anger.

"Atta girl," he smiled, struggling to sit up.

"Lay down," she put a hand on his shoulder to hold him there.

"Oh, baby," he teased.

"Get over it, you nut," she chuckled, smiling for the first time in years.

Within half an hour, the woods were illuminated by halogen lights and crawling with officers and technicians. Dani suspected everyone on the Tyler Police Force was there and probably most of the law enforcement from the county. She insisted on riding in the ambulance with Noah and they insisted that a doctor needed to examine her too so it worked out fine.

She wasn't too happy when the doctor ordered her put to bed in the hospital overnight, but found that all of her strength had abandoned her and she was too tired to argue. But when morning dawned, she was up and ready to go. Begging a set of scrubs from the nurse, Dani showered and changed, then went in search of Noah while her discharge papers were being drawn up. She found him down the hall, propped up in bed with Wylie parked beside him.

"Hey!" Noah's face lit up when she entered. Aside from a bandage on the back of his head, he looked pretty much like his old self. "My hero!"

"Stop," she blushed, moving quickly to his side and planting a kiss on his nearest cheek. "How are you?"

"Ready to get the hell out of here, but I'm a little underdressed," he laughed, peeking under his sheet for effect.

"Really?" a note of excitement crept into her voice as she sat down beside the bed. She was afraid they'd want to keep him awhile and the thought of going home alone was daunting.

"Don't let him kid you," Wylie said. "I thought he was going to assault the doctor this morning."

"Why?"

Wylie snorted. "Cause he told Noah he was going to keep him a few days just to watch him."

"Did you behave badly?" she smiled at Noah.

He gave her a wicked grin. "Depends on who you ask. I thought I exercised tremendous restraint."

"So you can go home?"

Noah scowled and Wylie answered for him. "He can go this afternoon, as long as his X-rays come back all right."

"Can you go?" Noah asked her.

"They're filling out my discharge papers now."

Noah frowned. "You're going to need her, aren't you?" he looked over at Wylie.

"I am," Wylie answered. "I can take her over to the station, then send someone back for you when you're ready if you want."

It was Dani's turn to frown. "Am I under arrest?"

Both men laughed.

"Hardly," Noah said. "Although I hear you did threaten to shoot a police officer. Not a good idea."

Dani grimaced. "I guess I did. But he wasn't wearing a uniform! I thought he might be Atkinson."

"Exactly why we forgive you," Wylie said.

"You frisked me!" she suddenly remembered.

Noah chuckled. "You held a gun on them, remember? I'd have done more than frisk you, I guarantee."

Dani frowned. "What?"

Wylie laughed out loud. "If he didn't shoot you on sight, you'd have been eating ice from the driveway."

"I plead temporary insanity," she groused.

"After what's been happening at your house, you'd have no problem getting people to believe you. That snake deal still has my skin crawling," Wylie observed generously. "Seriously, I went easy on you in my report and Huckabee's backing me up. Once I figured out who you were, I knew you were scared shitless. A common criminal, you ain't."

"So, I have to go with you?" she asked.

"You'll have to go to the station and make a statement, then they'll question you forever about shooting Caroline Crane. By then I'll be able to get out of here and come to your rescue for a change," Noah smiled.

It was dark by the time Wylie dropped them off at Dani's house, but she was glad to see lights burning through the kitchen window.

"I called an electrician," Noah read her mind, following her to the front door.

"Thanks," she said, almost overcome with weariness. She'd lost track of how many times she'd had to repeat the horrific tale of last night's adventure over the last ten hours. Every time she thought she was through, she had to go through the ordeal again with someone else, answering the same questions endlessly until she wanted to scream. Noah assured her it was completely normal, but his definition of the word escaped her.

Once inside, enveloped in the warmth of the now functional heater, Dani sank into the cushions of the couch and laid her head back, closing her eyes. She opened them again at the sound of a noise she didn't recognize and was shocked to see Noah moving the dining room table away from the window.

"It looks wrong," he said, seeing her stunned expression.

"Noah, you just got out of the hospital! I think that could wait."

He just shrugged and sat the table upright, then scooted it across the floor. Once he was satisfied that the room was back in order, he sat down beside her. "Well, it's over," he mused with a strange smile.

Dani attempted a chuckle.

"She had me fooled," he shook his head. "I never suspected it was her."

"Why would you?"

"I should have dug deeper into Atkinson's personal life," he said regretfully. "It was all there, I just didn't look in the right places."

"Well I don't know why you would have." Dani still had trouble believing a woman could have masterminded the whole thing.

As the pieces came together, they found that Caroline Crane had been in cahoots with Atkinson from the beginning. Even her marriage to Dr. Crane had been a part of the plan she and Atkinson hatched when she dated him in grad school in Lincoln, Nebraska years earlier. She'd skillfully manipulated all the players, helping them get jobs, arranging for funding, throwing soirees to tempt potential investors. She'd been the consummate front woman. She'd have gotten away with it, too, if she hadn't gotten so greedy. Or, if Dani hadn't been the one to buy Atkinson's house. Odd how a quirk of fate could throw such an enormous wrench in a plan.

"Did you hear they found Atkinson?" he interrupted her thoughts.

"No," she sat up straighter. "Where?"

"Not far from where Crane was. I guess it was getting so dark, I never saw him."

"Shit," she chuckled. "So all that time I was afraid he was still out there somewhere, he was dead?"

Noah shrugged. "What a waste of good fear, eh?"

"You never told me how they got to you," she turned so she could see him better. He seemed a little distant. Reserved.

"Oh. No I guess I didn't," he smiled. "I went for wood. You know that. But before I got there, I thought I heard something and turned back. I saw Atkinson run from the end of my driveway to the woods across the road so I chased him. Or maybe it was her. I never once considered there might be two of them. Anyway, Atkinson jumped me from behind a tree. He had a hunting knife that I managed to get away from him and stick him in the leg, but he got my gun and I had to hotfoot it into the trees to avoid getting shot. I still had my other gun, so I got that out and tracked him back near the shed. I got there about the time Crane went down and took a shot at Atkinson, but he got away. I ducked into the shed to make sure he hadn't gone in there and that's the last thing I remember until I woke up and you were there."

They were both silent a minute. Dani was still having trouble processing it all.

"Everything you did was just right," he said finally. "I'm just sorry I let her take me out. I should have been there for you."

Dani smiled weakly. "I'm just glad you're okay." Throughout the whole ordeal, the thought of his safety kept her going. If he hadn't made it, she wasn't sure she would have either. "They made an appointment for me with a shrink," she said.

He nodded. "See that you keep it. It hasn't really hit you yet, but it will."

He was right. The whole thing seemed like a horrible dream. Surreal. The thought that she'd shot a woman and killed her was completely beyond her comprehension.

"You need to go soak in a hot tub and get to bed," he tugged a strand of her hair.

Dani's eyes narrowed. The way he said it sounded like a prelude to goodbye. As if on cue, he got up and moved toward the stairs.

"What are you doing?" she asked.

He stopped and bowed his head, hand on the rail with his back to her. "I'm going to get my things." He waited a moment, but when she didn't answer, moved on up the stairs.

Dani stared dumbly into the blackened fireplace. It was over and he was going home. Just like that. He warned her. She hadn't moved when he came back down the stairs, duffel bag in hand, more than ten minutes later.

"Get some rest," he leaned over behind the couch and planted a firm kiss on her cheek. At the front door, he turned back. "We're still on for dinner tomorrow, right? It's Christmas Eve."

Dani forced her lips into the semblance of a smile. "Of course. Six o'clock."

"I'll bring the wine," he said. Then he was gone.

CHAPTER TWENTY SIX

Wishing she'd accepted the doctor's offer of a prescription for sleeping pills, Dani sat in the floor in front of the television trying to decide if she'd take another run at beating the alligator game in Bubblegloop Swamp or try to negotiate the lava pits and get to Mad Monster Mansion where she could turn Banjo into a pumpkin. She'd already been blown out of the sky repeatedly by Tie-Fighters and Mario Kart was no fun to race by herself. Desperation did strange things to people.

After Noah left, Dani had cleaned the house, taken a bath, finished a novel and built a fire. She'd rearranged the gifts under the tree and reorganized her pantry to make sure she had all the right supplies on hand for tomorrow night's dinner. Get some rest, Noah had said. Right. It was after midnight and she was fast awake.

When Bandit started whining and sniffing around the door, she felt a surge of panic, then realized there was no stalker in the woods anymore. Besides, in her cleaning frenzy, she'd forgotten to take him out. Glad for a chance to do something different, she paused her game and pulled on her coat. Rather than walking with him, she perched on the swing on the porch while Bandit skittered around in the front yard. He seemed intrigued by the snow.

"Bad habit," Noah's voice came out of the darkness and nearly knocked her off the swing.

She turned and watched him approach. Instead of his usual down jacket, he was wearing a black denim coat that reached to the ground. He looked like Kurt Russell's version of Wyatt Earp. "What the freak are you doing out here scaring me like that?"

A slow smile crept across his face as he ambled toward her. "Couldn't sleep. Mind if I sit?"

Dani scooted over and made room for him on the swing beside her. "You look nice," she said, noticing he'd removed the bandage and washed his hair. His beard was trimmed neatly and he was wearing dress slacks and a shirt and tie, although the tie was loose and the collar open beneath it. When the wind shifted, she caught the scent of cologne.

"Thanks," he smiled. "I had to put in an appearance at a company thing."

"Oh." Disappointment tugged at her heart at the thought of him going out to a Christmas party without her, not that he didn't have the right to do just that. In a few short days and weeks, he'd become the center of her world. Obviously, the reverse wasn't true. She stored that thought away for future reference.

"Why are you sitting out here?" he looked at her quizzically.

She opened her mouth to give a snappy answer, then closed it again as she met his eyes. Pretending required more energy than she had to expend. "I forgot to take Bandit out," she sighed and looked away.

"I think he's done now," Noah said, nodding toward the door where Bandit sat, shivering. "Mind if I come in? There's something I want to show you."

The idea that he thought he had to ask caused a sinking sensation. Reluctantly, she followed him to the door, then stepped inside as he held it for her. He made a dashing figure, even more so when he removed the coat and hung it comfortably on the coat tree. Once she'd done the same, she hesitated. "Want me to put on some coffee?"

"No," he turned to face her, still standing. "I want you to sit down on the couch."

Wondering why he was still standing in the center of the room, she did as he asked, then watched as he crossed to the tree and shuffled through the packages until he found the one he'd first placed there. Looking every inch as elegant as he had at the Rose Dance, he crossed the room and sat down beside her, still holding the package in his hand.

"It's after midnight," he said, as if that explained it. "Christmas Eve. I want you to open this."

Did she detect a hint of nervousness in his voice? With a trembling hand, she reached out and took the package from him, fumbling horribly with the wrapping.

"Wait!" he stopped her as she removed the paper to reveal what she'd suspected. A tiny jeweler's box. She looked up at him. "I should say something…" He looked totally perplexed and she had to smile. "No… just open it."

Dani was just as confused as he looked, terrified she'd lift the lid and find an engagement ring and equally afraid that she wouldn't – something she couldn't explain right now if her life depended on it. What she found when she snapped open the box threw her yet another curve. Sparkling in the flickering firelight was an enormous teardrop amethyst solitaire set in a smooth yellow gold band and encircled with diamonds. Eyes wide, she looked up at him in amazement, softening at the anxiety evident on his face.

"Noah, it's beautiful... but........." How could she ask him what it was? What it meant?

"You like it?" You'd have thought his future rested on her answer.

"Of course I..."

"Try it on! Here..." he took the box from her trembling hand and removed the ring, then slid it on the ring finger of her left hand. "Before you panic, remember that I'm no good at this. I've never done it before. Dani Jones, you have completely captivated me. You're the only woman in the world I can't imagine living without and I'd like very much to make you my wife. But if it's too soon for you to make that kind of commitment, I understand and I'm willing to wait, but I want you to have this because I'm making that commitment to you. I'm here for you, as long as you want me or need me. I'll stay here, I'll live next door, I'll fly you to the moon..............would you please say something before I make a complete and utter fool of myself?"

Dani didn't know whether to laugh or cry so she did both, wrapping her arms so tightly around his neck he had to loosen them after a moment just to get a breath.

"I guess you like it?" he pulled back far enough to look her in the eye.

"Noah, I love it......... I love you. And I want you to stay right here...and..."

"And?" his expression was one of infinite tenderness.

Dani took a deep breath. "And I'd be honored to be your wife."

That was all he needed to hear. In one swift movement, he scooped her up and carried her upstairs where they spent the rest of the night celebrating the holiday.

ABOUT THE AUTHOR

As with most things, PJ Nunn's career started out as something else entirely. She started out in retail then moved to property management. That led to teaching high school, then serving as a counselor and liaison to the local police youth services division. She also spent five years as chairperson of the Coryell County Child Welfare Board and spent years counseling abuse victims and serving law enforcement as a trauma counselor and consultant (something she still does today). When she moved to Dallas, a family illness caused her to leave a job teaching psychology at Dallas County Community College District to become a freelance writer, but found that a few favors she was doing for friends—writing press releases and setting up book signings—was better suited to her talents and her drives.

In 1998, she founded BreakThrough Promotions, now a national public relations firm helping authors, mostly of mystery novels, publicize themselves and their work. The business is thriving. PJ lives with her husband some of their five children near Dallas, TX.

Website: http://pjnunn.com
Facebook: https://www.facebook.com/authorpjnunn
Twitter: @PJNunn

Coming in 2014

January 2014 from Tidal Wave Publishing
No Such Thing as Ghosts: A Jesse Morgan Mystery - With only one really big case under her belt, Jesse's primed for more, but unfortunately, the publicity has brought kooks out of the woodwork. Byron is busy trying to get the security end of the business established so Jesse's left to handle the nutcases on her own.

When a call comes in to visit the owner of a local, exclusive restaurant, Jesse doesn't know what to expect. When he tells her he's afraid a ghost is stealing from him, she wants out and fast! She doesn't really want to tell him he's a nut and turn down the case outright, so she does what seems logical. She quotes an exorbitant rate, fully expecting him to turn it down. He writes her a check instead.

June 2014 from Oak Tree Press
THE PROTECTOR: A Shari Markham Mystery – Shari took leave of absence from the Dallas Police Department after she and her granddaughter Angel were in an accident during the capture of a serial killer. She returns to the job when another killer is linked to the college campus where she teaches in the law enforcement academy. It seems recent killings are somehow connected to a prostitution ring that's discovered in the campus computer lab. FBI Special Agent Luke Stanopolis, who left Shari to go back to Washington after the accident, returns to head the investigation with an undercover sting that goes bad. Will they catch the killer and bring their undercover officer back alive?